C000296048

MURDER FOR POLITICAL CORRECTNESS

NICK LENNON-BARRETT

FUNNY BOOK
PRESS

I dedicate this book to my mother Joanne, my number one fan

PROLOGUE

Carl dropped the key card on the floor, his heartbeat elevated as he glanced both ways down the corridor. It was so silent that he could hear his own breathing. He picked up the card and noticed his hand shaking; taking deep breaths his heart rate slowed, allowing him to swipe the card and get inside.

Alone in the hotel room, he thought about the events which had caused him to flee. Was that the right thing to do? He wasn't sure, but there was nothing he could do about it now. It was the guilt which played on his mind. He'd secretly wanted this to happen, he was a drama queen after all; yet in reality it was the worst thing that could have happened.

He paced the room, playing it back. What would be the situation in the morning? Would everyone know? What would they say? He didn't want to lose his job over this. He loved his job and was good at it. Besides, Walt had a major crush on him, so there was no way he would get rid of him – being *extremely* good looking had its advantages.

He thought he saw a figure at the window. He approached to pull back the vile net curtain when there was a tap on the door. It made him jump. On the other side of that door could be the one person he wanted to speak to. Forgetting the window, he rushed towards the door and opened it. His heat sank – it was in fact, the last person he wanted to see.

Thinking it best to just get this over with, he swung open the door and let them in. He could see how angry they were. The best thing to do was just shut up and let them have their say, but he couldn't do that. He lived for the drama. He apologised for the pain he had caused, expecting a mouthful of abuse. But they seemed calm. He got annoyed and laughed at how pathetic they were. Then they started to make wild statements which were clearly bullshit – they had to be. The thought that it was true was just too much to even contemplate.

Technically he hadn't done anything wrong. It wasn't his fault and he was going to make sure they knew that. The ridiculous claims were just their way of lashing out. They had been hurt, but they needed a reality check. This wasn't some ridiculous soap opera building to yet another dramatic cliff hanger. It was real life, and sometimes that was shit. They needed to deal with that.

He taunted them, laughed in their face, and called their bluff – they were pathetic. In his indifference, he was too slow to react when he saw the knife. The last thing he ever saw was the hatred in those eyes.

CHAPTER ONE

Detective Chief Inspector Fenton surveyed the scene, tiptoeing around the room, hoping to find anything significant, any clues as to what may have happened. He knew instinctively not to touch anything.

The room was dated. A musty smell hung in the air: not quite like damp, just a stale odour. The walls had a raised texture which took him back to the 1970s when touched and, although the room had seen a fresh lick of paint recently, there was nothing new or modern. Fifteen years on the murder squad, yet at times he still felt sickened. An elderly woman was slumped dead on the floor. The blood pooling implied she'd been stabbed in the chest, although there was no sign of a murder weapon. The victim was in front of a wheelchair. Based on the position of the body it was evident she had been sitting in the chair when she was killed. Fenton scratched around in his brain thinking about the correct way to describe her. Was it wheelchair-*bound*, wheelchair-*user*, *woman* in a wheelchair, or is it just woman and you don't acknowledge the existence of the wheelchair?

"It takes a right sicko to do that to a cripple, don't it?"

remarked Detective Inspector Lisa Taylor, entering the room. She scanned the place in seconds, like a hawk searching for its dinner. "And this place is a right shit 'ole."

Fenton smiled and shook his head. "Do we know who Forensics is yet?"

"Manning."

"Why are they sending her?" he said, trying not to sound irritated. "It looks like a straightforward murder to me."

"Is it? We don't have a suspect."

"Maybe it was the husband? Or one of her colleagues?"

"It's possible I suppose. From what I've picked up so far there's plenty of choice. This woman were not popular."

"What do you mean?"

"I can give you a quote if you like." Taylor took out her notebook. "She were an obnoxious old cow and I'm surprised it's taken this long for someone to off her."

"So how many potential suspects do we have then? Who felt the same way about her?"

"Seven."

"And how many have you interviewed?"

"Seven."

Fenton enjoyed having her on his team. She was direct and to the point or, to put it another way – northern.

Taylor was tall, lean, and athletic. She played squash regularly. Apparently, there was something therapeutic about constantly whacking a ball at a wall repeatedly. Fenton assumed there was some form of symbolism to it. This was a term he'd picked up from his eldest daughter. She said that there was always a hidden meaning behind everything a woman did, and men were just too thick to interpret those hidden meanings. He'd considered, for a brief second, challenging her logic, yet a quick shake of the head from his wife had saved him from yet another ear bashing diatribe. Fenton's wife had said she was going through a moralistic phase and in time she would get over it and develop a more cynical attitude like her father.

Fenton's eldest daughter had a similar look to DI Taylor; they both had short brown hair and piercing blue eyes that transfixed whenever you met their gaze. That was where the similarity ended, Taylor came from Bolton. She had a strong accent, which Fenton thought made her sound incredibly thick. However, he knew better than to stereotype based on an accent. Taylor had a razor-sharp mind and never missed anything; the slightest incriminating bit of evidence and she would find it. She was like Fenton and enjoyed being in the middle of the meaty police work, although he knew she also had the ambition to go all the way to the top. He was only too happy to help her in any way he could, which is why he had her on his team. Ambition and diligence did not always go together, yet Taylor was an exception.

Fenton regarded Taylor as like a much younger sister and he felt very protective towards her, like he did with all his team. One of his proudest career moments had been three years earlier when she was promoted to detective inspector at only twenty-nine – one of the youngest ever to gain that rank. She had been on his team for just over five years now and they had solved some extraordinarily complex cases. She had been very keen to join the murder squad and to be on Fenton's team. He had a reputation for getting results and this played into her ambitious side.

Fenton saw himself as a typical copper. Mid-forties, wife and three daughters. He'd been in the job since twenty-one, working his way up through the ranks, although happy to go no further than DCI. He liked to be involved in day-to-day policing and wasn't a fan of the photo shoots and press conferences that were a compulsory part of the higher ranks.

He felt he gave off a strong presence, not just because he was six-foot-tall, broad shouldered and kept himself in shape, or because of the subtle, well-spoken, London accent and dark chiselled looks of which his wife spoke. He saw himself as an average-looking bloke who you'd probably never glance at twice if you passed him in the street. He liked that. It was always best to not be someone who stood out. Despite what anyone says, standing out from the crowd was never a good thing. With adoration comes hatred; just ask any person in the public eye – celebrity, sports professionals and politicians were all testament to that.

Fenton had a quick mind and he liked having people on his team that he could stretch and challenge. When dealing with murderers you had to keep an open mind and be ready for the unexpected. Having done this job for many years, he knew that you could never predict how a killer, or the loved ones of the victim would react. Fenton had a strong intuition for killers. He could smell them. Not in a fetish way, not all killers had strange habits, although there had been a few over the years. It was more an instinct for the fear and lies which gave them away. He never let go of anything unless he was certain he was wrong – which, of course, was never.

He was proud of the fact he had an exemplary record of solving cases. Every murder case he had led on as DCI had resulted in a conviction – all except for one. DI Taylor was one of the few people who knew how much that case still troubled him. He had been going through some difficult family problems at the time. It was a frustrating case for everyone, and he had confided in her. He had blamed himself for his lack of focus. Whenever he had down time between cases, he would look over the old case files again, in the hope that, one day, he could finally solve it and give peace to the victim's family.

He loved to watch talented individuals grow – he had no

time for lazy arseholes. He'd develop and guide talent through the ranks. His protégés, he called them. In his own head, of course. He felt that saying so openly might make him come across as an egotistical prick, and the police service had no place for egos these days – not if you wanted respect from your superiors, subordinates, and peers alike. That had been a nugget of wisdom imparted to him by his old friend and mentor, Harry, whom he had met during training at Hendon. Harry was now more commonly known as Detective Chief Superintendent Beeden.

Fenton continued to review the crime scene. There was no sign of a scuffle. It also didn't look like there were multiple stab wounds. It would need to be confirmed by Forensics, but from what little Fenton could see, given how the body was slumped forward, she may have been killed from a single stab wound. That could imply she knew her attacker, as it would be impossible for someone to catch her unaware. The window was locked from the inside. The only other option could have been that the killer was waiting for her when she returned to her room. They had to look at all possibilities, but the lack of evidence to indicate a struggle, the more inclined Fenton was to think that she had known her killer. Although how much of a struggle could a wheelchair-bound woman in her sixties make? He thought again about what the correct term was.

"Is it wheelchair-*bound* or wheelchair-*user*?" he asked Taylor.

"I'm not sure – we're not supposed to use the word *bound*, are we?"

"Well, that diversity woman said not to, didn't she?"

"Yes, but the guy on the next course said we shouldn't be too politically correct, as it could be seen as patronising."

"That's true, but didn't the guy on the third course say it was important to engage with the individual or something like that?"

"Yeah, but then the fourth course..."

"Oh yes, that woman with the wobbly head, who looked like she was disagreeing with you all the time – what was it she said?"

"It's all about perception..."

Fenton clicked his fingers. "That's it – it's all about perception, so what you say, or what you don't say, could cause offence. I still have no idea what that means."

"Keep your gob shut and say bugger all, basically."

"Hmmm, not really me, is it?" Fenton clapped his hands and rubbed them together. "We have a dead woman in a wheelchair – well, not quite, because she's slumped on the floor now. How old was she exactly?"

"Sixty-four."

"Gertrude Longhurst?"

Taylor nodded. "Known as Trudie."

"Okay – we have a sixty-four-year-old woman, who was in a wheelchair. There is a single stab wound by the looks of things. That's for Manning to confirm."

"She'll probably say she's been shot."

"I don't see an exit wound, but you've got a point – don't you just hate people who have to be right all the time?"

Taylor raised her eyebrows.

"So, there's no sign of a struggle, or forced entry, but, again, that's for Forensics. The husband found her?" asked Fenton, ignoring the look Taylor had given him.

"Yeah – he's in a bit of a bad way though."

"Genuine?"

"Dunno. I've not had enough time with him yet. He was a colleague of the victim as well. They were all at the same conference."

"How many in total at the conference?"

"About twenty, and we've still not spoken to all of them."

"Well maybe we should have another chat with the husband first?"

Taylor nodded and they left the hotel room, leaving a uniformed officer on guard.

There was still something about the scene that disturbed him. For what appeared to be a brutal murder, it all seemed a bit too neat and tidy, so he doubted it was some random attacker. The scene looked a little too *organised*, as a psychologist would put it – although, after his many years attending crime scenes, Fenton still had no idea what that meant and regarded it as one of those annoying buzz terms – unfortunately, one which had never gone out of fashion.

An ear-shattering scream reverberated throughout the hotel. Fenton and Taylor rushed towards the commotion and found a woman screaming hysterically that her husband was dead. Fenton peered into her room and saw a similar scene as before, minus the wheelchair. The man looked middle eastern and was wearing a Muslim cap, which was usually worn for prayers. Was the man praying when he was killed? Fenton couldn't see a prayer mat. The victim was wearing what looked like pyjamas and lying on the floor with similar blood pooling and a wound to the chest. Fenton approached the body, bent down, and checked for a pulse. There wasn't one – he already knew that, but he had to be sure, and it gave the right image to the bereaved.

Fenton was on his phone immediately. "Gary, get me some back-up now, we've got another one."

Taylor was trying to calm down the hysterical wife by making shushing sounds that don't quieten a screaming baby and so would have little effect on a grieving widow in shock.

The woman was mumbling and wailing; generally making no sense. She kept letting out a blood curdling scream every few seconds, the kind which make your whole-body shudder. Fenton wanted to tell her to pipe down, but this was one of those *don't say anything* moments.

"I want every guest checked against the hotel register. Knock them all up if you have to." He fired off instructions to some junior uniformed officers who'd appeared as a result of all the screaming. "Get the guest and staff registers from the manager, and if he starts banging on about confidentiality again, tell him to speak to me. There's back-up on the way... what are you waiting for? Go!"

The officers scattered, looking bewildered and out of their depth.

"Bloody kids."

He signalled for Taylor to join him, so she left the sobbing widow for a second. "Get a female PC to sit with her. I need you to help me co-ordinate."

"I can't leave her on her own."

"Like I said, get a female PC."

"There aren't any here – I'll have to wait until back-up arrives."

"Right. Well, come and find me." He stalked off in the direction of the lobby, rubbing his fingers in his ears in order to regain full auditory function.

Fenton realised there was now a lot more to this than a domestic. Thankfully, he had only said that out loud to Taylor. He hated people to know when he was wrong, even though that wasn't very often. It wasn't that he saw himself as some arrogant twat, merely somebody who was right all the time.

. . .

When the back-up arrived, Fenton repeated his orders rapidly. "I want every guest checked against the hotel register. I want every person accounted for – now."

The police officers dispersed in all directions. This lot seemed to be more with it, which was something.

"Please don't let there be any more," he muttered to himself.

Fenton's wife had made her cottage pie with leeks sautéed in butter and then folded into the mash. He absolutely adored that meal. He could picture the crisp golden potato topping, taste the rich beef sauce and buttered mash. The thought of the smell was so intoxicating his mouth filled with saliva. He dismissed the thought that it might be a tad insensitive, when two people had just been brutally murdered and all he could think about was food. He had just finished a big case and was due some down time. He had been working late, wrapping up a few bits to pass over to the prosecution team when the call for this murder had come in. He'd called his wife to say he'd be even later, and she had promised to save him some and make sure the girls didn't demolish the lot. He knew he was being a bit thoughtless, but the reality was that people get murdered every day and he only got cottage pie every few weeks.

CHAPTER TWO

The third crime scene was even more brutal. Not the way it looked; it was practically identical to the other two. It was the feel of it. A young black man was lying on the floor with the same stab wound and blood pooling. Fenton was alone at the scene, aside from a uniformed officer who was stood by the door of the hotel room, looking the other way. Not everyone could handle this vivid expression of what human beings were capable of doing to each other.

Fenton had checked for a pulse to be certain, but there was nothing. The man was still warm, as were the others. Could that mean the killer was still in the hotel? Fenton was also curious as to why all the victims, so far, were on the ground floor. The hotel was only three floors, but given the proximity of all the murders, could all the victims have known each other? It wouldn't be long until they found out.

Fenton was crouched over the body when Taylor entered the room. She did the same quick scan of the crime scene.

"Do you feel it?" he asked her.

She nodded.

"They seem to change the goal posts so often now I forget, is it three or five for a serial killer?" asked Taylor.

"Three," replied Fenton, gloomily. "Although, technically this is a spree killer."

"That's not what the press will call it."

"Agreed. Well, that will be Beeden's problem to handle."

As Fenton thought about Detective Chief Superintendent Beeden, he knew that there was no chance he would get off this case. This was going to attract a lot of press attention. He knew the powers that be would want to give the right impression to the media by giving the case to an experienced pair of hands. Sometimes that exemplary arrest record could be a pain in the arse when it came to wishing for a bit of the quiet life, although Fenton was kidding himself; he'd be bored shitless within five minutes of having any form of quiet life.

"Well, all we need now is a few more from the other diversity tick boxes and we've got the set," said Taylor.

"How many minorities are there nowadays anyhow?" he asked, smiling. It was as if she had read his mind. "It could just be a coincidence, but we'll need to be ready for a rebuttal to the press when they start making their wild assumptions. Besides, there's only one minority now – the straight, white, able-bodied, atheist male, aged thirty to fifty."

"Will you be making that statement in the press release," she laughed.

"Best, we keep that one to ourselves!"

Over the next hour every guest in the hotel was tracked down, and every room checked. There had been no other murders: a relief in some ways but a concern in others. If someone had committed a spree of killings at this hotel, they could have then moved on somewhere else. Fenton was hoping he wouldn't be getting a call to say there was more bodies at another location. The team was already stretched just having three separate crime scenes on the same floor in one hotel. Fenton would need to check if the rooms could be accessed from outside, via the windows. There had to be a reason why all the victims were on the same floor of the hotel.

"Sir, Ms Manning from Forensics would like a word with you, when you have a moment," said one of the junior officers, appearing in the doorway.

Manning usually demanded Fenton's presence, so he doubted she had asked so politely. When he had asked her why she always requested his presence in such an aggressive way, she had argued back that it was not aggressive. If a man had done it, he wouldn't be asking these questions. She was a feminist and could speak to him any way she wanted; she was the expert and he needed to respect her. Fenton had a lot of respect for feminism. He had no objection to women in the police force, or indeed in any profession. He believed that a lot had changed over his years in the force, but he knew there was still more to be done. He also knew successful senior women in the police who had been very vocal about wanting to earn their way to the top, and not just be given it to meet a quota. It was about equality of opportunity, not looking good in the press when it came time to release the annual statistics. Manning, though, was not the type who merely thought that women should be given the same opportunities as men. She believed that, one day, women should, and would, rule the world.

That she was a brilliant forensic pathologist Fenton couldn't deny, despite her Rottweiler personality. She wore black-rimmed glasses and her hair was cut in a short, almost mannish, style. She was very tall, almost six foot and with a build to match. When he had first met her, he knew in an instant that this was someone you did not cross. The disturbing thing was that she had a sickly-sweet girlish voice which didn't correspond with her presence or personality.

"DI Taylor, nice to see you again – terrible circumstances of course," Manning said with a tone of relish. "Fascinating stuff for us scientists though. Three murders in one hit: you don't get too many of these anymore. Not so good for you though, Eric. I suspect you'd rather be at home watching the golf," she added, with a derisory snort.

Fenton smiled politely.

"Before you ask, Eric, I'm still making the preliminaries here and, as you know, that takes time."

She then launched into the same speech Fenton had heard a hundred times before.

"Policing is based on instinct, feelings and opinion which eventually may or may not lead to the truth. We scientists..." she continued, the arrogance up a notch, "don't have that luxury as we deal in, and pardon the pun here..." she gave the inane grin she always reserved for whenever she delivered what she thought was a joke, "cold, hard, facts!"

"Can you at least confirm how they died? We won't hold you to anything of course." Fenton added quickly.

"Well, don't quote me, but it looks like the cause of death for all three was a single stab wound to the heart. Of course, I'll know more after I've done the post-mortems. Should have the results within seventy-two hours."

"Try to make it quicker." Fenton snapped, without thinking. Manning glared at him. He smiled sweetly. "Sorry, but triple murder and all that. It would be good to have something when the press get wind of it. The last thing we need is Polly Pilkington poking her nose around, whipping up a press storm."

"Not a fan, are we, Eric? I think she's an excellent and talented journalist."

"You would." muttered Fenton, under his breath.

"I'm sorry, Eric? I didn't quite catch that."

DI Taylor, knowing her cue, flashed a smile and allowed

her eyes to dazzle at Manning. "Oh, nothing, Ms Manning. He was just reminding me of a statement I have to take."

Manning's cheeks flushed.

"Thank you, DI Taylor, and please call me Mandy."

"We'll let you get on with your work." Taylor scooped her arm around Fenton's shoulders and guided him out of the room. He too was starting to go red, but not for the same reason as Manning.

"Why do I have to call her *Ms Manning* and yet she calls me Eric?"

"Because you're a man!"

"And her name's Shirley, so why did she ask you to call her Mandy?"

"Must be a nickname or something," Taylor shrugged.

"I could think of a nickname."

"What would that be?" Taylor grinned.

"One piece of good news though, if you can call it that," said Fenton, deliberately diverting the conversation onto a direction of his choosing.

"Stabbed?"

"Yes, at least now we can share that with the rest of the team. I want the murder weapon found tonight." he said, in that authoritative tone men tended to use to reassert their authority after a metaphorical kick in the balls.

DI Taylor entered the hotel room where Fenton was seated making notes.

"The team are still checking for witnesses. I've got half of them looking for a murder weapon. It would help though if we had an idea what type of knife it was. Perhaps we should ask Ms Manning?"

"I'd rather stick pins in my scrotum," he muttered.

"What were that?"

"Nothing. We'll go back along in a bit and have another chat with her. In the meantime, what do you think?" asked Fenton.

"Well, at first when we just had Trudie I thought the husband was a certainty. It's still possible, I guess, just it doesn't make sense for him to kill the other two, unless it was to divert attention from himself, but that's a bit extreme."

"That's what's bothering me. It doesn't make sense. I believe we shouldn't rule out the husband as a suspect, or indeed the wife of the Muslim guy. Was the black guy married?" Fenton asked.

"No, sir, not that we know of. His name was Carl Davenport. The other two were both married, and their spouses worked for the same training company. They were both the ones who found the bodies."

"That isn't suspicious in itself considering that they were sharing the room with the victims."

Taylor nodded in agreement. "But you still have doubts, sir?"

"Yes, I do."

"It could be an inside job though, sir, someone else from the same company. Maybe they even planned it in advance, using the conference as cover. I think we should also look for any links between the three victims but also not rule out that it could be random and there may be more victims at other locations."

That was just what Fenton was thinking. He could understand Taylor's ambition, but felt her detective skills were so in tune to his own she'd do more for the police service in the field rather than sitting behind a desk, coming up with strategy and buzz words, or engaging policy makers in *dialogue*.

"I think we need to talk to the spouses of the victims. They've had long enough with the police liaison officers."

"Shall we go now, sir?"

"No. We have one more stop first as I need some more answers. I'm going to go with your suggestion. We're off to see your friend Mandy" he smiled.

Taylor rolled her eyes, smiled, shook her head, and followed him. Going down the corridor, Fenton stopped.

"Before we go into the lion's den, where are Brennan and Shirkham?"

"Interviewing witnesses I think, sir."

"Let's go and find them. I need them to do something for me whilst we talk to Manning."

Fenton and Taylor walked towards Detective Sergeant Gary Brennan and Detective Constable Emma Shirkham, who were engrossed in conversation and didn't notice their approach.

"Gary," Fenton said loudly enough to attract their attention. "I'd like you to speak to Elizabeth Jamal. Butter her up, but without using the words *love*, *darling* or *nice arse*. See what she has to say for herself. I want an alibi. Be subtle about it. If she's not involved, then remember her husband's just been murdered and we should be showing compassion. Pile on the charm and see what you can come up with."

"All right, Guv. Should I tell the liaison to do one in case she tries to interfere? I usually have better success when I'm not interrupted."

Fenton thought for a second. "If it's appropriate, maybe get her to go for some tea or something, so it doesn't look too obvious."

"No worries, Guv." Brennan trotted off, or lumbered would be a better description, given his short, stocky, frame.

Fenton turned to Shirkham.

"Emma, I'd like you to speak to Derek Longhurst. See

what you can find out. He's not making much sense at the moment, is he?" he asked, turning to Taylor for confirmation.

"No sir, but plenty of compliments about his wife between sobs. I think he seems to be the only person who liked the woman."

"Okay, Emma. You know what to do. I'll be along in a bit. Try and lose the liaison for a while as well if you can."

"Okay, sir," she replied, in her Irish brogue.

As she headed away down the corridor she appeared to be floating, her blond hair flowing down her back as if a wind machine had just started to caress it softly to the sound of a gentle purr. Male heads turned in her wake, as did that of Manning, who had just emerged from one of the crime scenes.

"Ms Manning, may I have a few words?" shouted Fenton, flashing a smile, as he strode up the corridor.

She narrowed her eyes and looked at him suspiciously over her glasses, which had fallen to the end of her nose. She always did that, probably in the hope that it would make men cower in her presence. Sadly, for her that didn't work with Fenton. He knew she had to indulge him as lead officer on the case.

"I am rather busy, Eric, you know."

"Of course, I apologise for taking you away from your work, which you do with such diligence."

Although she condescended people all the time, she did not like it when it was done to her. The expression on her face caused the words, *bulldog,* and *wasp,* to enter Fenton's mind.

"Cut the bullshit, Eric. What do you want?"

"First, you tell me all the victims may..." he chose to simulate inverted commas to emphasise the last word, "have been killed by a single stab wound to the heart. Any idea what size of blade we're looking for? We do need to look for a murder weapon now, you know. Also, are you sure each victim was stabbed just once? Finally, I see you are still working on Trudie Longhurst, any chance of getting to the other victims tonight?"

Manning looked furious. Fenton knew she saw this as her show and wouldn't be pushed around, least of all by a man. She drew breath but, before she could speak, Fenton continued...

"Oh, and please save us from the usual... *This isn't a television show or a film. These things take time, blah, blah!* Just answer the questions, please. This is a multiple murder enquiry."

Manning looked like she had been slapped hard in the face. She gave him a death stare and then made a point of turning to speak directly to Taylor.

"You're looking for a large-bladed knife, with two prongs at the end, possibly the type used for carving meat. There is one stab wound on each victim and death was very quick. From this you will be able to deduce, if it is not too difficult... that I have spent time with each victim. Now, if that is all, will you kindly leave my crime scene."

The last sentence was delivered as an order. Fenton chose not to rise to the bait; technically it was *his* crime scene. Instead he gave a mock bow.

"Thank you, Ms Manning. I'll send for you if I need any more information." and before she could respond, he was gone.

CHAPTER THREE

Taylor entered the room, causing Elizabeth Jamal to look up briefly before returning to sobbing into her handkerchief. Fenton had suggested to Taylor it would be better if they approached the grieving spouses in a delicate manner rather than appear to ambush them – an obvious statement: she let it slide. He'd also decided a boy/girl approach to both would give an indication of how they could play them later should they become suspects. He had gone to interview Derek Longhurst.

Taylor saw that Brennan was playing his Mr Smooth act to great effect; making reassuring sounds whilst he had his arm round Mrs Jamal. It seemed to have worked as she was far less distraught than she had been earlier. Taylor also saw that the police liaison officer had disappeared. Cups of tea were in front of them, so she must have returned and, somehow, Brennan had got her to leave again. Fenton was right: despite the feminist movement, flattery would still get you everywhere.

Taylor noticed that, despite Elizabeth's eyes being red and puffy, they were a beautiful deep green. Her face was round and friendly looking. She had blonde hair that had been pulled into a tight bun, but with none of the strict head-mistress look about her. She was pale but, as her husband had just been murdered, that was hardly unusual. Taylor thought she looked like a kind woman, albeit in a frumpy sort of way.

She went up to Elizabeth and Brennan, sitting down opposite them.

"Mrs Jamal, we spoke earlier. I'm Detective Inspector Lisa Taylor. Would it be alright to ask you a few questions?"

Elizabeth looked up and nodded.

"Can you just explain what happened up to the moment you found your husband?"

Elizabeth blinked and blew her nose into her handker-chief. Taylor thought she was either genuinely grieving or a damn fine actress. Elizabeth cleared her throat and began. She had a gentle voice which, although controlled, had a confidence about it. She had a soft Lancashire accent and spoke clearly and precisely. There was something else about the way she spoke – it was warm and embracing. Taylor suspected she was probably exceptionally good at her job. She'd checked and discovered she was the HR Manager for the training company. Here was a woman who people would feel they could confide in – before they found she'd screwed them in the latest pay review – but perhaps that was just Taylor's own perception of HR.

"My husband wasn't hungry. He was unwell and had decided not to join us for dinner. I met with everyone else and, after dinner, I called the room to see if he was feeling any better. When I received no reply, I went to our room to check everything was okay. It was most unlike him to be off his food, even when he's unwell. He eats constantly at home. I usually make those meals for four and he'll have three of the portions. Never puts on the pounds, of course, unlike me."

Taylor noticed Elizabeth was still talking about her

husband in the present tense but didn't correct her. She let her ramble off on a tangent for a while until she started to talk about things unrelated to her husband, the conference or even herself. Taylor would then gently steer the conversation back on track.

"Elizabeth" she said warmly, whilst gently taking her hand. "Am I okay to call you Elizabeth or do you prefer Mrs Jamal or Lizzie or Liz?"

"Elizabeth is fine, dear" she said, but, although she left Taylor's hand where it was, a brief coldness in her eyes suggested she felt Taylor was patronising her.

"Elizabeth, can you tell me what happened when you returned to the room?"

"Yes. I went into the room and saw Nadeem and all the blood and, and, and ...."

She became very distressed again, so Taylor left her to sob on Brennan's shoulder. She would have to approach this from a different angle.

———

Fenton entered another room. Derek Longhurst was sitting there, talking to Shirkham. Fenton looked around and smiled. Shirkham had got rid of the police liaison officer. Both looked up as he entered, and Derek managed a weak smile. Fenton studied him. The only word he could think of to describe him was *normal*. It was a word he disliked, as it was meaningless. It was like *nice*, which he had learnt never to use in relation to women, particularly regarding their cooking or clothes!

Fenton approached Derek and offered his hand. Derek stood up and shook it. A firm grip but not the sort men use to break your hand as a demonstration of their masculinity. Fenton deeply resented men who did that and wondered why they didn't just slap their genitals on the table and ask to compare sizes. As he stood up Fenton noted he was of average height and build. In fact, everything about him was simply average; the sort of person who just blended in. He had mousy brown hair, which had started to grey at the temples; the sort of look which can give men of a certain age a distinguished air about them; not with Derek. It made him look even more ordinary. He had dark features and, as Fenton met his eyes, he saw they were a deep hazel. It was the eyes which often gave people away; Fenton saw nothing in them to arouse suspicion, yet also nothing that said *my wife has just been stabbed to death*. Fenton found him more intriguing by the second. The more he studied him, and the more uninteresting he appeared to be, the more curious Fenton became.

"Mr Longhurst, I'm Detective Chief Inspector Eric Fenton. I'm sorry about your wife's death and don't wish to impose on you at this difficult time, but would it be possible to ask you a few questions?"

"Of course."

His accent wasn't Lancashire like most of the others from the conference, but it was still a northern dialect of some description. As a Londoner, Fenton could barely tell the difference between Scouse and Geordie.

"I appreciate you've probably been asked the same questions before, but can you just talk me through what happened in the moments leading up to the discovery of your wife's body?"

Fenton had to put his sympathy hat on. If Derek wasn't implicated, and, as the night progressed, it was looking more and more like that was the case, then he had just been through a terrible ordeal. It was best to play Mr Nice Guy for the time being – the other hat could come out later if required.

Derek said that Trudie had decided not to join the group for dinner, so he had gone on alone. He had eaten early, before most of the others arrived, then left to have a few drinks in the bar as it was quiet, and he wanted to unwind. Apparently, it had been a hectic couple of days at the conference. At about nine o'clock, he went back to his room to check on Trudie, and to see if she wanted anything to eat before the restaurant closed. That was when he found her. He explained that he had instinctively shook her to check if she was okay and then saw all the blood. It was at that point he realised she was dead and raised the alarm.

Fenton made copious notes. A habit of his. He checked and double-checked Derek's version of events. He tried to pinpoint the exact times when Derek left for dinner, left the restaurant and the bar. He also asked for names of anybody he had been in contact with.

"Am I a suspect?" exclaimed Derek.

"I'm sorry, Mr Longhurst, if it appears to look that way, but we have to check every detail whilst it's still fresh in people's minds. I hope you can understand that?"

Derek gave a non-committal shrug and Fenton continued to probe until he felt he had covered absolutely everything. He left Derek his phone number and told him to contact him if he remembered anything else, no matter how insignificant, then got up to leave. He signalled for Shirkham to stay with Derek and keep him talking. Fenton saw the police liaison officer returning with a tray of drinks. He told her to make herself scarce for another twenty minutes and she begrudgingly obliged, muttering something about cold tea.

Fenton leaned against the wall and gently closed his eyes. He needed to think and there was so much activity going on around him it was hard to block out the noise. He was in a corridor with various police and forensic officers milling about, so absorbed in their own tasks they barely noticed him. He heard the click of a door opening to his right. Taylor stepped out of the room. He signalled to her to follow him.

They milled their way through the commotion of people, ignoring anybody who tried to get their attention.

———

Taylor wondered where they were heading and was surprised at herself that she'd just fallen into line when her boss had signalled that she should follow him. She felt it reflected working in a male dominated profession – automated, almost robotic. The extremes she came across in the police force baffled her sometimes.

At one end of the scale were the chauvinistic knuckle-dragging morons. They rarely made it further up the ranks than uniformed constable. That was for two reasons. First, at least some level of intelligence is necessary to pass the sergeant's exams. Second, they seemed quite happy being able to beat the crap out of people with impunity, on the pretext that, "He resisted arrest, Guv." She could handle those types, usually by ignoring them.

The other type was the extreme opposite and she could always tell when they had come back from yet another training course. They would have new buzzwords. They were the sort who made her cringe and think the world had gone mad. She was fed up with them asking for an *information touch point* instead of a meeting. She assumed it might be some great new saying which had drifted across the Atlantic but was told that *meeting* was an offensive term and that people weren't supposed to use it in the workplace anymore. How it linked to diversity remained a mystery and she had no intention of ever seeking an explanation. She suspected the response would be completely ludicrous.

She also resented being asked if it was okay to call her Lisa or was her preference Miss or Ms Taylor? What annoyed her most was that, half the time, those junior to her, in trying to be so politically correct, missed the point that she was of a higher rank and therefore should be addressed accordingly.

———

Fenton walked into the hotel manager's office and asked the manager if they could give them a few minutes alone. The manager nodded and left.

"I think we need to start looking at other possibilities. For either of those two to have murdered all three people doesn't make any sense whatsoever, so there must be others with a more tangible motive."

Taylor was about to speak, but he continued.

"I mean, they aren't going anywhere so it's not like we can't talk to them again."

"Actually, sir, they're all heading back up north in the morning," said Taylor.

"Shit," said Fenton, rubbing his temples. He was tired and hungry. "Find me a room and get the key team together in half an hour."

The room was buzzing with about ten police officers of different ranks exchanging notes. Taylor had managed to commandeer one of the smaller conference rooms in the hotel basement away from the main action. It had the same stark sterile quality as the rest of the hotel. Apart from its grand lobby, the building lacked any character elsewhere. Fenton couldn't help thinking that whoever came up with the name Hotel Draconian had been taking the piss somehow. Either that or the decorators had. It couldn't have been a coincidence so he wondered why a company supposedly thriving with creativity would choose it for their conference. It wasn't dirty or untidy in any way. It just exuded something that could only be described – as Taylor had so eloquently put it – as a shit hole.

Fenton made his way to the front of the room, silence fell, and all eyes focussed on him.

"Okay everyone, now time is against us on this one. We have a hotel full of potential suspects. Remind me of the name of the company all the victims worked for."

"Training4All, Guv, with a number four instead of the word," said Brennan.

"What we have is three victims. One female aged sixty-four, who was also a wheelchair-user. One Asian man, thirty-nine, of Pakistani descent although he was born in Blackburn. He was a practising Muslim. Finally, we have a thirty-two-year-old male of Afro-Caribbean descent, who was also born in the north-west of England. Do we know where yet?"

"No sir, some people seem to think its Lancaster or Morecambe," replied Shirkham.

"Have we found any next-of-kin yet?" he asked generally

"Yes sir. We've got the local police handling that one," said Taylor.

"Good. Well, get them to find out as much as they can on the background. You never know, there might be a link."

"Sir, we've also found out that the last victim, Carl Davenport, was gay. It was common knowledge around the office, and he was open about it," added Shirkham.

"Emma, try and find out just how open he was with this sexuality. We shouldn't assume that someone who was open at work was the same with their family and we don't want the locals blundering in and causing a shit storm."

She nodded.

Fenton continued, "All three victims are quite different, but all appear to have been killed in the same manner, although we won't know this for certain until Forensics have finished. For now, that's the assumption we are going to work on, as time is against us. All these people are leaving at lunchtime tomorrow and we'll need to involve the local force in Preston if we want to interview anyone after tonight."

Fenton started to divide up the work amongst the officers. He told Brennan and Shirkham to return to Elizabeth Jamal and Derek Longhurst. He reminded them to be gentle as he felt they were both holding something back, although that was no proof either was involved. He told Shirkham to first ask Carl's colleagues about his background and who his closest friends at work were and then to report back to Taylor. The others were split into two teams. One was to get statements and full contact details from everybody in the hotel, not just those who were attending the conference. The other was to continue looking for the murder weapon. It was late and everyone was tired, but Fenton had given them a motivational kick, so everyone went off to get on with their work. He told them all to be at Kentish Town police station in the morning for a briefing at eight o'clock. The conference delegates weren't due to leave until noon, so he wanted to make sure he had everything he needed for the investigation to proceed before they all left London.

Taylor stayed in the room with Fenton. "Lisa, while you're waiting for Emma to come back to you, I'd like you to find out absolutely everything you can about this Training4All. We can't ignore the fact that all the victims worked for this company and my instinct tells me that's where we'll find the answers. If it was a random attacker, then I believe that at least one victim would have been from elsewhere. After that, talk to whoever Carl's best friend at work was."

Taylor nodded. "Where will you be, sir, so I can find you?"

"I'm going back to have a chat with Manning and another look at the victims before they're taken away."

"Good luck with that!"

Fenton smiled. "Oh, and Lisa, find out what this conference was about if you can, as well."

"Already done that, sir. The conference was called *Embracing Diversity*."

Fenton and Taylor walked into the hotel manager's office without bothering to knock; it was becoming their sanctuary away from the chaos. The manager was present and looked visibly irritated that his office was being commandeered yet again by a couple of whispering detectives. Another request to make himself scarce led to lots of heavy sighing and eye rolling.

"Is there a problem?" asked Fenton.

"I have a lot of work to do, you know. I do have a hotel to run here and guests to see too. This is the fourth time this evening I've been asked to vacate. It really is rather unacceptable."

"Would that be same hotel where three guests have been brutally murdered? I'd call hindering a police investigation as unacceptable," snapped Taylor.

The manager dutifully submitted.

"Perhaps if you spent less time gossiping in my office, you might be able to catch the triple murderer who's terrorising my guests." the manager muttered audibly, whilst walking out the door.

Fenton gestured to Taylor to take the seat. She looked down, arched her eyebrows, and shook her head. Fair point, Fenton thought. He was knackered so he flopped down without looking any further.

"So, are we still following the possibility that there could be a domestic angle, sir?"

"It's looking less likely, but I still don't think we're getting the whole story from either spouse."

"True, perhaps there were a bit of marital trouble they're keeping quiet. You know how guilty people act around the police, even when they ain't done nothing."

"Carl Davenport is the anomaly and we need to know more about him."

Fenton rubbed his eyes and ran his hand over his chin and realised it must be late, based on the level of stubble puncturing his skin – the curse of man. It took weeks to grow the sort of beard which gave the distinguished gent look, and the baby smooth, handsome look lasted for about four hours. Everything in between made you look like you've been dug up.

He glanced at his watch: it was almost four o clock in the morning, and he thought it best to call it a night.

"Make sure we have contact details for everyone, and I mean address, home phone, work phone, mobile, email – the lot. Then send everyone home."

Taylor nodded and left the room. Fenton looked around again and suddenly realised he was no longer hungry, just nauseous. With a vocal yawn and a stretch, he left the room. He decided to head straight to Kentish Town police station to check that the incident room had been set up. By the time he'd get home it would be time to turn around and come back again. At least this way he might be able to get some sleep.

CHAPTER FOUR

Fenton woke with a start as Taylor sat down opposite him.

"Briefing due in half an hour, sir, but we may want to make it quick as I've got someone coming in to give a statement."

"Who?"

Fenton was wide awake now. He was amazed that Taylor looked like she'd had a full night's sleep. One of the perks of make-up – even a corpse can look good!

"Woman by the name of Wendy Baxter. She works as trainer at Training4All. She were Carl Davenport's best friend. Well, according to her, anyway."

"According to her?"

"You'll see what I mean when you meet her. It could be useful though if you still think that Davenport's the key."

"What have you got from her so far?"

"Very little as she was so distraught."

"So why is she coming in now?"

"Well, apparently not only were she Carl's best friend, she's also known as the office gossip. It might come in useful for finding out a bit more about the spouses. I don't think we should give up on that angle just yet."

"I hadn't intended to," replied Fenton.

His brain had now kicked in and he was already thinking of questions he could ask Wendy when she arrived. A bit of flattery and false empathy and the gossipy types would tell you anything. Call it a stereotype if you like; he was just glad it was true.

"I had an interesting chat with Derek Longhurst before I left, as well," added Taylor.

"Go on," replied Fenton, bringing himself away from playing out the Wendy interview in his head.

"About Elizabeth Jamal."

Fenton was all ears; he still felt there was something he couldn't quite put his finger on with her. It all seemed a bit too perfect.

"Playing the grieving widow, is she? I think there were trouble in paradise."

"Is that what Derek said?"

Taylor nodded. Fenton thought of the possibilities. If Elizabeth had murdered her husband, then why had she murdered the other two? Unless she and Derek were in it together, so they could murder their spouses. Then where did Carl fit in, or was he just a diversion? But that didn't make sense either because, if this was what had happened, why on earth would Derek bring up Elizabeth's alleged marital troubles?

"Did you ask him what the trouble was?" asked Fenton.

"He didn't know. He just said it were a vibe he had from working with people for so many years."

Fenton raised his eyebrows. This just sounded like idle gossip to him. Men were worse than women half the time.

"How are they all getting back up north?"

"The coach is leaving at noon, but I know some of them are heading back sooner on the train."

"What about the spouses?"

"They both agreed to stay behind and leave with the coach in case we needed to speak with them again. Walter Channing agreed to stay behind and speak to you as well."

"Walter Channing?"

"Yeah – Walter, *call me Walt*. He owns the training company."

"Fine, but we'll see what we get from this Wendy first. It's going to be a nightmare involving the local plod every time we just want to check a few facts, so it might be worth speaking to the spouses once more."

Wendy Baxter was in her early thirties with a large round face and a frame to match. She had shoulder-length light brown hair cut into a bob, which only seemed to accentuate her rotund features. She had big brown puppy dog eyes which lit up with excitement owing to all the drama she had been caught up in. Fenton could tell she was the type who craved to be popular and probably had very few friends. She gave off the impression of being a very needy individual. She would probably be a very loyal friend, there for you in your hour of need, providing a shoulder upon which to cry. The downside was that the world and his wife would know your deepest darkest secrets within about ninety seconds. She came across as a friendly and warm individual, with a big heart and an even bigger mouth. Fenton would have to question her carefully as, whatever was said in this room, would be all round the office by tomorrow: the same office currently housing the only suspects.

"Carl always described me as the ultimate GBBF. Fact." exclaimed Wendy.

"What's that?" asked Fenton.

"Gay Boy's Best Friend," said Wendy, with a sarcastic sigh. "We were never keen on the term *fag hag*, so we came up with this one all by ourselves. Ain't it great?"

Fenton was already exasperated. This woman didn't seem able to grasp the concept that she was supposed to be trying to help with a murder enquiry. It seemed she saw the whole experience as some sort of audition for a trashy Reality TV show.

"You work at Training4All?" asked Fenton.

"Well, I always wanted to work in show-business, but I never seemed to have time to follow me dreams. I just love being around people, so I thought training were right for me. Maybe I'll even have my own company one day. It were something me and Carl talked about doing together."

That was the trigger for hysteria. Whenever Carl's name was mentioned she'd get highly emotional and cry out, "Whose GBBF will I be now?" Fenton was at his wits end with the vacuous self-indulgent woman. He was starting to wonder what the hell Taylor had been thinking about when she asked Wendy to come into the station. They were going to be here for hours and all they were going to accomplish was to provide Wendy with gossip fodder for the next decade. He wasn't usually this irritable but, having slept for only two hours, he was grumpy. He'd also missed out on his wife's cottage pie, although she had promised to make a fresh one that evening. She knew he preferred it fresh and apparently one of his daughters was taking his leftovers from the previous night to school for her lunch. With the thought of a good home-cooked dinner that evening he was able to keep a sympathetic look on his face whilst Wendy wallowed in self-pity.

"I know this is hard for you, but I wonder if you could tell us anything about the other two victims, Trudie Longhurst and Nadeem Jamal," asked Taylor. She spoke in such a kind and caring way, yet still with a firmness that would bring the conversation away from Wendy's trigger point for tears - Carl.

Wendy looked up and dried her eyes. She then launched into a full-scale rant about the other two victims' characters and any little snippets of gossip she knew about them. Fenton realised Taylor hadn't lost it after all and was glad Wendy had agreed that the interview could be recorded. He looked down at his brand new eighty-page notebook, knowing it still wouldn't have been enough – thank God for Fritz Pfleumer, inventor of the tape recorder.

Fenton and Taylor were summarising their interview with Wendy for Brennan and Shirkham.

"Did she say anything else about the car crash, Guv?" asked Brennan.

"Yes, that was interesting, and we'll need to verify everything as she could obviously sense we were interested, so I wouldn't be surprised if some of it was embellished. Apparently Trudie's first husband wrapped his car round a bollard, on purpose, which killed him instantly and left Trudie in a wheelchair for the rest of her life. She'd never had any children with her first husband and couldn't after the accident. Wendy has no idea if she ever wanted children."

"When was the accident?"

"That she wasn't sure about as it had been before Wendy had joined Training4All. She said Trudie had been with the company for ten years and married to Derek for the last five. They met at work apparently. She inherited three quarters of a million when he died, so there must have been an investigation of some kind. Emma, can you do some digging"

"Sure, what was Wendy's opinion on Trudie as a person?"

"According to Wendy she liked to belittle the younger

staff a lot. It was like a sport to her and there was a rumour that people used to take bets on whether she would break her record of having someone leave within less than an hour of starting."

"Although Wendy couldn't say who that person was, so make of that what you will," added Taylor. "Also, it was always the women. The men she liked."

Fenton continued. "She has been described as a very stubborn woman, who would never let anything go. Apparently, her feeble old woman act was just that. Although Wendy was complimentary in some regards and said that Trudie was good at her job, which was in the accounts department. Her job title was Customer Delight Manager."

"What's that?" asked Shirkham.

"Accounts Payable from what we could gather. Wendy didn't seem to know what she did on a day-to-day basis, just that she was good at it. The owner of the company, Walt, likes to give people special job titles. You want to hear what Wendy's title is – Performance Enablement Facilitator."

"Sounds like a drug dealer! Did she give us anything else?"

"The auburn hair we saw was dyed apparently and you could sense her presence by the smell of lavender."

"What about friends at work, Guv?"

"Walt and Elizabeth Jamal were the two she was closest to."

"That could be interesting?"

"We haven't established any link between Carl Davenport and Trudie yet, or indeed, with Nadeem."

"What about her marriage to Derek, Guv?"

"Happy, it would seem. Wendy felt that Derek was oblivious to the fact that he was married to..." he looked at Taylor.

"Satan's mother!"

"That's it... Satan's mother. According to Wendy, Derek is quite shy and introverted, which doesn't make any sense as he works as a trainer or performance enabling whatever, but Wendy informs us that some people are different when they are *on*. They were apparently very discreet about their relationship at work, although everyone knew Trudie wore the trousers."

"Sounds like she was a bit of a bitch, Guv."

"Yes, if we were just dealing with Trudie's murder then I'd say we'd have a nightmare on our hands, there would be no shortage of motives and suspects. However, we need to find what links all three of the victims and we have to work on the assumption that they were all killed by the same man."

"Or woman," added Shirkham. "You'd be surprised what women are capable of."

She had a point, although in his experience female murderers were lest gory with their killings, but he wasn't going to rule anything out.

Taylor was next and gave the team a rundown on Nadeem Jamal, from Wendy's perspective.

"He was born in Blackburn, although the family originate from Pakistan. Wendy was a big fan of his and she said he was kind and people were drawn to him for advice. She also said that, even though he looked like any other bloke walking down the street, he had a presence."

"What did she mean by that?" Shirkham asked.

"No idea. She couldn't really articulate any meaning. She just said *presence, you know presence*."

"What about his job?"

"He was a performance enabling... Right, going forward, can we all agree to just call them a trainer, unless we are talking to someone from the company."

Everyone nodded in agreement and Taylor continued.

"Nadeem was an exceptionally good *trainer*. He was also

particularly strong at winning new customers and getting repeat business. Walt was keen to have him out in the field as the face of Training4All."

"Tick boxing?"

"It would appear Walt isn't about the boxes. The trainers need to connect or something."

"And the marriage?"

"Happy, although there'd sometimes be an atmosphere if they'd had a row at home. Nadeem was the only thing that Elizabeth was giddy about, otherwise she was a straight talking and got the job done kind of person. Wendy described her as a bitch, as she'd given her a verbal warning for repeated lateness.

"Any friends amongst his colleagues?"

"He got on with everyone but worked regularly with Carl as their training style is similar."

"What does that mean?"

"We have no idea, and neither does Wendy it would seem. She kept saying *presence* again, so we stopped asking."

"What about his religion?"

"Well he was a practising Muslim, but this was more out of loyalty and respect for his parents. He wasn't overly strict about it, Wendy thought, and the loyalty was because they had supported his mixed-race marriage. Wendy said that Nadeem confided in her, but with a bit of probing that would appear to be...

"Bollocks," interjected Fenton. "The interesting part of the interview though was when she spoke about Carl Davenport."

"Wendy, I know this must be difficult for you and so far, you've been very helpful, but now we need to talk about Carl."

Fenton was now leading the questioning.

Wendy started to sob quietly. "I'm just going to miss him so much,"

"I know, I know. Did Carl have a partner at the time he died?"

"No, and I would have known as he told me everything and I mean everything," she said, raising her eyebrows, a slight smirk evident by the raised corners of her mouth.

"Tell me about him as a person, not when he was at work, but when he was out of work and the two of you would go out. Did you go out together?"

"All the time. He was a nice piece of eye candy to have on your arm and all the other GBBFs were well jealous. Fact."

"On your arm?"

"Well, you know what I mean. I'm nothing amazing to look at, although I've got a dead nice personality, but Carl had both. He were a lovely bloke and he were well fit. Over six foot and really muscled, which were all natural as he never went the gym that much and that was usually only to meet guys. He weren't your typical gay. He were dead straight acting, but it weren't an act with him, it were all natural. He was like a straight man who liked to sleep with guys in his spare time – he had a lot of spare time!"

"He had a lot of one-night stands?"

"Not really, that wasn't him. He were dead romantic. He said he hoped that he would see someone in the showers at the gym and would know there and then that they were going to get married. Isn't that dead romantic?"

"Sounds like he was a very special person," Fenton placated.

"Oh, he were, and he were always nursing a broken heart.

His relationships would always last for just a few weeks and then that would be it."

"Why do you think that was?"

"Well I did this psychology course once, so I know about these things?"

"What psychology course was that? An A-level?"

"Oh no, nothing dead boring like that. It were one of those weekend events where you find yourself and understand the real you and that of those around you.

"Oh yes, I know what you mean." *That isn't psychology you moron.* "Please continue..."

"Well, with men, there are three things that you need – looks, personality and a big cock."

Fenton choked on his water and Taylor slapped him on the back.

"It's true though, isn't it love?" she asked Taylor.

Taylor smiled and nodded, to play along.

"Well men don't have all three... ever. You're lucky if you get two of them. Well, Carl had the set. Fact. His problem was that he wore his heart on his sleeve and it were always getting broken."

"Nobody special that he might not have told you about?" asked Taylor.

"Are you even listening? I was the GBBF – I knew everything," she snapped back.

"Why don't you tell me about his work," Fenton interjected.

"What do you want to know?"

"Did you meet Carl at work?

"No, we've been friends for years and I got him the job at Training4All. Carl used to work in HR for years, but then made the switch to training. I knew Walt would hire him within seconds, so I put him forward when a job came up."

"Why would Walt hire him within seconds?"

"Err, because he was hot!"

"I see – carry on."

"Well, Walt also liked that he brought another dimension to the training and made it really fun. He was the one to suggest they get rid of PowerPoint in all training events. That made training people on how to use PowerPoint difficult, but we found a way."

"You trained people on how to use PowerPoint, without using PowerPoint?"

"I know – brilliant isn't it? That's how good Carl is... sorry, was." Her voice cracked.

"What about his other colleagues? Any enemies?" asked Fenton, to keep the conversation moving.

"None at all, he got on with everyone. He often helped Elizabeth out."

"In what way?"

"His HR background, so if she needed to prove she was right about something, then she would ask Carl."

"And was she right often?"

"Elizabeth is always right."

"What about Trudie?"

"What about her?"

"Did they get on?"

"Like I said, Trudie always liked the men as they'd fall for her act."

"You think her disability was an act?"

"Oh, no that was genuine, but I always knew something would happen to her one day."

"What makes you say that?"

"She was always pushing people too far and one day someone was going to snap."

"Any idea who that might be?"

"Take your pick."

. . .

Fenton knew they needed to find out more about the company Training4All. They had to do their interview with the Managing Director, Walter Channing before lunchtime. Fenton had met him the night before amidst all the chaos, although only briefly. He'd been particularly irked when Walt, as everyone called him, kept referring to Fenton as *dear boy*. All he needed from Walt was what the training company was about, what it did and how he ran it. He knew within those fleeting seconds the night before that, if he asked for a rundown on everyone who worked for him, he'd be there for hours and achieve nothing. No – he'd decided that, if he needed to know Walt's opinion on anything, then that would be a task he would have to delegate for his own sanity.

———

Training4All was an independent training consultancy located in Preston, Lancashire. Their aim was to provide blended training solutions to organisations to enable them to unlock talent and maximise the potential of their most important assets – their people. They also provided professional coaching under the strap line "Let us help YOU to become the Chief Executive of YOU." The company had been established for over twenty-five years and was doing very well with clients all over the country, ranging from small and medium enterprises to huge corporate giants. No job was too big, or too small. There were no problems, only challenges.

Twenty people worked in a huge open-plan office. It was felt that this was the right environment to encourage teamwork and bonding, as everybody was important at Training4All. The walls of the office were covered in flipcharts that gave the Golden Rules of building a winning team and motivation. With mottos plastered all over people's desks, Walter Channing was listed as the Managing Director at Companies

House, but to everyone in his company he was Chief Performance Enablement Guru. Walt also had his own personal motto, which inevitably had been adopted by most of his employees so they could get on board with Walt's way of thinking. "How can you share yourself with somebody else if you aren't comfortable just being you?" Walt had seen the motto on somebody's online dating profile and had loved the idea. It was how *YOU PLC* had evolved. Walt had described this person as an inspirational young man who had helped him to find his vision and set up Training4All. It was a wonderful story that everyone was told during their two-week team interaction event, whenever they joined the company. Walt felt that induction wasn't the correct term for such an occasion. It wasn't just an induction; it was a holistic socialisation process to enable the new team member to embrace a true sense of belonging from the beginning. Walt knew that his team got that.

As well as an open-plan office, there were two individual smaller offices and one large room. Walt liked to sit in the open-plan office and be amongst the action. He had a spare desk in the Finance Manager's office in case he needed to have some quiet time, although this was rare, and the Finance Manager regarded the place as his own office outright. He was also someone who would not accept a new job title. Walt wasn't particularly good at the numbers side of the business, so he had relented and allowed it to stay as it was. Elizabeth Jamal had then taken a stand and she remained as HR Manager as well. Walt hoped to convince them one day to have a job title which was more inclusive and engaging, but for now that task would remain in the *too hard basket*.

Walt, now in his early sixties, saw himself as a dashing gent who still had a full head of hair, granted that most of it had gone grey. He described his eyes as beautiful sapphires, which sparkled with the excitement of a small child whenever a creative buzz was circulating round the office. He had long delicate fingers that were almost feminine and people told him there was gentleness about his presence. He'd been fortunate not to inherit a middle-aged spread and he still possessed a splendidly slim physique of which a man half his age would have been envious. His whole aura was a mix of gentility and passion. He was childlike at times whenever he had a new idea and he often needed the staff to rein him in, so he didn't wander off on tangents and get lost in a creative blur. He found people were drawn to his warmth and enthusiasm. He had a thick Lancashire drawl that he was proud of. At times people suggested that he made his accent sound thicker than it really was – Walt simply scoffed at their jealousy. However, he did hold a degree in drama and theatre studies.

The other office belonged to Elizabeth Jamal; the HR Manager, although, as it was a small company, she doubled up as the Office Manager as well. Most people tended to have dual roles at Training4All, except for the Performance Enablement Facilitators, who were always either out with clients or coming up with new and wonderful learning interventions in the other room, known as the Creation Room.

The Creation Room was where the magic happened. The walls were covered in whiteboards and it was where the ideas grew into learning innovations. Anyone could put an idea down, and they would have the opportunity to run with it. Walt was never out of the Creation Room. He was one of the few sixty-year-olds to move with the times. He knew that, come sixty-five, he would keep going until they literally had to carry him out. He even wanted to be buried with a pack of dry wipe markers.

Training4All was described by Walt as a working environment which was always buzzing with excitement and energy. A fun place to work. It was important that everyone said good morning to all their colleagues. Walt was thankful the business was in Preston. He'd considered London in the early days; the money was there. However, the thought of being subjected to involuntary molestation and assault whilst crammed into a metal snake moving slowly through tunnels every morning made him shudder – no, according to Walt, Preston was the place to be.

———

Fenton turned off the tape. From Walt's interview, he realised he had only learnt one thing – the guy was a prick!

CHAPTER FIVE

Fenton was sitting in his dark green Vauxhall Astra with Taylor crawling through the London traffic. It was a humid October morning and he was starting to bake. The windows were firmly shut to block out the noise of yet more road works. Even after living in London all his life it still baffled him why utility companies had such a strong aversion to the art of communication. A road would be dug up causing complete chaos for weeks whilst the gas companies did some underground works. After normal service had resumed for a few days, the road would be dug up again, this time by an electric company.

Fenton had decided he didn't want to speak to Elizabeth or Derek again and had let them return home. Following the interview with Wendy, they felt they now had a good background to each of the three victims, albeit a biased one. If Trudie had been the only one murdered, then it would have been likely they'd have had about twenty suspects. They needed to be certain, though, that they were looking for only one killer and only one motive. Preliminary forensics were needed quickly so a strategy could be planned. Fenton had opted for the direct approach. He felt Manning might be less likely to say *piss off* to his face than she would have been on the phone. He'd brought Taylor along, as Manning was always less bolshie when she was in the room.

They arrived at the lab and got out the car.

"You need to get the air conditioning fixed. I'm sweating like glass-blower's arse," Taylor grumbled.

"It works fine. It just eats the fuel, so I always make out that it's broken."

Fenton burst into the lab and was annoyed to see Manning was working on a corpse that wasn't one of his.

She didn't even look up before bellowing, "Robes."

They already had them on, as they were well versed in the etiquette for Manning's lab. She no doubt knew this, but her tone had ensured that an atmosphere lingered like something pungent and unappetising, and it wasn't the dead body.

"I haven't finished with your three yet and if you'd bothered to call, I could have told you that and saved you a wasted journey."

There was a sense of finality in her tone. It insinuated that the conversation was not going to proceed any further. Fenton disagreed with the sentiment and chose to ignore it.

"I'll just have anything you've got, thank you."

"I have to do these in order. Just because you've got a serial killer on the loose doesn't give your case precedence over these other poor souls." she gesticulated with her arm around the room, but Fenton noticed that only one body was out on display, the one she was working on.

"Who said anything about this being a serial killer?"

"As I told you last night, Eric, all three victims have had a stab wound to the heart. It appears that death was instant in all cases. Until you find the murder weapon, I can't be sure, but all three victims have been stabbed with a similar instrument based on the wounds being identical at first inspection. Now I'm no detective but it stands to reason that all three have been killed in the same way, at a similar time, in the same hotel and therefore by balance of probability, by the same person."

"We deal with reasonable doubt in policing."

She glared at him. He suspected that if she had any supernatural powers he'd be melting in acid. Most supernatural beings would shoot sparks or lasers out of their eyes; with her it would be acid.

"Now I might be wrong, but I understood you had to kill three times to become a serial killer, and, look, we have three bodies." She swept her arm across the room and held up three fingers.

Fenton wondered what the hell she was referring to as there were no other bodies in the room. The technical term for their killer was a *spree killer*, but he wasn't going to correct her and risk antagonising her further. They needed her input so they could push the case forwards.

"I want a preliminary report on my desk by four, Ms Manning. I will need to share your findings with my team."

Manning gave Fenton her death stare again and a sweet sickly smile to Taylor, before walking towards her office.

"By four, Ms Manning," he shouted as she slammed her door.

Fenton was steaming and marched straight past his car over to a coffee stand.

"She's taking the piss now. She must have known about the similarities of the stab wounds last night. What is wrong with that woman?"

"She likes to play power games. Let her have her little ego

trip. We've got a lot of good background now because of all the extra interviews. It could be useful. At least we can start casting the suspect net wider now."

Fenton knew she was right and was glad it was nobody else who had seen him lose his temper. It wasn't like him to do that, but that woman could push all the wrong buttons.

Coffee in hand, Fenton started to calm down. He knew he had a briefing that afternoon and then he was going to give the team an early finish for all their hard work the night before. He was also looking forward to his wife's cottage pie and found himself salivating at the thought on the way back to his car.

"Oh shit!"

He turned and saw Taylor looking at a copy of the *London News*.

"Shit, shit, shit, shit," she kept saying.

"What is it?" asked Fenton urgently.

She held up the paper showing the headline.

"Bollocks, bollocks, bollocks."

There, staring him straight in the face was the one thing he didn't want to see.

POLICE HUNT DIVERSITY SLAYER

———

"Sorry, love, it's going to be another late one. You and the girls enjoy it... No, it's okay I'll just grab something here... Bye." Fenton replaced the receiver. He was livid.

"Any idea how she got hold of it so quickly?" asked Taylor.

"I have an idea, but no proof of course."

"Interesting how the press seemed to know it were the same killer for all victims before we'd even issued a press release."

"Exactly!"

"It's not a serial killer though. This is just going to cause panic."

"Well it's going to be referred to as a serial killer now by everyone. This is just what she wants – drama and panic."

Taylor left the room and Fenton slumped back in his chair. He surveyed his office and wasn't sure if he'd used this one before. They all looked the same. Magnolia walls that were covered with notice boards full of multi-coloured drawing pins. A few obligatory Metropolitan Police posters, with one in prime position offering free 24/7 telephone counselling to help you with work-related stress. Fenton had never bothered to call one of those help lines. It wasn't that he thought it was beneath him, he just believed stress was an integral part of the job. It was his strongest motivator. He already knew that this would be a stressful case. It was still less than twenty-four hours since the murders had occurred, and he knew he needed a quick result. Polly Pilkington had already called requesting an interview. She was kindly told to take a running jump – in fact, she was told to piss off and crawl back into her hole, but she'd caught Fenton at the wrong time and he was annoyed that she seemed to have his private mobile number.

He regarded people like Ms Manning as just an annoying fly which tended to bugger off after it had finished buzzing round your head for a while. Pilkington was different. She was like a wasp, the insect that stings you for absolutely no reason, and will keep stinging you again and again, for the simple reason that it could.

―――――

Polly Pilkington worked for the *London News*. It was a rival to the *Evening Standard*. One of those free papers that's thrust into your hands every evening, regardless of whether you wanted it or not.

She was a true North Londoner. She'd been born in Camden and was still there. She owned an expansive loft apartment overlooking Camden Lock. She had natural blonde hair cut short and, despite what people said about her looking boyish, she knew she was pure femme. Anyway, they soon changed their opinion when they got to her chest, which was gigantic; and all natural despite the rumours, which were all bullshit. Why was it assumed that there is no such thing as a natural blonde, with natural big tits? She wasn't afraid to use her feminine charms to their full extent in order to have men eating out of her hand, and a good few women as well: flattery and big tits got you everywhere. Her perfect hourglass figure and healthy orange glow were what made men stop and stare. She had her own spray tan machine and had saved thousands on salon bills within the first three months, as she used it daily. Polly always wore business suits as she felt this gave her a more intimidating look. She no longer wore anything in black as, during one of their many confrontations, Fenton had remarked that the suit, her bleached blond hair and orange skin made her look like a bollard with a warning light ablaze on top of it. He was the only man whom she couldn't bend to her will. Maybe he was an arse man; she didn't regard her arse as one of her best features.

She'd started her journalistic routes at the *Camden Echo,* and it was one story that secured her a role at the *London News.* That was the reason Fenton despised her.

She knew of Fenton's exemplary record at the Metropolitan Police. Every murder he'd been assigned to as DCI, he'd managed to solve. He was leading the case on the murder of a young boy, whose body had been discovered in Camden Lock. It appeared the poor boy had been strangled and then dumped. There were no witnesses, no forensics and, as far as she could ascertain, no suspects.

Pilkington had discovered Fenton's wife was pregnant with a son. Shortly before the murder occurred, there were complications and the child had died late in the pregnancy. Pilkington had obtained the hospital report and the trauma of the miscarriage had also meant his wife had to undergo a hysterectomy. There would be no more children and Fenton had three daughters. He must have been gutted not to have his male heir. Despite what they say, every man wanted a son.

Fenton had been brought back early from compassionate leave as the Chief Superintendent wanted someone, he could trust on such a sensitive case, according to Pilkington's source. Fenton had thrown himself into the case, although he failed to secure an arrest.

Pilkington believed that the police had made a mistake using him to lead such a critical investigation, just because he had an exemplary record and was good PR. The man was obviously emotionally unstable. She felt it was her duty to report it to the public.

————

POOR POLICING IN CAMDEN LOCK KILLING
Polly Pilkington

Police are still no closer to finding the person responsible for the brutal murder of six-year-old Jack Davies. The young boy was abducted and strangled before being dumped in Camden Lock two weeks ago. No arrests have been made.

Concerns from poor Jack's family were heightened earlier today when it emerged the lead detective in tracking the killer, DCI Eric

Fenton, was assigned the case whilst on compassionate leave following the still-birth of his own son. Sources close to the case have confirmed that there is no forensic evidence and no witnesses have come forward. As time passes, it is understood the police privately believe they have little hope of ever catching Jack's killer. It is thought vital evidence from early in the case has been lost due to procedural blunders by the investigating officers.

It is rumoured DCI Fenton will soon be removed from the case as it is thought he is not the right man to lead the investigation forward. A source close to the investigation said, "He's in a deep depression since the death of his son. His focus on the case has become very lax. In cases like these the first few days are crucial, and a lot of errors were made. I doubt now if we will ever find Jack's killer."

Jack's family were not available to comment on the latest developments, but a close friend of the family said, "Clearly they are devastated to think that Jack's killer will never be brought to justice."

———

Fenton had regarded the Pilkington article as a personal attack. He had refused to give Pilkington an interview regarding the case and when she had persisted, he had given her a piece of his mind.

"It's people like you that are taking up valuable police time. Time which could be spent trying to catch the killer."

"Do you think you're the right man to lead the investigation considering your own recent loss, DCI Fenton?" she asked.

"If you call this police station again, I'll have your arrested for obstruction of justice, you obnoxious bitch." He slammed down the receiver.

Just twenty-four hours later that article was in print. The local news channels picked it up and before long the matter was national. Fenton was kept on the case. However, with press intrusion at every corner, the investigation stalled and in time the case was wound down. It would never be closed. Fenton had promised the parents that, one day, the killer would be brought to justice, although to this day they remained at large.

Fenton saw the value the press could bring to policing and was always willing to give statements or interviews if it meant jogging the memories of potential witnesses or hitting the conscience of the killer, or whoever might be hiding them. He didn't particularly like rolling families out in front of the cameras, but it had been crucial in breaking several cases in the past.

What he didn't like was the sort of journalism Polly Pilkington adopted. She was a ruthless and overly ambitious individual who would stop at nothing for her story. She was always careful never to lie blatantly, only to sensationalise the truth for maximum effect. Fenton had a suspicion that she was in cahoots with Manning, who was leaking the stories. Fenton had tried numerous times to get a different pathologist, but she was the top one in his area and, despite being an egotistical cow, she was good – much to Fenton's annoyance.

This latest scoop of Pilkington's had Manning all over it, but there was no proof. This time though he was determined to find it; first he had a killer to catch.

———

POLICE HUNT DIVERSITY SLAYER
Polly Pilkington

Police in London are hunting for a serial killer. The perpetrator struck at a "diversity" conference at the Hotel Draconian near London Euston station.

Last night, three bodies were found brutally stabbed to death.

Police have no leads and are not working on the assumption that the cases are linked. All three victims were killed in the same way and within a similar timeframe, so this just highlights the ineptitude of the investigating team. The victims were also at the same conference, work for the same company and are all from minority groups.

The oldest victim, Trudie Longhurst, 64, was a wheelchair user. A Muslim man, Nadeem Jamal, 37, and a Black man, Carl Davenport, 32, were also slain. All three were employees at Training4All, a training consultancy based in Preston, Lancashire.

Sources close to the police reveal they are concerned that the investigation is not assuming these murders are linked and there is a fear there may be more victims as the "diversity slayer" aims to complete the set. There are currently nine protected characteristics within UK equality law. It is unsure who could be next.

This comes after the recent case of Peter Goode, 42, who murdered his son's Pakistani girlfriend as he did not want them to marry. Goode was sentenced on Monday to life imprisonment but could be free to kill again in as little as 15 years.

No leaders of the three main political parties were available for comment on this latest hate crime last night. With the current Parliamentary session due to close in six weeks' time, it is still not known if the Prime Minister will announce tougher sentencing measures in the Queen's Speech, despite pressure from the Leader of the Opposition and general public to take stronger action against violent criminals.

CHAPTER SIX

The Leader of the Opposition described himself, privately, in two words – *smooth bastard*. He had charm, charisma and was desperate for power. The public adored him, as they usually did whenever something bad happened and their venom was targeted at the serving Prime Minister. The advantage to being on the other team was that you were an unknown entity, and when the competition had delivered nothing but catastrophic fuck ups, something different gave hope to the masses.

He was a young leader at thirty-five, with a working-class background, vastly different from previous leaders. The party had felt that, by electing him as their *face*, they would look *real*. What they didn't realise was they were electing an extremely ambitious individual who was not going to play the part of puppet. His predecessors had allowed themselves to be controlled by the political elite at the top of the party. They had paid the price at the ballot box. Things were going to be different this time. He was calling the shots and he was going to be the next Prime Minister.

The only flaw in his plan was that the election was three

years away. That was if the current Prime Minister could hold out that long. The government's majority was now down to single figures. It was steadily decreasing as by-elections and defections ate away at it. The likelihood of being able to force an election was becoming ever nearer. It was a motivating thought. He longed to get out on the campaign trail and show the public that things would be different this time. It wouldn't be the same old bullshit, just wearing a different coloured rosette.

With his dashing good looks, he had it all and enjoyed the fact that his counterpart, who was another young leader and only three years older than him, looked completely worn out. The public suspected the age gap was closer to twenty years and there was much speculation in the press that the Prime Minister had lied about his age. He'd had to publish his birth certificate to refute the claims. That had been an enjoyable few days. It was amazing the drama that one little anonymous phone call could create.

The Leader of the Opposition liked to keep fit, which he did at his local Council gym. It was good to be seen by the public, and not be seen to be splashing his wealth around. He'd made millions in property development, but his East London dialect, which he took speech lessons to maintain, made people feel as if he was one of them. He saw his personal trainer away from prying eyes and played into the vacuous mindset of the public. It was amazing how quickly a photo could become viral when you *accidentally* mopped your brow with the bottom of your t-shirt, after running 10km through the streets of London. His abdominal muscles now had their own fan page on social media.

He was reading the article by Polly Pilkington, as he did his PR for the day, by using the exercise bike at his local gym. He knew her by reputation. They had never met in person, and she had barely mentioned him in her articles, but he knew she was not a fan of the incumbent at 10 Downing Street. This meant they had something in common. Did she feel strongly enough for it to be a common enemy? His brain whizzed into gear. The fact that three people had been brutally murdered was irrelevant, sad, but still unimportant. The article had given him a potential opening to put further pressure on the Prime Minister. Jumping off the bike he snapped instructions into his mobile phone, ordering his minions to converge on party headquarters. He had a plan and he was going to need Polly Pilkington's help to execute it.

―――

OPPOSITION SUPPORT TOUGH CRIME MEASURES
Polly Pilkington

The Leader of the Opposition has come out in support of tougher crime measures, particularly when dealing with hate crime.

"We will be looking to bring in swift new laws to tackle this abomination that is polluting our society once we are in government, but the Prime Minister must act now. How many people must be violently killed before he realises that his crime measures don't go far enough?"

He was speaking in response to yesterday's exclusive article that revealed the police are looking for a serial killer. The killer struck two nights ago at a conference, murdering three people from minority groups.

"The upsurge in hate crime is abhorrent. I will be raising these grave concerns from the public at Prime Minister's Question's tomorrow!" he added.

Police are still nowhere near identifying a suspect, as concerns mount that the killer will strike again.

"I've had eighty per cent of my bookings cancelled. I wish the

police would do something. This is concerning, people are scared,"
exclaimed the General Manager of Hotel Draconian.

The investigation is being led by DCI Eric Fenton, 45. Sources
close to the investigation tell us that he refuses to believe this is hate
crime related and may even be working on the assumption that it is
some form of "domestic." It is rumoured that if Fenton does not appre-
hend a suspect within the next 48 hours then he will be removed from
the case.

Five years ago, DCI Fenton, failed to catch the killer of a young
boy who was strangled and dumped in a London canal. At the time he
was grieving for the death of his unborn son and sources close to the
investigation claim that vital evidence was lost due to DCI Fenton
failing to steer the investigation, caused by his lack of focus. The killer
is still at large.

This raises the question about whether an officer with this history
should be leading such a high-profile case. It is evident that a hate
crime motive should be where police attention is focussed, otherwise
more families will be devastated when yet another killer, being hunted
by DCI Fenton, escapes justice.

The Leader of the Opposition smiled as he read the article.

"What do you think?" he asked his chief minion, or
Personal Assistant as was his official title, or was it Executive
Assistant these days? He made a mental note to check the job
title; he didn't like to be made to look like he didn't give a shit
about his staff. It wasn't good publicity.

"Very good, sir," came the standard reply.

"I think we need to pile on the pressure ahead of PMQs.
A bit more PR is needed."

The minion got out his notebook and gave an attentive
look. The Leader of the Opposition knew he was taking the
piss, but he was a top-class minion, who had the contacts.

"I think what we need is a photo. Perhaps I could be seen talking or even hugging a crippled child. Of course, I will be outraged that the press has witnessed such a private moment!"

"Okay, sir, I'll get it arranged."

"Hold on a minute. What colour do you think the child should be?"

"Sorry, sir?"

"Well, it would be good to kill two birds with one stone, so to speak. Why not more than two birds? Why don't we use a teenager who is aware that they're gay, and perhaps they could be Muslim as well, and female? Although it would be good to have the set. Maybe she could be pregnant, in a civil partnership and be about to undergo a sex change once the baby is born?"

"I don't know if we could find someone who ticks all those boxes before noon."

"You're right, I suppose. Just the crippled child then." He clicked his fingers prompting the minion to rush off to arrange the photo shoot.

Maybe I should check what his name is as well whilst I'm checking the job title.

———

The Prime Minister was irritated. His opposite number was scoring political points by using a triple murder. He didn't like the dirty side of politics and resented the fact this made him look weak to the public. It was a vicious cycle. Something would happen and the media would jump on it, creating hype. The public would then demand a response and you were expected to react immediately with no thought about the implications of what you were suggesting. That was not how people worked in business. You didn't just jump into things without well-thought out planning and discussion, as well as consulting experts. However, if you didn't react in the moment you were considered weak. That was the advantage of being the Leader of the Opposition. You could promise anything as you were never going to be held to it. By the time the next election came around, people would have forgotten all the promises. If you were in power and you acted rashly then you were punished when it went wrong. If you took time to think about the best course of action, then you were punished for being ineffective; you literally could not win.

The Prime Minister tossed the newspaper to one side and rubbed his eyes. Studying himself in the mirror he was reminded again that he was looking old. Seven years in the job had taken its toll. To become Prime Minister at thirty-one was something he was immensely proud of, and now the man in the mirror resembled a pensioner.

His dark brown hair was greying at the temples, although this didn't give him the same distinguished look as his counterpart. It just made him look like some seedy geriatric. The creases under his eyes were now more apparent and what were once doleful brown eyes, as described by his mother, now looked beady and shifty. No wonder the public were getting turned off. Would you trust someone who was a dead ringer for a crypt keeper to run the country? There was still a lot of progressive policies he wanted to introduce before he handed over the baton.

One of his secretaries entered the room. "Excuse me, sir, your car's here to take you to the Commons."

"Thanks," he said, not really paying attention.

He knew it was going to be a bloodbath today. He knew there was only one way to fight the mudslinging and that was to throw it back. He was determined not be forced into making snap policy decisions by the other side. He had also wanted Prime Minister's Questions to become a more professional affair and to stop all the jeering and children's playground antics but trying to control over six-hundred people was no easy task. It was also difficult to not get swept up by the theatrics, and today was going to be a circus.

———

CRIME AGAINST US ALL
Polly Pilkington

The Prime Minister refused to be drawn into important policy decisions on law and order today. He stated he had "The utmost confidence in the police that they will bring the killer, dubbed the diversity slayer by the media, to justice."

He deflected questions from the Leader of the Opposition regarding the hate crime motive for these murders. "It would be wrong to make such speculations whilst the police investigation is ongoing." He also took a swipe at the press. "The press intrusion with this case could reduce our ability to provide a fair trial, which could result in a triple murderer being set free."

The Leader of the Opposition was quick to scorn these comments. "This man is so out of touch with the public he isn't fit for office."

With a general election potentially three years away, pressure mounts on the Prime Minister as he clings to power. Last week's by-election saw the government's working majority now reduced to five. With more by-elections due in the coming weeks, following several MPs standing down, due to various scandals, there is an increasing possibility that the governing party will soon have no outright majority, and a no confidence vote is highly likely.

There was still no word from the Prime Minister on what we can expect to see in the Queen's Speech, which has now been moved back to its traditional November slot. Rumours close to the Prime Minister suggest that a big policy announcement is in the pipeline but, when pressed on this, he refused to discuss the matter further.

Meanwhile police are still no further along in their investigation. The lead officer, DCI Eric Fenton, 45, refuses to speak with the press or ask them for any help. He now only has 24 hours to reach a breakthrough, or rumour suggests, he will be removed from the case.

———

The Prime Minister knew it was going to turn nasty but felt he had held his ground well. He was having a meeting with Detective Chief Superintendent Beeden who was updating him on the case. Not usual protocol, however, this was an unusual case. He also wanted to have one up on his counterpart who seemed to be far more knowledgeable about this case than he should be, given his position.

"I don't want to interfere with a police investigation, but the press is making it very difficult."

"You're right, Prime Minister, the investigating team are following every lead. We're hoping for further forensic detail imminently," replied Beeden.

"Are you working on the hate crime angle, or is that just a press storm?"

"It's one of several lines of enquiry."

"Is there even any proof that it's a hate crime, or is this Pilkington woman creating a panic for her own personal gain?"

"She's certainly fuelling the fire, sir."

"Perhaps it's just some random killer, which doesn't fill me with a lot of confidence, or the victims were just unpleasant people, and somebody snapped?"

Beeden smiled. "That's another possibility Prime Minister."

"What about this talk of changing the lead detective? I understand he has an exemplary track record, except for one unfortunate case."

"I have no intention of removing DCI Fenton from this case. He's one of my best officers and I could think of nobody better to lead the team. It's all just rumour-mongering and I'd ignore anything Pilkington says."

"Bit difficult when I keep hearing her quoted across the Commons."

———

That evening, the Leader of the Other Party appeared on a national news channel to voice his opinion about the murders. He felt he could bring a neutral approach to the escalating controversy. Unfortunately, and much to his dismay, the PR department had scheduled the interview to air at the same time as *Cake Shop Hell* – a new reality TV show where overweight individuals were forced to work and live in a cake shop for three months. Their every move was monitored and each week the two that cracked and ate the most cakes would be put to the public vote. This week the national hero, Debbie, had been on an eating binge after an argument with one of her competitors. Ten million people tuned in to watch her survive the public vote. The rest of the population were enjoying the weather, as it was still twenty degrees, in October. Nobody bothered to watch the news.

CHAPTER SEVEN

Fenton massaged his temples as he scrutinised the pile of newspapers in front of him. The story had now gone national, although it was Pilkington leading the assault and making it personal. He banged the desk in anger. He knew he should be getting ready for the briefing, but he couldn't help it. He was drawn back to the articles, scouring them, looking for anything that would give him proof that Manning was the leak.

Bringing the unsolved murder of a young boy back to the forefront was what really got to Fenton. It wasn't fair on the family. They had never blamed him, and they had assured him that they knew everything had been done to catch their son's killer. Fenton still visited them each month to see how they were coping. Nobody on the team knew that he did this, not even Taylor. Beeden knew about it, but that was due to Fenton's respect for his boss. He didn't want any backlash coming back on him. Fenton wasn't doing anything wrong and the fact Beeden knew about it would mean that if the press found out, it would be quickly dealt with. Fenton had kept promising himself to look at the Davies case again, but there had been no let-up in caseloads for some time. Normally he would be juggling a few cases at once but, due to the number of murders and the high-profile nature of this case, the Chief Superintendent had assigned Fenton, Taylor, Brennan and Shirkham, with a dozen other officers and support staff, solely to this case. They wanted a quick result, or at least a suspect – and they wanted it yesterday.

His gut instinct was telling him that there was more to this than just random chance, but the pressure came from above to treat it as a hate crime, so that's what he had to do.

"Eric, this is starting to get out of hand. The bloody politicians are poking their noses in now," grumbled Chief Superintendent Harry Beeden.

"I have an idea where the leak is coming from, sir, but it's difficult to prove."

"Forget it. Concentrate on the case. We'll worry about the leak later. Last thing we need is a bloody complaint as well."

"Yes, sir."

"So where are we now with the investigation?"

"I'm going to take some of the immediate team up north to speak to all the employees again at Training4All. It could just be an inside job."

"Not very likely, if it's a hate crime angle."

"I'm not a hundred per cent sure that it is hate crime, sir."

"Yes, well, keep that to yourself."

"Sir?"

"Come on, Eric, you've been in this job a long time. Image is everything in policing."

"I thought it was to maintain law and order, sir."

"Eric, you've never struck me as the naïve type!"

"We have a briefing shortly. Would you like to sit in?"

"I'll leave it in your capable hands Eric."

"Okay, sir," Fenton replied, getting up to leave.

"Don't make it personal between you and Pilkington."

"Bit late for that, isn't it?"

"I trust your instincts, Eric, so follow them if you must, but keep it quiet. I want the hate crime angle followed publicly. Image and politics are at the epicentre of policing."

Fenton nodded and left. At first, he thought his old mate was taking the piss, but he'd seen that look before, so knew he was deadly serious. If Beeden was putting the pressure on Fenton, then it could only mean one thing; someone even higher up the ladder was putting the pressure on Beeden.

Fenton was back in his office with Taylor, Brennan and Shirkham. He wanted a quiet word with them before he spoke to the whole team.

"The four of us are going to head up north straight after the briefing. Emma, can you sort us out some accommodation? We'll drive up in my car so we can discuss the case on the way in private."

"Just the one night, sir?" asked Shirkham.

"Better make it two but make it a flexible booking in case we can get back quicker. Gary, when we get up north, I want you to work on Wendy Baxter."

"Oh, cheers, Guv."

"She's a gossip who knows everyone and everything about that company. If it was an inside job then, she'll know who hated who, who was screwing who and probably who the murderer is! Plus, she's got no alibi."

"Is she a suspect, Guv? You can't be serious?"

"Deadly. She's a suspect until proven otherwise. We're not a jury, it's guilty until proven innocent with everyone. You'll need to butter her up. This is your trademark, so you're the best one to talk to her. A bit of flattery will get you everywhere."

"Hopefully not everywhere, sir. I do have some standards, you know."

"Judging by the WPC from the other week, I doubt that very much," scoffed Taylor.

"How the hell do you know about that?" replied Brennan, blushing profusely.

"Can we leave the soap opera for Training4All," snapped Fenton.

Brennan and Shirkham went to leave the office and, just before he opened the door, Brennan turned around with an inane grin on his face.

"What?" asked Fenton tetchily.

"How about a group hug?"

"Piss off," replied Fenton, shaking his head, and laughing.

Fenton and Taylor were left alone.

"Lisa, I need you to do something for me quietly."

"Prove Manning is leaking to Pilkington?"

"Am I that transparent?

"No, I just know you won't let go of anything."

He gave a non-committal shrug.

"Maybe I can catch them together being cosy?"

"I really don't care what they get up to, but they obviously do, otherwise they'd be more open about it. At least if she's shacked up with Pilkington, she might stop fawning over you."

"I doubt that very much, sir," she replied tossing her hair.

Fenton chuckled. It was the first time he'd laughed or smiled in what seemed like ages. The case was only a week old, yet it felt like months had passed by. This was normal on cases that stuttered in their early days, although still frustrating for everyone. He was sure their killer was now thinking they were safe up north, but he wasn't going to rule out some random nutter in the capital either, just in case.

Fenton called everyone together and looked at the incident board. There were quite a few new additions since the last briefing, which was hopefully a good sign. He'd had to tell his wife he was going to be away for a couple of nights, so he may miss his youngest daughter's birthday party. She'd told him not to worry and that she'd be so busy with all her friends that she wouldn't notice anything. Fenton knew this wasn't strictly true. When they're toddlers maybe, but when they're ten they did tend to notice things.

"Right, what do we have on the other unsolved murders within the M25?"

Brennan, who was in his usual jovial mood, got up and started to recite from his notebook...

"There are two possible cases that may have a link."

"Out of how many?" asked Fenton.

"Forty-six."

Fenton gestured for him to carry on.

"Both were stabbed, and they came from minority groups."

"Talk us through each one."

"The first was a nineteen-year-old black woman, who was found dumped on Hampstead Heath. She was found by two men who were out for an evening stroll."

"At what time?"

"Three o'clock in the morning!"

Everyone laughed.

"There's no sign of any sexual assault or robbery, and the investigating team have not been able to find a motive." He pointed to the case details on the board.

She looked exceptionally beautiful, even in death, although Fenton suspected that there was no link to his case.

"The next one was a gay white male who was stabbed in a shop doorway. No sign of sexual assault or robbery again with this one."

"Where was this one?"

"Soho."

"Any witnesses?"

"No."

"Naturally."

Brennan closed his notebook and sat back down.

"Forensics?" Fenton asked, looking at Shirkham.

She got up and made her way to the front. "They believe that the murder weapon could be the *World's Sharpest Knife*."

"What?"

"The *World's Sharpest Knife* has two prongs at the end, and they are used in the kitchens at the Hotel Draconian. Apparently, you will only ever need *one* knife for the rest of your life. Despite that claim, Forensics have seized a dozen from the kitchen and will be running tests on them later today. The manager was not best pleased when we seized all his knives. He said he was going to make a complaint."

"Bollocks, a complaint's the last thing we need."

"Apparently Manning was her usual charming self when she ordered them to be seized."

"That request should have come through me."

"She went to the Chief Super."

"Did she now. Right, carry on."

"The families of the victims keep asking when the bodies are going to be released so they can arrange the funerals."

"What's Manning said?"

"'I'll release the bodies when I'm satisfied that we have everything we need. We are dealing with science here,'" replied Shirkham, in a fantastic impression of Manning.

The incident room was now falling about in hysterics.

"Settle down now everyone," shouted Fenton, although he couldn't help grinning himself.

"Manning said she wants to examine Trudie's body again. She's not completely satisfied with the angle that the knife went into the heart. It's different to the other two."

"Perhaps because she was sitting in a wheelchair and the others were standing," replied Fenton sarcastically.

"I questioned that and was told that I wasn't a scientist."

"Typical. When is she going to examine the body again?"

"Tomorrow at the earliest."

"Is she taking the piss? Tell her I want that body examined today. There might be something crucial that we can use when we're up north."

There was a murmur amongst the other officers following this statement. Fenton gestured for Shirkham to sit down.

"I'm heading up north with Taylor, Brennan and Shirkham. I want more investigation into these other two murders, so they can be ruled in or out as soon as possible."

He was pacing backwards and forwards as he was talking. He noticed everyone was following him with their eyes, like they were watching a tennis match. The tenacity with which he was pacing, though, must have been making them feel dizzy. This was confirmed when a junior officer fell off her chair. Everyone ignored her out of politeness as she stumbled back to her feet looking dazed.

"We're dealing with some form of hate crime angle here." The words felt bitter as they came out. "There are one of two possibilities. It's some random attacker, and these other cases might be linked, or it was an inside job within Training4All. I want a briefing here on Monday morning. I think we could all do with a Sunday off, so knuckle down for the next two days and you can have it."

The briefing ended and everyone went back to their desks

working at twice the speed they were prior to the briefing. This was a usual response after a briefing had re-energised people, although it was also because the words *day* and *off* are more motivating than the word *beer*.

Taylor, Brennan and Shirkham stepped forward.

"Get yourselves home and pack a bag. Hopefully, we can crack through everything and be back by Saturday. I think we could all do with Sunday at home as I suspect we'll have a lot to look at on Monday morning. Be back here in two hours ready to go."

They all left quickly, as getting across London and back in two hours was more challenging than climbing Everest. Fenton always had an overnight bag, which was good for a couple of days in the office, so he knew that he had some time to himself before the long schlep up the motorway to Preston.

———

POLICE TRACK DOWN DIVERSITY SLAYER
Polly Pilkington

The lead police officers in the Diversity Slayer case travelled to the north-west of England earlier today as the hunt intensified for the serial killer who committed three brutal hate murders just seven days ago in a London hotel.

All victims were employees of Training4All, a training consultancy based in Preston, a small city in Lancashire. Police now believe the killer is a fellow employee. With a company housing such a diverse workforce, there are grave concerns that the killer will strike again in order to complete their set of "protected characteristics" under equality law.

The police are still stumped as to which of the equality strands the killer has already crossed off their list, with all three victims covering at least two. The big question is not if the killer will strike again, but when!

Despite the lack of any development, the case is still being led by DCI Eric Fenton, 45. Sources close to the police claim that the investigating team are very despondent with the way Fenton is leading the investigation. It is known that Chief Superintendent Harry Beeden is a close friend of Fenton, and this is likely to be the reason why Fenton remains in charge of the case. It is believed that, should a breakthrough not occur by next week, then Fenton is highly likely to go.

The Leader of the Opposition has responded to the lack of progress in the case with grave concern.

"It is deeply troublesome that a suspect has not yet been identified. I also strongly believe that when the suspect is apprehended, an exceptionally light sentence is likely, given this government insists on a wishy-washy approach to law and order."

The Prime Minister is yet to respond to these latest allegations about his soft approach to crime and was unavailable for comment earlier today.

Meanwhile a survey has been commissioned to gauge public opinion about suitable punishment for the Diversity Slayer, if they are ever brought to justice.

———

Polly Pilkington surveyed the article again and reclined on her aubergine-coloured chaise longue with a glass of Merlot, stretching her body so her back arched, giving her a sense of absolute pleasure.

The sun was still streaming into her loft. It was a beautiful October evening and she felt good. The sales of the paper were up dramatically, and her editor had congratulated her personally on what he described as excellent intuitive journalism.

It was only a matter of time before she was promoted,

he'd told her. She'd acted delighted at the prospect, but this was merely her steppingstone to the nationals. She had no intention of staying at some low-budget free newspaper that most people would line their cat litter trays with tomorrow. The longer this case remained unsolved, the happier she was. If she brought everything crashing down around Fenton's ears, then that would be job done. Men are bastards and deserved to be treated with absolute contempt. Her mobile rang. She sat up, glanced at the screen, and clicked it open.

"Hello, darlink. Did you see the paper?" she asked with a purr in her voice. "I know... thank you for letting me know about the trip up north, darlink. It's always good to keep ahead of the nationals... I know, darlink. I know. My editor is delighted. Stupid moron thinks I've got a long-term future with the paper." She cackled with laughter. "It's a shame I can't see you this weekend, but I know you have to work... Bye now, darlink."

She ended the call and sank back, taking a generous gulp of wine.

Oh, life is good!

CHAPTER EIGHT

Fenton hadn't seen the *London News* as he had left the capital in the morning and it didn't hit the streets until the afternoon. The team were bickering amongst themselves about who was going to be the one to tell him. Nobody fancied hearing the word bollocks a hundred times in their ear.

"Get the newbie to tell him," suggested one of the officers to his colleague.

"She already fell off her chair in front of everyone. It would be a bit cruel to have her break this to the boss as well," she replied.

"I wouldn't call it cruel."

"What would you call it then?"

"Character building!"

———

The journey to Preston had been largely uneventful, Fenton thought. Alarmingly clear roads. It was astonishing how warm it still was. Brennan was driving Fenton's car, with the occasional back-seat interference about the air-conditioner wasting fuel. He liked to look green; in all honesty he was just a tight arse with three expensive daughters.

Shirkham had phoned ahead and arranged with the local police force that they would head straight to Training4All. The local DCI had seemed relieved that they weren't being asked for much involvement. He had given the impression that a triple murder with national press attention was not very welcome and the less they had to do with it the better. This was Fenton's preference. He was very respectful of local police forces, but they usually didn't have the experience or manpower to support large murder investigations. It wasn't unusual for them to call in the Metropolitan Police to support cases which happened on their territory. Fenton had once spent a month in Harrogate, investigating a double murder. The team he had worked with had been excellent, but without the experience, there were lines of enquiry which were missed in the early days. Still, they caught the killer and Fenton was then back home; it was the longest he had ever been away. He'd been out of town before on investigations, but he was usually back every weekend. That case had been all-consuming without a single day off in a month. Fenton hoped this case wouldn't turn out the same, which is why he had got in early with giving the team a day off. There was no way of predicting when the next one would come.

Fenton had decided that he wanted to tackle specific people on the Friday and wanted to go to the company offices to do this. Elizabeth Jamal and Derek Longhurst were off on bereavement leave, so he would speak with them the next day. Wendy Baxter was at home, signed off with stress. She'd wanted bereavement leave; apparently GBBF was not listed as eligible in the company policy.

Brennan was to go to Wendy's house alone and see what he could get out of her. Fenton added that he might also like to return the next day to speak with her personally. The fact that the DCI wanted to speak with her could make her feel far more important than she was. Brennan was to allow her to ramble on about trivial bollocks as there might be something hidden in the drivel. Brennan had remarked that the only bollocks he was concerned about were his own.

"Gary, you can deal with the hysterics today and I'll get the facts tomorrow."

"Cheers, Guv, really appreciate it!"

Fenton wanted to speak to the company owner, Walter Channing and Peter Gleeson who was the Finance guy. He also had Jeremiah Tool on his list, who was the IT guy. They had all missed dinner on the night of the murder and technically had no firm alibi, along with Wendy Baxter. It was a good starting point, and except for Walter and Wendy, they were in professions other than training. Fenton and Taylor were to tackle the three interviews and Shirkham was to confirm alibis of the other eleven members of staff. Everyone had been asked to be on site, where possible. This had apparently not been a problem as it was company policy not to deliver training to their clients on a Friday. Walt had stated that this was the day of the week when learners would be leaving the learning zone and their own socialisation needs would become their dominant state – which Fenton translated as nobody learns anything on a Friday as their brain has already checked out for the week and they are too focussed on getting shit faced in the evening.

Fenton had scheduled interviews for the following morning with Elizabeth and Derek. That way he could potentially be home to spend the evening with his family for his daughter's birthday. He would still miss her part in the daytime, although his wife was better skilled than him at handling two dozen ten-year olds who were high on fizzy drinks. Of course, it was dependent on everything going to plan, which in his experience, was usually wishful thinking.

Walter Channing gave off the aura that he was hosting a cocktail evening. He appeared to find the whole experience of being interviewed rather exciting. Fenton's initial thought that he was a prick had not abated. Looking at Walt, he couldn't see how he could murder anybody, but he'd been surprised by killers in the past. Failing his emergence as a suspect, he felt that standing in front of him was just a thinner, more delicate, older, and male version of Wendy. Fenton guessed that here was another gossip, so he would let Taylor lead the interview. Fenton could see himself getting irritated by the guy's lack of focus. It was like he was auditioning for *The Nutcracker*. Another stereotype was walking and talking in front of him; or in Walt's case, floating and gushing.

"Such a terrible, terrible, business," said Walt.

Fenton had heard him talk before, yet the deep Lancashire accent still threw him. The voice didn't match the person in front of him.

"As the only victims came from your company, we can't rule out the fact the killer is also one of your employees," stated Taylor.

Fenton was all for the direct approach.

"How awful. How absolutely, ghastly," was Walt's dramatic response. "I can't believe it. I won't believe it. It's just unspeakable. Nobody here could do something so heinous. I know these people. They're like my own children."

Fenton suspected this was going to be another load of waffle, only to come away with bugger all that would progress the investigation. He wondered how Brennan was getting on with Wendy, and if she'd tried to jump him yet. He smiled, then realised this would be inappropriate given the nature of the conversation that was going on next to him, and his serious face resumed.

"Can you tell me your whereabouts at the time of the murders? That would be between eight and nine thirty? The same time everyone were at dinner," asked Taylor.

Fenton could tell Taylor was also irritable from the brutal way she was firing off the questions. He knew she couldn't stand people who found murder enquiries an opportunity to perform some dying swan routine.

"Dear God," exclaimed Walt, clutching his chest in a dramatic fashion. "Surely you can't suspect me?"

"Just answer the question, Mr Channing," replied Taylor, making a point of visibly raising her eyebrows.

"I must have been at dinner with the others," he spluttered.

"You've already told us that you missed dinner that evening as you had a private engagement."

"Ah yes, well it's a bit delicate, my dear."

"Just tell us his name, so we can verify your alibi."

Fenton was, for a rare moment, shocked.

"That's very presumptuous of you, dear."

Taylor raised her eyebrows again, and her mouth twitched upwards at the side.

Walt gave a sheepish grin. "I must ask for discretion."

Taylor nodded.

"I'll just get you a number," he said, before floating out of the room.

"That was a bit close to the bone, wasn't it? What if you were wrong?" asked Fenton.

Taylor repeated the same look she'd given Walt just a few seconds before.

He nodded his head in agreement, barely able to suppress a smile.

. . .

Peter Gleeson had some physical similarities to Walt, but that was where it ended. They were similar height and build, although Peter was in his forties, and he looked like an accountant. Fenton had deduced this as he felt that the man looked incredibly boring and, based on looks, he didn't think this was who they were looking for either. This time Fenton led the questioning.

"Where were you between eight and nine thirty on the night in question?"

"I was in my room, alone. I hadn't been feeling well, so I skipped the evening meal as I wanted to try and shake off my lethargy before the trip back the next day." He also had a Lancashire accent, albeit subtle and, thankfully, he had a full vocabulary, unlike Wendy.

"When did you become aware of what had happened?"

"I woke up to Elizabeth's hysterical screams."

"So, you weren't aware of Trudie's murder, which was discovered some forty minutes prior to the discovery of Nadeem Jamal?"

"Evidently not, if Elizabeth's screams woke me."

He seemed a bit too cocky and confident for Fenton's liking. "When did you discover that Trudie Longhurst had been murdered?"

"That was much later." He sighed, looking bored. "I came out of my room and heard that Nadeem had been found dead. I had no idea at the time that foul play was involved. It was only about an hour or so later that one of your officers knocked on my door and asked to take a statement. She told me that three bodies had been found and that you were treating them as suspicious. Naturally, I then assumed one of these had been Nadeem and, after I told your officer all I could. I then went to speak with a colleague, and she informed me of the whole grisly affair."

"Which officer was it that interviewed you?"

"I'm sorry, I don't remember the name. It was a lady and I believe she had an Irish accent."

"DC Shirkham?"

"Yes, that sounds right."

"The same officer who is outside talking to the rest of your colleagues right now."

"Sorry, I didn't notice anybody when I came in."

"And the colleague?"

"Wendy Baxter."

"Okay, that will be all, Mr Gleeson. We may wish to speak with you again."

Gleeson shrugged looking like he didn't give a shit. He stood up and left the room.

"Right, we have a suspect," stated Fenton.

"You're not serious?" replied Taylor.

"Probably not, but he's the only one so far without an alibi. Of course, that's if Walt's little dalliance turns out to be true."

"Still, I doubt it very much."

"Me too, but if we get nothing else then at least it gets the Chief Super off my back, thinking that we've got nothing." Fenton stretched and yawned. It was already mid-afternoon, and his stomach was rumbling, which was a distraction. "Let's speak to Jeremiah Tool and then meet Gary and Emma for some lunch."

"I think they call him Jez."

"Jez Tool? Poor bastard, I'd stick to Jeremiah if I was him."

Jez Tool looked like a thug. Tall, broad physique with bulging muscles and tattoos plastered on every available patch of visible skin below the neck. He wore a tight black T-shirt that showed off his frame, with his crew-cut hairstyle and a nose that had been broken at least once. You couldn't not feel intimidated by him. Fenton wondered if he drove a motorbike and then remembered he did. Taylor had done her homework on everyone they were going to interview. He also lived alone in a bedsit; so perhaps Peter would become number two on the suspect list. Although Fenton was never one to make sweeping assumptions, it was bloody hard not to, with a guy like Jez sitting opposite you. Fenton was to lead the questioning again, which was probably for the best; Taylor seemed distracted.

"You told my colleague that you were in your room between eight and nine thirty."

"Well, I weren't hungry, so just chilled out in me room, like."

"When did you hear all the commotion?" Fenton was starting to feel like a parrot.

"I popped out for some fags about nine. When I came back, I saw the police all over the shop."

Fenton sat up. *This was new.* "You left the hotel?"

"Yeah, but not for long, about half hour."

"Where did you go for cigarettes?"

"A shop near Kings Cross station."

"Bit of a walk, when Euston station is closer."

"I wanted some fresh air, after being in conference room all day, like."

"And you didn't notice anything when you left."

"What do you mean?"

"Well, the police were already on the scene by that time. I'm surprised you didn't notice anything."

Fenton could feel his pulse racing. The rush he got when he knew an investigation had suddenly switched from meandering, to going full pelt again.

"I'm not very observant, so there could have been loads of police cars outside."

"That will be all then, thank you."

Taylor looked like she wanted to ask more, but Fenton shot her a look that told her to keep her mouth shut.

Jez looked a little confused that the interview had been brought to such an abrupt halt and left the room looking bewildered.

"What was that all about?" asked Taylor.

"I need more information before I speak to him again."

"You know that only me, you and two uniformed officers were at the scene until Nadeem's body was found, so he may not have seen anyone."

"Bollocks. Didn't think of that. But surely you'd notice a patrol car outside?"

"A police car parked up in London is hardly going to get noticed."

"It should, if you're not from London."

As Fenton left Training4All with Taylor he started scanning his emails on his phone. Although at first irritated at this reliance on technology, he had found that he now couldn't live without it.

"You've got to be joking," he bellowed, causing Taylor to whip round.

"What is it?" asked Taylor. The urgency evident in her voice.

"Who do you think? Another article in the London News from that bitch," replied Fenton, exasperated. "She knows we're up north interviewing potential suspects, and she hasn't wasted an opportunity to put the boot in again! Where did she get that from, I wonder?"

"Maybe one of the team mentioned it? She might have called?"

"Well whoever it was is getting disciplined."

"But nobody else knows we have a leak. We're not a hundred per cent sure, that's why we haven't shared it with the rest of the team."

His rage boiled. He knew Manning was feeding information to Pilkington. He couldn't prove it. He'd put Taylor on the case, and he knew it would take time, but he was impatient. He was doing something that he always told junior officers not to do. He was making it personal. It would never take away the guilt of the unsolved case, but to give Pilkington a taste of her own medicine would give him a smug sense of satisfaction. In fact, that was an understatement. It would make him happier than a pig in posh shit. If Manning could take a fall as well, then so much the better. Law and order didn't need people like that involved with it. Such over-inflated egos moved the focus away from where it should be – the victims.

CHAPTER NINE

Fenton, Taylor, Brennan and Shirkham were having lunch, although it was now almost five o'clock, so it was more like an early dinner. They'd opted for a quiet table at the back of the hotel restaurant and, due to the time of day, they were the only patrons in there. This suited Fenton as he wanted to discuss the case, and he wouldn't put it past Polly Pilkington to be lurking somewhere. Fenton had already had a minor tiff with the waitress when she presented them with the *dinner* menu. Taylor had kindly explained to him that dinner was lunch in northern. Fenton had then been the perfect gentlemen and apologised. This was something he had learnt when working on the case in Harrogate. If you're ever rude to a northerner, you apologise and most of the time they will gratefully accept and tell you *not to worry*. Fenton knew that such an approach did not work in London. Firstly, most people didn't notice if you were being rude because that was the default. Secondly, if you try to apologise to anyone, they will assume you were some form of lunatic and flee in terror.

"Have you seen this?" said Fenton, passing his phone to

Brennan and Shirkham. He was still fuming. They scanned the Pilkington article.

"How did she know?" asked Brennan.

Taylor looked at Fenton, who nodded.

"Keep this to yourselves, but we think Manning is leaking information to her," she said.

"Are they on together or something?" asked Shirkham bluntly.

"No idea, perhaps they're acquainted some other way," was Fenton's pessimistic reply.

It was wrong to make such assumptions, he knew, but why else would there be information passing between them? He knew that Manning was very well off, and Pilkington was hardly in a position, at a free local paper, to start dishing out fistfuls of cash. These were the only two reasons Fenton could think of that made people loose with their tongues: money or sex.

"Are you all right, Gary?"

Fenton noticed Brennan was pulling an odd face and had seemed to stop the repeated shovelling motion that tended to ensue whenever food was placed in front of him.

"I've never known the thought of girl-on-girl action to put me off my food before," he said pushing his plate away and feigning a look of disgust.

Everyone looked at each for a moment and then started laughing. It was what they needed after a week of the investigation going nowhere, and then everything suddenly going at a hundred miles an hour in one day. They were all exhausted; Fenton knew they still needed more. Now they were acting on nothing but circumstance and gut feeling, an excellent combination for policing, but not enough to convince a jury. The case was a long way from concluding, but at least they now had a few people who could be considered as potential suspects.

"Emma, anything new?" asked Fenton.

"Not really, just confirmation of all the alibis. It appears that, except for Walter Channing, Peter Gleeson, Jeremiah Tool, Elizabeth Jamal and Derek Longhurst, everybody else was at the dinner for the whole meal, and Wendy Baxter was also away for part of the meal, of course."

"Okay, so we have six possible suspects then," Fenton stated.

"If it was someone from the company," added Brennan.

"Well, that's all we have to work on at the moment."

"There's still the possibility that the other two in London could be linked," remarked Taylor, although she sounded doubtful.

"Don't sound too convinced," Fenton remarked sarcastically. "Let's look at the six."

"I think we can rule out the two spouses, as it doesn't make any sense for them to have committed all three murders and, even if they worked together, what's Carl got to do with it?" said Shirkham.

"Fair point, but let's just back-burner those two."

"I think we can rule out dear Walt as well, provided his alibi checks out," added Taylor.

"Have we done that yet?"

"I've got the team in London looking at it."

"Good."

"What's his alibi?" asked Brennan

"He was entertaining a male escort, or gentlemen friend that he helps financially, as he put it," quipped Taylor.

"Stupid thing to lie about, we'd only find out if it was bollocks."

"That leaves Jez Tool, who's top of the list for me, then Peter Gleeson, who was a bit too arrogant for my liking," summarised Fenton. "Not forgetting Wendy Baxter of course. I see you are still in one piece, Gary."

Everyone laughed, apart from Brennan.

"Only just, but I don't think she's the one."

"She worked her magic then."

"Hardly," Brennan snapped back, blushing. "It's just the woman is totally incapable of keeping a secret. If she had anything to do with it, she would have told me. I mean, she told me pretty much everything else about all the backstabbing and in-fighting at Training4All."

"Not all group hugs then?"

————

Brennan had spent the day with Wendy Baxter. They'd had tears, drama, laughter and lots of leg and cleavage.

"Oh, Officer Brennan, I forgot you were coming today. Please forgive my satire," came the greeting as she opened the door wearing a nightgown that left little to the imagination, especially when she was wearing something about four sizes too small.

Brennan opted not to correct her Freudian slip and merely beamed his cheeky grin at her, causing her to giggle and invite him in. He breathed deeply to steel his nerves before stepping inside.

"Why don't I make us both a cuppa, while you get yourself dressed? I'm sure I can find my way around your kitchen."

Looking disappointed, Wendy nodded and went off to get changed. Brennan busied himself in the kitchen, making sure it took as long as possible, hoping that when she reappeared, she would be wearing something that resembled clothes or, at the very least, had tried to cover up some of her modesty. He wasn't a shy man and he could turn on the charm when he needed to. The team saw him as a bit of a joker and he played up to that role, but first and foremost he was a professional.

Even if Wendy had been like a catwalk model and thrown herself at him, he would have still batted her away. Not that he went for catwalk models. He wasn't someone who was driven by aesthetics. Given the job he did, all he wanted was to go home to a woman who could make him laugh.

Wendy emerged, framed in the doorway. Brennan noted that she looked like she was going clubbing, not sitting down to talk about the murder of three of her colleagues, one of which was her best friend.

"Do you have somewhere to rush off to?" asked Brennan innocently.

Wendy looked slightly perplexed at his question. She recovered quickly. "No, not at all, Officer Brennan, I'm all yours."

"Wonderful, then we needn't rush. I wouldn't want you to get upset. I know it's been a difficult time for you, and please call me Gary."

Brennan was turning it on now. He hoped that she was so gullible that, if she was a triple murderer, he'd have a full confession in no time.

"Oh, thank you, Gary," she exclaimed with a smile and a wink. "Shall we go through to the sitting room? We'll be more comfortable in there?"

"Sounds perfect."

She beamed and led the way.

He rolled his eyes and looked up to the heavens, mouthing *help,* as he followed her.

Brennan wanted to get the tears out of the way first. They were inevitable. He asked her more about her friendship with Carl. It was like turning on a tap. She became hysterical very quickly. A bit too rehearsed, but he needed to give her the benefit of the doubt. He believed that Carl was a very close friend of hers and she was upset by his death, but he also suspected that she was loving the drama of it all, and the fact that she was at the epicentre of it.

"We were like soul mates," she sobbed. "You don't have to sleep together to be soul mates, you know. We understood each other better than anybody else."

Brennan knew she had a point but, from what else he'd picked up from other people, Carl did indeed care very much about Wendy as a friend, although Brennan suspected that his idea of a soul mate would have lumps and bumps in very different places. Carl probably found Wendy to be a comfort in between the many breakups she had already spoken of when Fenton had interviewed her. Brennan did wonder if she saw Carl as much when he was enamoured with his latest squeeze. In the same way that most friends bin you off as soon as they are getting regular orgasms.

"I know this must be very difficult for you." he added, soothingly.

After a while she managed to stop sobbing and spoke openly about their friendship. They would spend at least one night in the week and one weekend evening together, every week, whenever Carl wasn't travelling with work. They always had a holiday together each year as well. Brennan decided against asking if this was also their routine when he was dating somebody. He knew it was best not to pull at that thread with Wendy; he needed to keep her as focussed as possible.

"He used to have a boy's holiday each year as well."

"Was that with any colleagues from work?"

"No, these were friends he'd had for years."

"Where did they usually go?"

"This year they went on a gay cruise round the Caribbean. Of course, they wanted me to go with them, but it were men only."

"Did he do a lot of men on holiday? Sorry, I mean men-only holidays?"

"Usually one a year. His friends were quite keen on them."

Brennan thought it was more likely that Carl wanted a week off every year.

"Was there anyone in particular who he would be away with on his business trips?"

"Not really. Depended on who were available. He used to be away with Nadeem a bit. They got on well and had a similar style of training. It were Walt who paired them up. They had the biggest clients like, so they were in London, Edinburgh, and Bristol all the time. If they were in northern cities, they'd come home as Nadeem didn't like being away from Elizabeth."

"How was Nadeem and Elizabeth's relationship, from what you saw?" asked Brennan quickly, pleased she'd given him such an easy opening to steer their conversation elsewhere.

"They seemed happy. They didn't see much of each other at work though. She weren't keen on him being away all time. I think it caused tension or summat. Nothing out of ordinary though. Why, do you think she did it?"

"No, it's just that it's good for us to have a clear picture of the victims so we can look for possible motives."

"You don't think it were someone random then, like it said in the paper? You think it were someone from our company?"

"I didn't say that. We just need to check every possible avenue."

Brennan was aware that the roles had suddenly switched, and he needed to steer things back, without her realising – hardly a challenge. He opted to pull out the trump card straight away.

"Tell me a bit more about Trudie."

It worked. Her eyes narrowed.

"Well, I don't like to speak ill of the dead, but what an absolute fucking bitch. Sorry, Gary."

"I've heard worse." He smiled.

Wendy giggled.

"She constantly got on everyone's tits. If it had just been her that were murdered, anyone could have done it. Except for her husband."

"Why's that?"

"He thought the sun shone out of her arse, but she were a complete bitch to him. Just like she were to everyone else."

"In what way?"

"She were just vile – I mean vile to everyone. I know this is wrong to say..." oddly, there was a sense of relish in her voice as she uttered those words, "but she wanted the world to pay for the fact that she were in wheelchair. She were very bitter about it."

"Was she always like that?"

"I'd never known her not to be. Apparently, she were happy with her first husband. I wouldn't know though, I never met him."

Brennan wanted to discuss the employees, other than her and the spouses, who had no firm alibis for the time of the murders. He didn't want it to be obvious though, or it would be round the office the next day. He begrudgingly decided to ask her for her opinion of every employee at Training4All. It was the safest approach, and he settled himself in for a long day.

Wendy spoke of Walt with enthusiasm and passion. The same way everyone had. It was getting tiresome. The youthful energy, love for learning, holistic dynamics of team synergy and every other cliché in the book. Although, it wasn't a book – it was a learning tool!

"He's quite lonely though," she added.

Brennan woke up at that comment.

"He has his special friend – we all know it's his partner. I think they have a business arrangement that stops them from getting too close, which is a shame, as he's a lovely bloke."

"What sort of business arrangement?"

"I believe they started out as escort and client, but it's developed to another level. I reckon there's more deepness to it, kinda spiritual."

"Can we cut the platitudes now please?" he snapped, without thinking.

Wendy's face crumpled. She looked very hurt.

"I'm sorry," he said, gently patting her knee.

This was the signal she'd evidently been waiting for, as she lunged for him. Even though Brennan was a trained officer and he could look after himself, no training prepared you for an eighteen-stone woman trying to mount you without warning. Her hands were everywhere, and he had to think fast. A little voice, the Guv's, told him she was crucial to the case, so he needed to use his brain and not his gut instinct.

"I think we need to keep things professional, Wendy, or I could lose my job," he said wrestling free

"Nobody would know," she remarked moving in again for the kill, her arms open, ready to lock together around her prey.

He jumped up quickly.

"I have my professional ethics, Wendy, surely you can understand that."

The term seemed to have the desired effect. It was an easy strategy to adopt. Find a person who spends their whole day spinning platitudes and bullshit and then do just that, bullshit them. They'll fall for it every time.

"Of course, Gary, I understand. I have ethicals an' all. I know it's hard for some of me clients sometimes to fight normal urges. I insist that we keep things proper."

"I knew you would empathise with my predicament," he said flashing a smile.

For a lad who'd been raised on the estates in East London, he was impressed with the amount of crap that could spew from his mouth at a time when his genitals had retreated into his body in trauma. It wasn't that Wendy was unattractive, it would just be completely unprofessional, and she would then no doubt sell her story to the *London News*. Perhaps Brennan was over-stretching here – he just didn't want to get mixed up in any of Wendy's drama, other than what he had to as part of the investigation.

Wendy had got the message and then carried on talking about her colleagues. Brennan hoped that now she'd made her move that would be it, but he kept a safe distance and sat with his hands by his sides, palms flat to the chair, ready to leap to sanctuary if need be. He was starting to get bored again, when suddenly she started to talk about Jez Tool. He'd zoned out and only heard the words *mean bastard*.

"Sorry, Wendy, could you repeat that please?"

"People say that Jez looks like a right mean bastard, but he's a gentle giant really."

"In what way?"

"Have you met Jez? He can look a bit intimidating. Well, he's sweet really. I've never seen him get angry, to be honest."

"Does he have any close friendships at work?"

"Not really, he just does his job."

"You've never met with him socially?"

"Only when we have work parties. He always comes to 'em – unlike Peter. Now there's a real arsehole."

"Is this Peter Gleeson, the Finance Manager?"

"Yeah, he never comes to any parties. He's a miserable twat at work and don't even say hello to you if you bump into him in the kitchen. He won't even do Walt's training."

"What training is that?"

"Walt has some compulsory courses that he likes everyone to do. Not just the Performance Enablement Facilitators. They're linked to our core job compensatories. Is that right?

"Competencies?" he offered.

"That's it, the ones that everyone has to do."

"And he won't do any of them?"

"Well he did a couple. He refused to do the diversity awareness course."

Brennan was suddenly interested. "What's involved with that course?"

"Well, its odd days here and there. Walt wanted everyone to do it. The problem were when you've got a load of professional trainers in one place, they can be quite critical. Walt kept changing the course content and asking everyone to do it again. Him and Peter had a huge row, and Peter told him to let him know when he'd decided what he wanted on the course, because until then, he weren't attending."

"What did Walt do then?"

"He came up with the away conference that we just had. He thought it would be good for us all to be away together for a couple of days. Peter point blank refused to go, but Walt got Elizabeth involved and I think she gave him some kind of warning."

"What sort of warning?"

"I dunno. Elizabeth's quite strict on the confidential thing."

"So, Peter obviously attended in the end?"

"Yes, but he weren't keen. I'd say he had more reason than Jez to kill anyone."

"What makes you say that?"

"Well, I know Jez used to belong to that group. His family have got a bad background, but Peter was very openly nasty about the whole diversity thing."

"What group did Jez belong to?"

"I don't know the name. It were one of them far right politics groups. I think he gave all that up though when his dad and brother went back to prison for armed robbery!"

CHAPTER TEN

Fenton and Taylor were having breakfast. Fenton was taking advantage of the all-you-can-eat buffet – well, it was paid for and he was away from home. Taylor went for the porridge and fruit option. You'd think this would have brought about a sense of guilt as he devoured his second plateful of lumberjack breakfast, but it didn't. When you're away from home it didn't count, he told himself. That might also explain the ample frames of most long-distance lorry drivers; perhaps they channelled the same view as Fenton.

Brennan and Shirkham had returned to London the night before. Fenton had asked for more detail about the political group Jez had been affiliated with. He thought it best not to tackle Jez directly; if he was to become prime suspect, then they didn't want to tip him off before they had anything concrete to hold him on. He also intended to find out more about Peter and Walt's altercation. He suspected a good start would be his interview with Elizabeth. He had decided to speed up time so that they could get back to London earlier than planned, mainly owing to the Pilkington article. Taylor was to interview Derek at the same time.

"Try and get a bit more about Trudie's relationships with the rest of the staff. It will be interesting to see if Derek has a different perspective. We can then work on one of two assumptions – he's deluded or lying."

"How are you gonna approach Elizabeth?" asked Taylor

"I can take a different approach this time. We have a plethora of suspects now that are as diverse as the victims."

"The old charm hat going on?"

"Naturally." He smiled.

"I bet she won't give anything away about Peter and Walt."

"The old professional ethics thing?"

"I expect so. HR People are bit anal about the confidentiality thing, so much so that their own team don't know what's going on half the time."

"Yes, well, she better not try that with me."

"We'd struggle at the moment on what we've got to get a warrant."

"True, but I'll make out that's in her interests."

"Be careful, she's a very shrewd woman and she'll see you coming from a mile away."

"Yes, but I'm an arrogant twat who likes to get my own way."

They both laughed. Fenton just managed to stop himself from spraying beans and scrambled eggs everywhere.

"What time do you want to head back?" asked Taylor.

Fenton glanced at his watch: it was just after nine. "No later than midday, I think."

"I'd better head off and get a cab."

"I can drop you."

"No, it's in the opposite direction, and you need to have another breakfast yet."

He grinned, his mouth bulging with food.

"You look like a very content gerbil," she smiled.

———

Derek was giving Taylor a tour of his home. At first, she was pleased that he'd volunteered an opportunity for her to have a look around his home, but every room came with several anecdotes of his life with Trudie. She glanced at her watch. They'd already been walking round for almost an hour and she was aware that time was against her if she was to get a lift back to London. The last thing she needed was a delayed train ride surrounded by drunk northerners. Of course, she would vehemently stand up to any anti-northern comments made by southerners; however, in her capacity as a fellow northerner, she could describe these drunk yobbish morons accurately – gob shites!

The house was nothing spectacular, although it had character. It was obviously the home of two people who had led very full, yet separate lives. Even though effort had been made to integrate the lifestyles of the people that lived here, there was still a sense of this is yours and this is mine. A tad unusual after five years of marriage.

Derek's office had resulted in a ten-minute lecture. The walls were plastered in top ten lists covering many different topics: *How to give managers the edge*; *How to adapt to change*; *How to use empathy in a performance review*; *How to inspire people with your vision.* There was a particularly long-winded one; *How to look inside yourself and take charge of your own learning.*

He also had a mirror covered in Post-its that seemed to be affirmations. She suspected Derek would absorb them each day, reading them aloud before he went to work. She noticed a few of the affirmations were replicas from those seen around the Training4All office. He was probably one of those types who spent an age each morning gazing adoringly at his own reflection before reading the final, most important affirmation that was in prime position. The one that would give him his sense of purpose for the day ahead – *I'm the only me there is therefore I'm special*.

One glaringly obvious fact was that this was Trudie's home, except for Derek's office. Her presence was everywhere, and you wouldn't automatically realise that Derek lived here. Taylor suggested they make their way back to the kitchen, as she didn't want to keep him too long.

"Can you tell me about Trudie's relationships with her colleagues?"

"Anyone in particular?" He was trying to act like this hadn't sparked his interest, but she knew from his body language that it had.

"No, just generally."

"Well, I won't lie to you. She wasn't the most popular person in the office."

"In what way?"

"In a highly creative environment there are always a lot of strong characters, but my Trudie was the strongest. She didn't suffer fools. She had a gentle side that she only showed in private. She always kept it professional at work."

Taylor noticed he was starting to get teary, so she pushed the conversation on, rather than let him wallow in it for too long. There was something about the man that was slightly nauseating to her. She kept this to herself. The man was grieving after all.

"Was there anyone in particular that she had an altercation with?"

"I'd say she had a run-in with everyone at one time or another. I know it sounds terrible, but I think it's important to be honest with you."

"I appreciate that. I know it must be difficult for you." She resisted the urge to pat his hand as she suspected Derek would see this as condescending, which of course is exactly what it would be. "What about more recently?"

"She had a few rows over the last month. She had a major run in with Elizabeth. She had a bit of a tiff with Walt, and she was always rowing with Peter. He was her line manager."

"Why don't we start with Elizabeth? What was all that about?"

"I'm, not a hundred per cent sure. Elizabeth likes to wave her confidentiality banner a lot. I think it had something to do with that. An invoice came in for coaching of a staff member or something. Trudie wanted to know who it was going to be assigned to. She refused to say who it was, and they had a blazing row."

"Do you know who it was for?"

"You'll have to ask Elizabeth. I'd get a warrant or something. She acts like she's guarding national security, instead of a handful of personnel files."

"Was that a typical disagreement between the two of them?"

"Usually, anything that hindered Trudie in her work would get her steamed up."

Taylor thought for a while. She really needed to find out about Trudie's relationship with Jez. Derek hadn't mentioned him. It wouldn't be easy to hoodwink this guy; he was very astute, and she didn't want to arouse any suspicion against one person just yet.

"Can you tell me about the disagreement with Walt?"

"That was something or nothing. I believe she gets fed up with sending various payments off to a selection of men. I really shouldn't say any more. He is my boss."

"He won't know it's come from you."

"Well, Walt has been known to enjoy the company of young men. He has some regular guy who lives in London, although he's not so young anymore. He often has payments going off to a variety of guys, some on the other side of the world, especially Thailand and a lot to Eastern Europe. We don't ask any questions. Trudie would get annoyed that suppliers would be paid late as those boys always got their money first. That was the main thing they would have any disagreements about. She'd built up good relationships with suppliers and Walt's bits of trade undermined that at times, she felt."

"Does anyone else in the office know about this?"

"Everyone, although Walt likes to think he's discrete."

"What about her relationship with Peter?"

"Well, he was her line manager. She'd get annoyed if he asked for something that messed up her day. She was a meticulous planner, and Peter is quite disorganised. He'd always be stressed with deadlines, like most accountants. Very clever, but no people skills. They just didn't get on from day one."

"A personality clash?"

"Personalities don't clash, behaviours do!"

Taylor repressed the need to sigh deeply, roll her eyes, and if she was completely honest, slap the self-righteous prick round the face.

"So, their behaviours clashed?" she said, through gritted teeth.

"Don't worry, it's a common misconception. Yes, they have a different working style and at times it just wasn't compatible. No menace there, just not a good match."

"So why put them together?"

"With a small company, everyone works together to some degree."

Derek started to busy himself making more coffee. He'd asked Taylor if she wanted one. She declined and asked for water. The strength of the coffee she'd had when she arrived meant it was unlikely, she would sleep for another forty-eight hours.

"What were Trudie's relationships like with the other victims?"

"Nadeem and Carl? She didn't really have one. Most of the trainers are out a lot. I'd never seen them row. I know she thought Carl was a nice young man. She always felt sorry for Nadeem being married to Elizabeth."

Taylor noticed that he had referred to himself and his colleagues as *trainers*. This pleased her. "Any particular reason?"

"Not really. She didn't like Elizabeth. The feeling was more than mutual."

"You work as a trainer as well, so are you away a lot?"

"No, because of Trudie's situation, Walt was very understanding. I would tend to take the local clients. I'd rarely be away overnight."

"Are all the other trainers away a lot?"

"Nadeem and Carl took most jobs in the south. They were away a lot together. Walt paired them up as they have training synergy."

"Is it normal for two trainers to go to one client?"

"Not always. They would often have jobs in the same city and travel together."

Taylor made a note of this. It was something that had been mentioned before, yet nobody had really investigated it. If they were good friends, then it was possible that they could have had a common enemy. It was still possible that Trudie was just killed for good measure, as apart from her husband, nobody liked the woman.

Taylor made her way through every member of staff, asking Derek about Trudie's relationship with them. It was mind-numbing and she was getting fed up with Derek's patter. She kept zoning out and hearing snatches of conversation peppered with phrases like *get on board, top-down and best practice*. After what seemed like an eternity, she was miffed to find out that Jez was the only other person that Trudie seemed to like. She was aware he lived alone in a bedsit, so would always cook him casseroles or numerous other concoctions. According to Derek, Trudie had treated Jez like a son and was extremely protective of him. Fenton would not like this development.

Taylor asked Derek about his marriage to Trudie again. She wanted to steer the conversation onto her first marriage and thought this would be a good tactic. Derek gushed about how they had found each other at Training4All and how he had seen her gentle and vulnerable side, which she hid behind a tough exterior. More like a steel-plated bomb shelter, Taylor thought.

This had made him fall in love with her. He had courted her in an old-fashioned way. He never mentioned about Trudie being in a wheelchair and Taylor thought it best not to raise it. Besides, it wasn't relevant, although it must have caused their lives some difficulties.

The downside to talking about his marriage to Trudie was it caused him to launch into an array of childlike sobbing. Talking about how he had lost his soul mate, and how his life would be so difficult to move forward. When he calmed down, which took some considerable time, she steered the conversation back on track.

"You were both married before?"

"Yes. Trudie's husband died in the car accident, which left her in a wheelchair for the rest of her life. My wife died after a long illness."

"I'm very sorry."

She thought that Trudie's first husband had committed suicide. The reports were clear that it was no accident. Maybe he'd meant to take Trudie with him? Now was not to the time to raise it. She'd investigate it later.

"It was so fortunate that we found each other." The tears came again.

Taylor decided it might be best to call it a day. She wasn't going to get any more out of him today and she needed to get back to London with Fenton.

"I'm sorry to have caused you distress, Derek." She got up to leave. "I'll let myself out. Do you know when you'll be returning to work?"

"Walt has told me I can take as much time as I need, but I can't even think about it until after the funeral."

"Of course." This time she patted his shoulder, which caused him to break down further.

"Do you have any idea when I'll be able to start arranging things?" he said through gasping sobs.

"We're hoping everything will be passed to the coroner in the next couple of days, so we'll know more then. I'll call when I hear anything. I'll see myself out." She scooped up her bag.

Outside the front door she could finally exhale deeply. She made a note to herself that if they had to interview the spouses again then she was swapping with Fenton and taking Elizabeth next time.

————

Elizabeth Jamal's home was clearly lived in by a loving couple, Fenton thought. A couple who lived together as one – as Walt would put it. Fenton wasn't automatically offered a guided tour, so he used the old ploy that it helps the investigation to know as much about the victim as possible. She'd evidently found this plausible and given him a whistle-stop tour of her home, barely giving him a second to glance around a room before she was ushering him on to the next.

Nadeem's Muslim heritage was visible, but it was subtle and fitted with the style of the home. The place obviously had influence from both of them. There was a box room that was used as an office. Although there was a lot of training material, there were also Elizabeth's employment law books. There were no whiteboards.

The place was beautifully decorated throughout. It struck Fenton as odd that someone as plain and dowdy as Elizabeth would have her home like this. She barely spoke as showed him around her home. Perhaps it was all still too raw for her, thought Fenton, but he needed further information. He was hoping to have final forensics the next day. His budget had been increased due to the press attention of the case, so he was able to leapfrog to the front of the queue. It had given him a smug sense of satisfaction when Manning hadn't been able to use her customary, *I must do these in order,* excuse.

They settled in the kitchen and Elizabeth made tea for them both. He'd have preferred coffee, as even though there was allegedly more caffeine in tea, it didn't have the same psychosomatic jolt that coffee did. The case was already taking its toll and they were only just over a week in. The fact that he had gone straight from one big case to another didn't help. It was best to have some down time after a big investigation. You could recharge and get the old case out of your system. In his tiredness he opted to just go straight for it with his questioning. He expected floods of tears, but he surmised that he might as well get these out the way.

"I know this must be difficult for you, but could you tell me about your marriage?"

She looked slightly taken aback for a fraction of a second.

"What would you like to know?"

"How you met? Your work together? Your relationship at home? Anything that you think will give me a better picture of the man your husband was?"

"Why do you need to know this?" she asked coldly.

"It's helpful to have as much background on the victims as possible. It can help in trying to ascertain motives. I need to know as much about your husband as possible. Obviously, you will be able to provide me with the most insight."

The false flattery was not going to work on Elizabeth Jamal. She was a very sharp, worldly-wise woman. Her eyes narrowed in a way that said, *I know what you're up to.*

Fenton chose to ignore this and took a gulp of his tea, which was scolding hot, so it removed a layer of skin from the roof of his mouth. He could feel himself perspiring yet didn't react or take his gaze off her. His professionalism and masculinity were to remain intact.

"I suppose you'll be asking Derek similar personal questions?"

"My colleague is speaking with him at this very moment."

This statement seemed to relax her, and she spoke candidly about her marriage. Fenton noted that she didn't become emotional at any time. It was as if she was reading a script. He'd seen this before. People who were hysterical at the start suddenly became numb. It probably wouldn't hit her again until the funeral.

They had met at work. Her marriage was an incredibly happy one; a joyous wonder, she described it as. His family had been reluctant at first about a mixed-race marriage. They were eventually won over. Nadeem had never been strict about his religion and had only maintained his faith out of loyalty and respect to his mother. There had been no desire on both sides to have children, so this had never caused any tension, although Nadeem's family had been pushy to start with. Fenton wondered if he should ask about his routine around prayers, given he was wearing a cap when he died, but it didn't seem like a necessary question given her description of his commitment to his heritage and faith. Perhaps he had been praying and didn't use a mat or had put the mat away and left the cap on before being confronted by the killer. In reality, it would only matter if that was the reason he had been murdered.

She spoke about Nadeem's work. They rarely had to deal with each other on a professional basis, as he was out of the office most days. He was often away from home, but she knew this was part of the job.

"He would often be away with Carl Davenport, one of the other victims, wouldn't he?" Fenton asked.

"What's that got to with anything?" she snapped back.

"Nothing, Elizabeth, I just heard that there were often assigned together as they had a similar training style or something?"

"That's quite true. They both enjoyed experimenting with new training methods, such as active and intensive short bursts or training bites as they are more commonly known. Their game-based learning was also immensely popular."

Fenton smiled and nodded. He sipped his tea again making that essential slurping sound necessary to also take air into your mouth, so it cooled down the beverage. He had no idea what she was going on about – bites that burst? What kind of training courses did people do these days? He let her prattle on for a while.

"What was your husband's relationship like with the other victim, Trudie Longhurst?"

"Frosty and tolerable, I'd say. The same as everyone. The woman thought she owned the company. It's terrible what happened to her, but I'm not surprised that somebody finally snapped."

Fenton declined to probe further on this. The woman may have been obnoxious, but someone had stabbed her to death.

"How about your relationship with her?"

"The same. I tolerated her. She had no understanding of confidentiality."

"In what way?"

"She wanted to know everything. Personnel details are private. She had no business asking, and I told her as much."

"Was she after anyone's details in particular?"

"It varied. There was nobody specific if that's what you mean." Her cold manner had resumed.

"Can you tell me about the disagreement that you had with Peter Gleeson, a few days before the conference?"

"Spoken to Wendy Baxter, have you?"

Fenton said nothing and held her stare.

"It was a private and confidential matter, officer. I'm afraid I can't give you any more information."

"Do you not want us to catch your husband's killer?"

"How dare you?" she shouted. "Of course, I want my husband's killer caught. This was an internal matter that has nothing to do with my husband's murder."

"Why don't you let me decide if it's relevant?"

"I'm sorry, DCI Fenton, but unless you have a warrant, I will not compromise my professional ethics. Surely you can understand that. I do believe that the police have them as well?" she scoffed.

"Please calm down, Mrs Jamal."

"Mrs Jamal now, is it? What happened to Elizabeth?" She was starting to get hysterical and Fenton had no idea what had made her suddenly flare up. "I thought you were looking for some serial killer whose murdering people from minority groups?"

"I wouldn't believe everything you read in the papers." He was irritated, although kept his voice soft and controlled, as he wanted her to calm down. There was still more he needed to get out of her.

"But these three victims cover all of the six original protected characteristics in law. Isn't that a motive?"

"There have been no other cases that we can link. Serial killers are very methodical and would want the whole set."

"But they've got the whole set – well, the main six anyway."

"Please explain," asked Fenton calmly.

"My husband was a Muslim, and Asian and male, so that's three. Religion, race and gender, yes?" She held up three fingers and carried on before he could answer. "Carl was black, gay and male, again three. Race, sexual orientation, and gender. Trudie was disabled, elderly and female. Disability, age, and gender. Again three. That covers the main six, and three each."

She held up three fingers to emphasise each time she said three, evidently making sure that he was clear what three was. Her manner implying that she thought Fenton was below average intelligence.

"There are now nine protected characteristics," he added calmly.

"Don't you think I know that? I work in HR. The three new ones have been broken out from gender so technically it is still just six. Your killer is clever, that's how they've done it. With having each victim being from three individual minorities, it is too much of a coincidence. I didn't think the police believed in coincidences?"

"You've obviously put a lot of thought into this."

"It's my job. I know diversity and equality like the back of my hand." She waved her hand at him.

"Surely the gender issue only applies to Trudie?"

"Men are covered by the law, as well you know. Don't you police know anything?" Her patronising tone was starting to piss Fenton off.

"Then if that's the case, the fact that your husband and Trudie Longhurst were heterosexual would also be covered. This would then give them four protected characteristics."

He held up four fingers. He couldn't help himself. "Carl Davenport remains on three." He repeated the gesture. "So, there is no logical pattern."

He sipped his tea, maintain eye contact.

Elizabeth went noticeably quiet. He was right. She couldn't argue it. She burst into floods of tears. Fenton tried to calm her down. He gave up after a while and left her sobbing. She'd reverted to type – come out fighting, and if that fails, wail like a banshee; the men will flee.

Fenton wasn't sure what had suddenly made Elizabeth flare up like that and then crack so quickly. She had come across as cold and uncaring, that didn't bother him; he'd seen people act in a similar way when they were grieving. She'd obviously put a lot of thought into a reason behind her husband's murder. This had possibly helped her to rationalise in her own head. She had a solid theory, but Fenton had just shot it down in flames. He hadn't thought about men being covered by equality legislation, and he hated being made to look stupid. He hadn't meant to upset her, although he'd fired back a good point on the sexual orientation argument. If this had been the killer's motive, then they weren't doing a good job. Serial killers weren't usually stupid. Yes, killing people in cold blood isn't the most intelligent thing to do, yet the meticulous planning usually warranted a degree of intellect – so that was Wendy ruled out.

This case was still not making any sense. Looking at the murders collectively was causing a monumental headache. When he got back to London, he would split the team up, so that each group looked at each murder individually. Then they would look for patterns. He wasn't convinced that it was totally random. He still regarded Jez Tool and Peter Gleeson as prime suspects.

He had a late meeting scheduled with the Chief Superin-tendent for when he got back to London – so much for dinner with his family! It was also unusual for Beeden to work on a Saturday, so it was clearly important. He would have to convince his boss about breaking the investigation up. He was going to need more officers, and for the first time, he hoped that Polly Pilkington was about to publish another damming article. You couldn't beat a bit of media pressure to squeeze more funds out of the budget.

CHAPTER ELEVEN

DEATH PENALTY DEBATE
Polly PIlkington

Pressure is mounting on the government to table a motion for a debate on the re-instatement of the death penalty. The Queen's speech is due in less than a month. It is believed that the Prime Minister is being forced to consider the option.

There is support from the Leader of the Opposition, who states, "I don't advocate that the death penalty should be brought back without vigorous discussion in the House of Commons. The time has come for the matter to be discussed and the Prime Minister should not be afraid of what our neighbours in Europe might think. Our society has been blighted by brutal murders in recent times, and it's clear that our current justice system is not enough of a deterrent."

The Prime Minister refused to comment on the matter, and no senior cabinet minister would be drawn on discussing the proposals. Sources close to the government reveal that despite overwhelming public support for the death penalty to be re-instated, it is likely that the government will cave into pressure from Europe, conceding that the matter is not up for debate.

This debate has been promoted by the recent triple murder in a London hotel. Three victims were brutally murdered, simply because of their disability status, religion, race, or sexual orientation. The police are still nowhere near to identifying a suspect, despite a recent trip to Preston, Lancashire where Training4All, the company all victims were employees of, is located. A substantial number of the investigating team travelled up north last week, in what was believed to have been a breakthrough. However, DCI Eric Fenton, 45, returned empty-handed, still no closer to solving this heinous crime.

Sources close to the police admit that they are still trying to ascertain a motive for the murders, which seems abundantly clear to the rest of us. They should be focussed on identifying potential suspects and not trying to deflect that this is yet another despicable hate crime. It is also believed that police will not be issuing a warning to members of the public that the killer might strike again. It is not known for serial killers to suddenly become dormant after a multiple one-event slaying. It is now only a matter of time before more lives are brutally lost.

A recent survey confirmed that 85% of the public are in favour of the death penalty being re-instated for hate crime murders. It is now just a question of whether a government breathing its last will be able to ignore the public's demands for much longer.

———

The Leader of the Opposition was content. His plan was working. With more by-elections due any day, the government would soon have no outright majority. He would be able to force a no confidence vote, provided he could get the smaller parties onside. He knew that they were against the death penalty in any form, so he would have to use a different tactic with them. Initial conversations had already been held about forming a coalition to give some of the smaller parties a real voice in parliament. The truth was, he had no intention of forming any coalitions, he wanted an outright majority and he was going to get it. This government was now on its knees after years in power. Victory was so close; he could almost taste it.

If the public was really in favour of bringing back the death penalty, then he had been seen to be supportive of the issue from the start, and most importantly, before the Prime Minister. If the whole thing went belly up, then he'd been careful to only ask for the matter to be debated. That way, the current government would get the blame if there was any backlash. So far, the media were largely supportive of there being a grown-up debate about the topic. It had been a long time since it last happened. Parliament looked vastly different now, as did the country. There were some media outlets who would never be onboard with even discussing it and others who wanted to stop all the chatter and start hanging people for minor traffic violations. They were the worst, as they could stoke up an ugly and vocal side of the public. That would then fuel the other extreme side of the debate, who believed that psychopathic murderers were just misunderstood and needed a hug and some group therapy. It was the grown-ups in the middle, who thought adult discussion was the right approach. Although most of the British public really couldn't give a fuck and were more concerned about whether the good weather was going to hold out for weekend, so they could squeeze in another barbecue before the shitty autumn weather arrived.

The next few days and weeks would be interesting. He had to be careful not to be overly pushy on the death penalty issue. It didn't matter one jot to him. A few dead murderers were nothing to lose sleep over, even if they got the odd one wrong. The odds of murder convictions being overturned were limited now anyway, especially with the emergence of DNA evidence. That was certainly what the more logical side of the pro death penalty debate were pushing as their angle anyway.

He was hoping that the Prime Minister would make a statement soon. He didn't want to risk shooting his mouth off during a heated debate in the House of Commons. It was always a danger. The smell of the green leather was intoxicating, and he visualised himself up there taking the questions himself one day, instead of that smug-faced little prick. Some people were born for power, and that's what this country needed, someone to take a stranglehold of it, and drag it into the future kicking and screaming. The death penalty might seem like a step back, like something out of the dark ages, but politics was all about image. If he supported the public on this, then they were so gullible that they would support him on some of the more extreme sweeping reforms that he had planned.

He got up, stretched, and began pacing round his office muttering to himself. Talking through how he was going to handle the questions when he next faced the cameras. The story was national now. Polly Pilkington was getting all the scoops and he liked to use the local angle of her being London based – convenient too! She was a woman you wanted as a friend not an enemy. He'd seen her personal vendetta in every article against that DCI Fenton bloke. There must be some bitter history between them. He wondered what it could be and had contemplated having someone dig around to find out, but perhaps this was one of those situations when it was best not to know the full story; it would be easier to claim ignorance later.

———

"Is this woman serious? She never even asked to speak to me, did she?" the Prime Minister asked his secretary.

"We never had any calls from her, Prime Minister.".

"I thought not. Have you seen this so-called survey?" he said brandishing the newspaper. "Look at the bottom in font so small that you need a microscope. This was a survey of a hundred people, blah, blah. A hundred people? That's eighty-five people in favour of the death penalty out of over sixty million. Hardly eighty-five per cent of the population now, is it? Where did they even survey these people?"

"I could try and find out," offered the secretary.

"What's the point? She'll only find out and start gunning for me more than she is now, instead of this poor Fenton bloke."

The secretary nodded and left the room.

The Prime Minister rubbed his eyeballs, so they made that satisfying squelching noise and yawned. He was tired. He was about to lose a string of by-elections and move into minority government. A general election did not have to be called for another three years, but he knew that as soon as he no longer had the numbers, a no confidence vote would be called by the snake who sat opposite him every day. The smaller parties would be needed to topple the Government and he was aware that the Leader of the Opposition were already canvassing that group. The advantage to the Prime Minister is that that smaller parties didn't trust his counter-part either, but if a vote was called, they would likely abstain. This would still bring in the numbers to topple the Govern-ment and trigger an election. There was no way he was going to let that happen. He'd lose by a landslide. The Prime Minister knew how politics worked in this country and if he went to the public now, he would face a crushing defeat. However, he knew the public had short memories when it came to the ballot box and if he could cling on, things could look quite different in just a year, let alone three.

He had to think fast and react. It was no good being seen

to be playing catch-up all the time. He had to wrong foot him; go one better. He wouldn't just propose to debate the death penalty as part of some boring *motion*, he could introduce a bill in the Queen's speech. That would wipe the smug look off his face. This would mean the debate being pushed for could still happen, but if the House of Commons was in favour of reinstating the death penalty in some form, they could move swiftly into legislating. The Prime Minister knew it was unlikely that the House of Commons would vote for the death penalty to come back, but it would look more decisive to the public and could bolster his approval ratings, which were currently in negative territory. He'd play it safe for now; he wasn't going to wade in with this suggestion straight away. He wanted to see if the public were really in favour of this, rather than just eighty-five carefully selected people that still lived in caves. He would need to do some discrete polling by way of asking his MPs to find out what their constituents really thought about the whole debacle that was playing out in the press. He would make sure it was brought to everyone's attention how minute the sample size had been. He wouldn't do it personally as it would look petty, but he had someone in mind, who would love the drama of raising the issue.

With the press, he'd use the angle that some important issues had been raised and that more thorough research into public opinion was needed. That way he could use that argument with his own MPs, some of which were vehemently opposed to the death penalty and believed that it shouldn't be even be discussed; that conversation belonged in the last century. They had a point. Even though the death penalty had remained on the statute book for a few offences, including treason until the late 1990s, nobody had been executed in this country since the 1960s. Did they really want to go back to that time? Most liberal countries had moved on from such draconian measures, but it was something which bubbled up every now and then. You had to be seen to placate the public, even if you thought they were idiots. After all, it was the public who put you in power.

He was getting excited by politics again. If he could score some political points, then even better. He felt that it might be prudent to get the inside track on the police investigation. It was highly unethical to go behind the back of his Home Secretary but needs must. He needed facts to throw at the Leader of the Opposition. All he'd get through official channels was image and spin. It was the real police investigation he needed to know about, and there was only one man who could give him that.

———

The Leader of the Other Party appeared on *Newsnight* to discuss the findings of the survey. Debbie was up for the public vote again. She survived, albeit with a reduced majority. Debbie was still the bookies' favourite to take the title, although fellow competitors had started narrowing the gap. Twelve million viewers tuned in. The *Newsnight* figures weren't high enough to register on the BARB scale.

CHAPTER TWELVE

Fenton was sitting in his office bewildered by what had just happened. Upon returning to London he'd received a very mysterious phone call, asking him to attend an important meeting that he wasn't to share with anyone. He'd been stunned to find himself facing the Prime Minister who had asked him about the case in detail. In all his years in policing he had never heard of politicians becoming involved with police investigations, with perhaps the exception of the Home Secretary, but even then, Fenton never got to meet them.

The Prime Minister had probed Fenton on how the investigation was proceeding and he'd kept to the official line. They were looking for a serial killer with a hate crime motive. Only when the Prime Minister offered up alternative scenarios did Fenton talk more candidly. He explained how they had narrowed things down to two possible suspects and his team were carrying out further investigations. They were confident of having enough for an arrest within days.

He asked Fenton about Polly Pilkington's personal attacks in her articles and he explained the history. He informed the

Prime Minister that he suspected a leak was coming from inside the Police and that's why she seemed to know how the ins and outs of the investigation, sometimes before even they were aware. When quizzed about whether he knew who the leak was, Fenton kept quiet. That was something he had shared with only Taylor, Brennan and Shirkham. He didn't want to risk a slander case when he had no proof.

The Prime Minister had asked him to keep their meeting private. He had respected this wish and hadn't even told Taylor, or his wife. He was starting to forget what his children looked like. He was up and out before them every morning, and they were already asleep when he got home. With weekend leave now cancelled, he wouldn't see them properly until the case was over. He only saw his wife because they shared a bed. She'd politely told him that she and the girls were getting bored of cottage pie. Every time he asked her to cook it, he had been kept back at work. She'd promised to do one of her best when he could guarantee he'd be home. Even though a conclusion to the investigation seemed a long way off it gave him something to look forward to; it was the smaller things in life!

Taylor knocked on the door and he signalled for her to enter. She was holding up a copy of the *London News* with a look on her face that said trouble.

"What now?" he groaned.

"Forensics have come in."

"Brilliant."

"I'd save your enthusiasm." She tossed the paper at him.

He scanned the front page, which was dominated by another Polly Pilkington article; the new daily normal. When he finished the article, he was raging.

"When did we get hold of these?" he fumed

"That's it sir, we haven't!"

"You mean to tell me the forensic results have appeared in the press before we got hold of them?"

"Exactly."

"That's all the proof I need. Get your coat, and don't tell anyone where we're going, I want to turn up unannounced."

Taylor left the room. Fenton was feeling a plethora of emotions – joy, and anger vying for prime position. This was the proof he'd been hoping for. He had to think carefully about how he was going to play this. His wife had mentioned the phrase *bull in a china shop* all too often and he had her voice ringing in his head as his instincts kicked in. He needed to be the consummate professional and tactful in how he addressed this gross breach of confidentiality. As he grabbed his jacket he thought about how he could bring it up and there were many ways he could play this, but after years of her jibing at him, he knew the reality of how he was going to handle this situation; his wife's voice of warning pushed out of his mind.

He burst into Manning's lab with a grin fixed on his face. She looked a little startled at first; however, the typical stony expression was soon firmly ensconced.

"Eric, I wasn't expecting to see you."

"Can we speak somewhere privately please?"

"Of course, we can use my office."

He'd never seen her look so flustered. It was a wonderful feeling. Fenton and Taylor followed her into her office.

Fenton had never been in Manning's office before. He found the place devoid of any soul. There was no feminine touch, no trace of personality. The atmosphere gave the place a sense of cold and caused him to shiver. It was vastly different to the clean, new, and modern lab outside, although the lack of character was identical. The shelves were covered with medical books and journals. Nothing else would have given the indication of who used the office. He thought it was unusual for a woman not to put her mark on her personal space. Taylor moved offices all the time, depending on where the investigation was, but she still had her little trinkets that went everywhere with her. Granted women didn't tend to mark their territory by urinating round the desk; however, something usually gave an indication that it was their space. It made him think that Manning was either very lonely, or very secretive about her private life. No doubt the latter.

"Can you explain how the press have got hold of your report before the investigating team?" asked Fenton bluntly.

"I'm sorry?" replied Manning, not giving anything away.

"I was just surprised to read your forensic report in the *London News*, rather than in the usual manner... Like when you send me the official report. So, tell me Mandy, what the fuck is going on?" *Oops, didn't mean to swear!*

Manning's eyes narrowed. "Please do not use that language in my office, or I'll have to ask you to leave."

"Sorry, Ms Manning."

"That's not what I was referring to."

"Nice try – just answer the question," he said flopping down on the chair.

"What are you implying, Eric?"

"Would you like me to spell it out?"

"Evidently."

"I think, no, sorry, let me rephrase that, I know that you have been leaking information to Polly Pilkington."

"How dare you," she replied incredulously. "I am a professional. I would never speak to the press without being asked to by the investigating officer."

"Well, how did she find out before we did? You're the one who wrote the report."

His tone was getting increasingly patronising and he was pleased to see that it was continuing to fluster Manning. He noticed that Taylor was finding a patch of dust on the carpet interesting, probably to avoid pissing herself laughing – so much for sisterhood.

"Not got anything to say, Lisa, or are you just the witness?"

"Keep her out of it," bellowed Fenton.

Taylor went to speak, but Fenton held up his hand to stop her. She held his stare for a moment and then went back to her dust.

"There's a good girl, know your place. God, you've got her well trained, Eric."

"We're here to talk about you and the fact that you have hindered my investigation from day one by talking to that woman."

"What proof do you have?"

"Apart from what I've just mentioned. Well, the photos of the two of you in bed together should be back from the developers soon."

Taylor gasped.

Fenton realised he had gone too far.

Manning's rage disappeared from her face, only to be replaced by a smug grin.

"Get out of my office, and my lab, DCI Fenton."

"Not before we have discussed the implications of this report."

"Try reading it, get out – now!" she screamed, but keeping the cat that got the cream look on her face.

"But, but, but…" Fenton spluttered.

"I can have security remove you if you wish?"

Knowing he was beaten and knowing he needed time to calm down, he left, slamming the door behind him before Taylor had chance to follow him.

.   .   .

"Manning has made a formal complaint, Eric," said Chief Superintendent Harry Beeden with a severe tone to his voice.

"You've got to be joking. She's the one that's been leaking…" He was spluttering out the words. It was unlike him to be flustered, but Beeden held up his hand to stop him.

"Sit down, Eric, please."

Fenton did as he was told. He explained calmly about the report. He described his first suspicions, and lack of any evidence, emphasising that the press getting hold of the forensic report before he had seen it was proof that the leak couldn't have come from anywhere else.

Beeden held up the forensic report and explained that it had been overlooked by one of the junior team members. He questioned why Fenton hadn't held a briefing since his return from Preston. Fenton explained that he was waiting on the forensic results to do a full briefing and asked to see the report. Beeden passed it to him and waited patiently whilst he read the report in detail.

"Well, at least one good thing has come out of this," he said when he'd finished reading.

"What's that?"

"This proves that there could be more to it. Why would she have been killed differently to the others? There has to be a reason."

"Eric, I want you to keep up with the same line of enquiry."

"Sir, but surely you can see from this?" He'd stood up and was waving the report.

"Sit down, Eric."

He did, exhaling loudly.

"Eric, I know you've got a good instinct for these cases, which is why I've kept you on it, but there is a lot of press attention and with this death penalty debate looking more likely by the day –"

"You're not serious?" he interrupted.

"It's just a rumour for now, but momentum is gaining. Most of the nationals are following Pilkington and running surveys of their own, with larger sample sizes."

"She's only doing this for her own career."

"I know that. She's scooping all the big players and the news channels on this, and before you interrupt again, you've not got enough proof. Now, I can slow down this complaint working its way through the system. Make an arrest, Eric, and quickly, or I won't be able to keep you on the case. If you feel there is something more to it then by all means investigate it but do it quietly. We have to be seen as taking this hate crime angle seriously, whether that is the true motive for these killings or not."

"Thank you, sir." He got up to leave, but Beeden gestured for him to sit again.

"Rumour has it that the Prime Minister is keeping a close eye on this case personally, but that's nothing for you to worry about. I'll deal with the politics and the press; just don't piss anyone else off."

Fenton nodded feeling slightly guilty about not mentioning his private meeting with the Prime Minister. He felt that might be the last straw for Beeden, and he would almost certainly throw him off the case if he found out. Something that would never happen, and Fenton would keep his word and never tell anyone.

"I think an arrest is imminent, sir. I have two, or maybe even three strong suspects. I just need a little bit more time. It's still all circumstantial."

"Circumstantial is enough for an arrest. Bring them in."

"I'd rather not be releasing them a couple of hours later and being made to look an incompetent prick by Pilkington."

"You need to stop this vendetta, Eric. Nobody blames you for the Davies case."

"I do, sir."

"Solve this one quickly, Eric, and I'll give you Taylor, Brennan and Shirkham to reopen it."

"What if it wasn't a hate crime?"

"Get a conviction and nobody will give a damn what the motive was."

Fenton smiled, he'd known Harry a long time and it was good to know that the old Harry was still there behind the image side of high-level policing.

"I'm always the consummate professional, sir."

"We'll see about that. I want you to give an interview to Pilkington and try not to lose it."

Fenton buried his head in his hands, shaking and laughing with the sheer irony of the situation.

Beeden couldn't help but laugh as well. "You can hold off until you've made an arrest, but I want that within forty-eight hours."

Fenton nodded and got up to leave. "It's good to see the old Harry still lurking in there somewhere."

"He always will be here Eric. Keep me updated."

Fenton was back in his office absorbing how much had happened in one day; a private meeting with the Prime Minister, he'd finally told Manning what he thought of her and he'd been offered the opportunity to re-open the Davies case. On the other hand, he had to give Polly Pilkington an exclusive interview, but life tended to be mixed bag.

The way this case was going, who knew what else could happen in the next two days, or who they could arrest as a suspect – this investigation was becoming more dramatic than a soap opera. Not that he watched such tripe, but his wife was a fan, so occasionally he had to feign interest.

"Come in," he shouted in response to a knock on his door.

Taylor, Brennan and Shirkham entered and sat down. He explained his meeting with Beeden and about the complaint from Manning. There was to be no recourse against the junior officer who'd missed the report. Fenton took full responsibility for the blunder.

"Are you still on the case, Guv?" asked Brennan.

"Yes, lucky for you." He smiled. "We need to drop the Pilkington and Manning thing now."

"We know there's something going on though."

"Maybe we can come back to it later but, in the meantime, Beeden's said we need to make an arrest within forty-eight hours."

"So, do we go for Jez Tool, Peter Gleeson or Wendy Baxter?" asked Shirkham.

"I think we can rule out Wendy for now. I can't be arsed with the wailing victim act and the last thing I need is another complaint. We need to find out as much as we can on the other two. I want to know what the confidential matter between Elizabeth Jamal and Peter Gleeson was. Emma, get a warrant or something. Whatever it takes. Let the locals deal with it. We haven't got time to be bombing up and down the motorway. Not until we're going to make an arrest, anyway."

"Yes, sir."

"Gary, do you know what that political group was that Jez Tool belonged to?"

"Apparently it's called FREE, short for Far-Right Extremist Enigma."

"Extremist Enigma?"

Brennan nodded.

"But that name doesn't make any sense."

"What does about this case, Guv?" Brennan shrugged.

"True but find out that it's not some sort of ironic piss-take before we take it seriously. Now I need to have a quiet word with DI Taylor."

Brennan and Shirkham both nodded and left the room, leaving them alone.

"You all right, sir? You look knackered."

"Nothing that a good night's sleep won't fix."

"Then slip off for bit. I can hold things here."

"Nice idea, Lisa, but I've got too much riding on us making a break and quickly."

"A good home-cooked meal will do you good."

"Not much chance of that; anyway, she's away for the weekend at her mothers with the girls."

"Then takeaway and twelve hours' sleep."

The idea sounded wonderful, but he had some other pressing matters he wanted to deal with first, to move the case forward. He'd thought long and hard about what he was going to do next and Taylor was the one he could trust the most.

"Just between me and you this is, Lisa."

She gave him a look as if to say that it didn't need saying, but he felt by saying that, it would emphasise he was treading into dangerous waters. The kind that could prematurely end or at the least severely damage a career. Only his though: he would never do anything that could threaten hers.

"I still want to go for Manning and Pilkington."

"What do you need?"

He breathed a sigh of relief, as he thought he might have to spend some time convincing her.

"It's a bit unethical."

She shrugged.

"I want proof that they're screwing."

"What, literally?" she joked.

"Whatever it takes."

"Just one question though. What if they're not?"

"You don't think Manning's the leak?" he asked sarcastically.

"No doubt that she is. They may just be friends, or some mutual backscratching is going on. If you'll pardon the pun."

"Do lesbians scratch backs?"

"Dunno, sir, it's never come up in conversation with any lesbians I know."

"I think it's doubtful that they are just friends. I couldn't see what Pilkington might be able to offer Manning as a friend."

"At least if we catch them together it proves they're more than passing acquaintance. I'll save the bedroom shots for Gary."

He nodded, not really listening. He'd zoned out again. He vaguely knew that she had stopped talking. This was something she did, allowing him to come back into the room in his own time and negating the need for her to sound like a parrot. This period of silence would usually cause him to be aware that his attention was needed elsewhere.

"Beeden says I have to give Pilkington an interview."

Taylor laughed.

"It's not funny."

"Oh, it is."

He smiled. In some weird masochistic way, it probably was very funny – he'd laugh later, if he survived the interview without using the words *bitch* or *Manning*.

"I'm going to hold off until the arrest. I'd like you in with me though."

"To give you a kick under table if you get too gobby?"

"Something like that."

Taylor left, leaving Fenton alone. Within two days he was going to have a suspect in a cell downstairs, even if it was just circumstantial. He suspected that Tool would be using legal aid, unlike Gleeson, who would no doubt have some smart-arsed lawyer who would have his client back up the M6 within the hour. Unless something major came his way then he'd focus on Tool in the first instance. It was cruel, but Jez looked the part and would make it easier to fob off the press for a while. They don't like their killers to look like accountants, let alone be one – it was boring and didn't sell newspapers.

It would be inevitable that Pilkington would break the story. If he could make the arrest tomorrow, Saturday, then she wouldn't get the chance as her paper didn't publish on weekends. A small victory of course, but needs must when the devil...

He was going to take Taylor's advice and head home to recharge himself. He hadn't shared with the others about reopening the Davies case, although it had never been closed to him. Whenever he got a spare moment, he would go over the case notes in the vague hope that something glaringly obvious would be staring at him.

He put a call in to Taylor and told her to schedule a briefing for the next morning at nine o'clock. He was going to go home. He wanted a full intelligence file on this FREE group by then, and a warrant for the personnel files of all Training4All staff. What he didn't tell her was that he was going to make a quick detour on the way home. He made a phone call asking the other person if he could drop by and speak with them. They agreed. It was something he should have done days ago.

CHAPTER THIRTEEN

Far Right Extremist Enigma (FREE): a small political party, was formed to protect the interest of the common man. The founder and chairman, Mr Bill White wanted to create something that reached the people who felt like they didn't have anyone listening to them. Bill had changed his name by deed poll and only his nearest and dearest were aware that he was once Lesley Timpson. Bill felt that the name didn't have quite the same impact as his adopted pseudonym. It also might make him come across as a bit fruity, which was not the impression he wanted to give. Not that there was anything wrong with being fruity, it just wasn't a rumour he wanted to carry into adulthood. Having that name as a child had made life unbearable at school. Now, he was playing with the big leagues and those wankers at school were all working on building sites. It was the only advantage of old classmates making friend requests on Facebook – you could see that the people who made your life miserable at school had basically amounted to nothing. There was something strangely satisfying about that.

Bill was married with eight children. He felt that the

more children he had, the more manly he would appear. He believed that humans should take their lead from the lion in the jungle and it was the one who produced the most cubs who became king of the jungle. Once he took his virility to extremes and horrified the delivery team, after child number seven, when he tried to mount his wife immediately after the birth, but found himself covered in placenta.

After that incident, Bill always let his wife have a cooling off period before impregnating her again. She was currently pregnant with their ninth child. Impressive, you might think, even more so when you found out that she was twenty-five years old. Bill was only two years older. His first two children had been born out of wedlock. There wasn't anything rebellious about it, they just weren't old enough to get married at the time. Bill wanted to have even more children but was planning to stop when his wife was thirty. Their eldest child would be able to have their own children by then and it was important to Bill that none of his grandchildren were older than his own kids – that would be weird.

Bill liked to think of himself as a bit of a rebel, which is why he set up FREE. He had got a taste for power when he had been the leader of THE GANG at school. They had selected this name because they felt it had a mysterious edge to it, as nobody would know what sort of gang they were. It was a collection of misfits who were bullied by other kids for having certain quirks, oddities, or fruity names. One of the teachers had described Bill and his gang as an extreme enigma. This had stayed with Bill until he had set up FREE and he used it in the name.

Bill chose to add *far-right* to the name, as this explained the geographical location of their headquarters – they were based in East London. The name must have worked as it attracted people. As word spread, numbers swelled and soon the party had topped one thousand members – more people than had been in Bill's school. He was enormously proud and told his wife he wanted to celebrate this achievement by making her pregnant again. It was then that she told him it wouldn't be possible to get pregnant for at least six months. Bill protested that this was a dig at his masculinity. His wife pointed out that she was unlikely to fall pregnant for the next six months as she was already three months gone and not even Bill was virile enough to impregnate a woman who had ceased ovulating.

FREE meetings were always a lively affair. People boasted about their recent criminal activities, although the most extreme thing anybody had done was beat up old ladies and school children for pin money. This was, of course, not advocated by Bill, and was not in the party's manifesto. It was just that the party seemed to attract a few unsavoury types and Bill wasn't sure why. He didn't commend this type of behaviour and he often had to calm down some of the group when they got a bit restless. There would often be talk about pummelling blacks and gays. Bill found that these bold statements from some of the group rarely turned into action. The few that had been less talk and more action had forgotten that in this day and age, grown men, no matter what colour a person is, or what they did in bed, simply wouldn't put up with that kind of crap any more, and tended to beat the living shit out of anyone who attempted to bully or intimidate them. Bill was still mystified as to why he attracted so many yobs to his East London based enigmatic party.

FREE didn't have a manifesto at first as Bill didn't know what one was.

"It's what changes you would make to the law if you were Prime Minister, Lesley," his mother had said one afternoon.

"Mum don't call me Lesley, it's Bill now. Dad calls me Bill."

"You're not too old for a clip round the ear."

Bill thought that he probably was but decided not to test his mother. His ear was still ringing from the last time he'd back-chatted her.

The manifesto idea had got Bill thinking. He had to come up with some bold and controversial ideas. The sort that would get people's juices flowing and swell membership further. This was his only source of income at present and party funds were badly depleted, partly because Bill had a small football team at home, and a wife who couldn't go out to work as she was always pregnant.

There had been calls from some of the more vocal elements of the party that there should be a ban on certain sections of society from being allowed to gain membership. Bill was aware this was now illegal and the last thing he needed was a legal challenge to the validity of his party. He was a man of principle, but he was also a man with little disposable income. FREE wasn't about excluding people. It was about protecting the interests of the common man. It didn't really matter where that man came from. It was about brotherhood. The only group he'd wanted to exclude was women, but his wife and mother had put the kibosh on that notion. Bill knew when he was beaten, literally, so women could now join as well.

He decided to come up with ten things he would do if he was Prime Minister. It seemed like a good number and it would mirror that of some of his competitors.

———

FREE MANIFESTO

1. Protect the interest of the common man (and woman).

2. Free education for everyone on low income, even when you have left school.

3. Death penalty for all murderers and anyone that does anything that's not normal to a child (can't spell that big word).

4. Legalise all drugs, except heroin, crack, the date rape drug, the legal highs which keep killing all the kids and dope, because it stinks.

5. Free housing for people with more than five children.

6. Increased welfare for people who support the interests of the common man (and woman).

7. Ten extra bank holidays, which means everyone will be allowed to get their dole money early.

8. Allow people to have twenty minutes porn viewing during the working day, with use of a private office.

9. Get rid of TV licences and have adverts instead.

10. You must live within twenty miles of the football team you support, or you will go to prison for ten years.

———

Bill was immensely proud of his manifesto. He felt that the FREE message needed to reach people outside Plaistow. He had a few northerners in the group, one guy was from as far north as Tottenham but, if he was going to be Prime Minister, he needed people who lived outside the M25. He liked the idea of living in Downing Street and wondered if they had enough bedrooms for all his kids. He remembered Tony Blair having to move next door and he only had four kids. Perhaps they could knock a few walls down. Well, if he was Prime Minister it would be up to him.

He made a website, well, a Facebook page, and started to generate interest in FREE. He wanted a real website, with a logo and everything, so he recruited a volunteer website manager. This was how he met Jez Tool.

Jez had been in London visiting his brother in Wormwood Scrubs, and his father in Maidstone, his uncle in Pentonville and his mother in Holloway. The judge had put them into prisons as far away from home as possible. Jez told Bill that, this way, when they were released for the umpteenth time; all the friends they had made in prison would be unlikely to venture too far north without coming out in a cold sweat. This may mean the possibility that they would go straight. The judge also felt Jez needed a break and had said he was a bright lad, with a misguided loyalty to his family.

They were a nasty bunch but, in the past, had merely been shoplifters, shed robbers, car vandals and benefit fraudsters. It was a right pain in the arse if you were a victim, but they were still petty criminals, nonetheless. The judge had branded them as this when he last sentenced them to a spell inside. They'd robbed a post office with a banana in a brown paper bag. He'd given them a few years apiece and got them as far away from Jez as possible, Bill thought. Sadly, Jez was too blinkered to see this and spent most of his weekends in London on prison visits and attending FREE meetings. Bill was pleased to have Jez's company and put him up on the sofa. His wife grumbled at first but, one day, walked in on Jez when he was getting out of the shower and, for some reason Bill couldn't quite fathom, she'd never complained since.

Mrs White had a minor crush on her new house guest. Even though nothing had happened between them, yet, the thought that a man existed who appeared endowed enough to be able bring her to a state of ecstasy, without touching her at this time, excited her. Especially after giving birth eight times, she thought her orgasming days were over. She'd resigned herself to the fact that her lady area now resembled a log flume.

Sex with Bill was exciting again, purely by the wondrous use of her imagination. She'd fantasise about what Jez Tool could do to her with his, well, tool. Her vivid thoughts took her to places that made her writhe in absolute unadulterated pleasure and screaming abandon. She'd never known her spine to be so flexible. She made sure that she bellowed the house down whenever Jez was on the sofa, and then act all coy in the morning as she prepared his breakfast, well, poured out the cornflakes into the best bowl – the one with only two chips!

———

Bill was ecstatic at his new active sex life and the noises his wife was making as he ploughed her. He'd started measuring his cock regularly, convinced it was getting bigger; well, why else would she be screaming the place down? The neighbours had called the police once under the impression that someone was being murdered. It was one of the proudest moments of Bill's life when the police burst in as he hit the vinegar stroke.

Jez spent time building the website and membership continued to grow, much to Bill's delight. The tenth child was now on its way so the increased revenue would come in useful. The ninth child had been a huge eleven-pound bundle of joy. Following the release of Jez's family from prison, his visits became less frequent and Mrs White spent the rest of her twenties either pregnant, or with Bill writhing around on top of her trying to get her there.

Jez had let his FREE membership lapse and, when his family were put away again, this time for armed robbery with a courgette, Jez gave up on them and only visited infrequently out of a warped sense of duty. He had other interests that took him to London at times, although Bill wasn't sure what these were. The judge had got his way in the end and, with his mother, the ringleader as far as the judge was concerned, in Durham, she never got a visit. Jez never had an excuse to go there.

———

"What is this FREE? Should I be concerned?" the Prime Minister asked his secretary.

"I don't think so, sir. They seem a bit low rent to be honest."

"Never heard of them. Sounds like they don't know what they want or what they are doing. Bit like the opposition really," he laughed.

"Yes, sir."

"I mean they could have come up with a better name. Talk about an oxymoron."

"Should we have the intelligence services check them out?"

"I think they're rather busy at the moment and these people appear to be rather inconsequential."

"As you wish, sir."

———

"Who is this FREE? Sounds like a bunch of knuckle-dragging twats to me," remarked the Leader of the Opposition to his chief minion.

"You've described them to a tee, sir."

"Get the intelligence bods to check them out anyway."

"Erm... we can't do that, sir."

"What do you mean?"

"Well, only the Prime Minister can do that, and he already regards them as irrelevant so won't sanction it."

"How do you know this?"

"A little bird told me."

"Been screwing his secretary again, have we?"

"Erm... well, I, no, well..."

"Feel free to fraternise to your heart's content; just don't go giving away my secrets at the same time."

"Don't worry, sir, I'm not the one with the loose tongue."

"Yes, well, find out what you can about this FREE thing anyway. It may come in useful later."

"Certainly, sir." He left.

He should really find out the chief minion's name. Not out of some duty as an employer, but if the minion was rogering the Prime Minister's secretary he had suddenly become an incredibly useful minion, instead of the usual fodder.

————

Nobody knew what the Leader of the Other Party thought about FREE as, although he had recently made an appearance on *BBC News*, Debbie was up for eviction again and the entire nation was gripped to see if she would survive the chopping block for a third time. To everyone's delight, she did, and she vowed to avoid temptation as she was doing this for her fans. Her popularity intensified overnight, and the bookies stopped taking bets on her winning the grand prize – a lifetime supply of cakes!

CHAPTER FOURTEEN

Fenton was picking at an inedible microwaved cottage pie. He missed his wife's home cooking a lot; aside from that, he missed her and the girls more than anything. Even though he hadn't seen much of them these past few weeks, the fact that they were at home had been somewhat reassuring. They'd now gone away for the half-term break and the house was very empty, even when he did manage to make it home.

Taylor's suggestion of a takeaway and twelve-hour sleep had been a great idea. The takeaway had not happened as he'd showered and lain down on the bed and fallen asleep immediately. He'd woken at seven and ventured down to his local café for a builder's breakfast – it took half an hour to eat. It still wasn't enough though, so he was eating the cottage pie he'd bought for lunch. He picked around a bit more, looking for the bits that were masquerading as meat, then tossed the rest in the bin.

He glanced at the wall. It was almost time for the briefing, which had been pushed back to ten o'clock because there was, yet another tube strike and people were having to literally walk into the office. He was well prepared, as having such a long sleep had made him very alert. He was hoping that someone was going to come up with some evidence which sent them one way or the other. By the end of this meeting he would need to make a final decision about whom he was going to go for, Peter Gleeson or Jez Tool.

Everyone sat facing the incident board. Fenton familiarised himself with anything new that had been put up. Taylor had briefed him earlier on any developments. He didn't like surprises, although he hoped for one this morning which would force him in one direction or the other. He turned around and noticed that Brennan was absent from the briefing. Before he could question his whereabouts, all eyes fixed on him and the room fell silent.

"What we have is two suspects and a lot of circumstantial evidence. We've got enough to bring them both in, but nothing that would stick in a court of law. I doubt they were both in it together, so what we need is something that will tip the balance towards either Peter Gleeson or Jez Tool. Let's start with Gleeson. Emma, what have you got for us?"

Shirkham got up and Fenton took her seat. She was sitting at the front and only needed to move a few inches to take Fenton's position, but she still managed to do this with a gliding motion that entranced the men. Taylor's face showed a look of amusement.

"Peter Gleeson had a disagreement with Elizabeth Jamal a few days prior to the conference and was given an informal warning for his conduct. He was refusing to attend the conference, referring to it as *fluffy bullshit*, and failed to see why the support staff needed to attend, when it was aimed at the performance enablement facilitators. Sorry... trainers!"

Everyone laughed.

"Why did he go then?" asked Fenton.

"The warning would have become a formal one had he not, and he didn't want an active warning on his file."

"Looking to move on then, is he?"

"It seems that's a strong possibility, but he wasn't about to volunteer that information. He also has a strong aversion to diversity training. It's compulsory for all staff at Training4All, which he doesn't object to. What he does object to is that they keep changing it and then making everybody do it again. It appears the course has undergone seven revamps in two years, and Peter isn't the only one grumbling about it."

"Is Jez one of them?"

"Not that we've heard. He's not the vocal type though."

"What was Gleeson's relationship like with the victims?"

"Well, he was Trudie's line manager and there was definitely some issues there, although that's nothing unusual. I never met the woman and even I could see the appeal of throttling her. The only thing between the two men was that it was Nadeem's wife who gave him the informal warning, and Carl was the one who was delivering the diversity training course. He was known for thrusting the gay agenda down people's throats, if you'll pardon the pun, quite a lot."

More laughter.

"In what way?"

Fenton smiled as Shirkham raised her eyebrows.

"Well they used to spend an equal amount of training time looking at each of the protected characteristics. A day on each to be precise."

"A day?"

"Yep, the course took two weeks! Then it was reduced to two days with half an hour on each, plus a load of other stuff about the law and Walt's vision for a better future. In the end, it was cut down to half day and included one case study, which was always on sexual orientation."

"Do we know what the case study involved?"

"Something about how the term girlfriend and boyfriend might offend homosexuals in the workplace."

"What a load of bollocks."

"That was the point Carl was trying to get across. It was a brainwave that Carl and Walt had together during one their sessions in the *creation room*. Let me just get the exact quote." She flicked through her notebook and then found what she was looking for. Putting on her serious face, she cited, "It's politically correct to be against political correctness."

"And it took them seven attempts to come up with that?"

"Yes – training is an evolutionary process."

"That come from Walt?"

Shirkham nodded.

"Thanks, Emma."

She took her seat as Fenton stood up. He had to shush the team as they were giggling like children. Fenton wasn't sure if it was what Shirkham had said, or her delivery style which had been very entertaining – probably a combination. She had held their attention throughout her debrief and that wasn't because of how she looked. The team respected her, and it was a shame that she had no desire to go further up the ranks.

The team had quietened down so he began.

"Right, if we are to focus on the hate crime angle and assume that Peter Gleeson is our killer then we only have a possible motive for the murder of Carl Davenport. Perhaps the conference just tipped him over the edge. Was it at the conference this politically correct drivel was thought up?" he asked, looking at Shirkham.

"Yes, sir – it was a *thought shower* conference," she said, with disdain.

"Good, but if he killed Nadeem Jamal to get back at Elizabeth then it doesn't add up, unless he just lost it and went on a killing spree. As for Trudie, well, anyone could have killed her in all honesty. I mean, I'm surprised she lived that long if everything we've heard about her is accurate. The only concern now is this forensics report. It appears that Trudie was killed in a different way to the other two. Not a different weapon, just a different way," he added to reduce the murmuring that had suddenly broken out.

"The two men were both stabbed in the heart by a double-pronged knife. The murder weapon has not been recovered, and it appears there is no way of knowing how many knives are missing from the hotel kitchen as they don't count them. *I'm running a hotel not a prison.*"

His impression of the hotel manager caused great amusement – hosting briefings was often like a stand-up routine in order to keep all the brains engaged. Besides, he had to up the ante after following Shirkham.

"Both men were standing, and their killer stabbed them, it appears face on. Trudie however, was sitting, obviously, but the killer came at her from behind, still killing her with the same type of knife and with a stab wound to the heart. Death was a matter of seconds for each of the victims. The way Trudie was slumped on the floor signals that she toppled forward, rather than was pushed, and the forensic evidence indicates that this was after death. Perhaps it means nothing, other than the fact that our killer had a conscience about looking the old woman in the eyes when they stabbed her. It's for us to find out and quick."

"Perhaps she was first, and the killer didn't get enough of a kick out of it the first time so changed tactic for the second and third," piped up one of the junior officers at the back.

"Good suggestion," acknowledged Fenton. "We know that Carl was killed after Nadeem as traces of Nadeem's blood were found on Carl's body. We have no forensic evidence of where in the sequence Trudie was killed. Manning has finished her reports and the bodies have been released to the families. I'd like details of the funeral arrangements please, so we can ensure we are represented, if I can't make it myself."

He signalled towards Taylor, who got up and stood at the front. Fenton took her seat.

"The second suspect, Jez Tool, was a member of the political group FREE. Now from what we can make out, they seem to be all words and not much action, but this could just be a front as there were some very unsavoury types who identify themselves as members. Jez was alone in his room at the time of the murders and was only aware of anything going on when he returned from his visit to the shops, by which time all the bodies had been discovered and the place was buzzing with police. Jez has a couple of arrests on record but no convictions or cautions. It appears to be more association than direct involvement in any violent crime."

"The family are still inside?" Fenton asked.

"Yes. He's still known to make regular visits to London, often staying in the Kings Cross area. He doesn't stay with Bill White, founder of FREE anymore."

"We need to look into the Kings Cross thing. That can't be a coincidence. Have we interviewed White?"

"Yes, nowt of use though, sir. We spoke to his wife as well, as Jez usually stayed at the family home when visiting."

"What did she have to say about Jez?"

Taylor stumbled over her words for a second and Fenton wondered what had flustered her.

"She didn't say anything of use, other than that he stayed on their sofa occasionally."

"Did we check with the hotel manager about what time he left and came back?"

"Gary's doing that now."

So that's where he was, Fenton thought, as he stood up and swapped places with Taylor. He was annoyed that this important fact hadn't been checked earlier.

"We still have a leak somewhere within the team, and I don't just mean the team within this room. I mean the whole team."

Fenton had regained control of the room and was a little bewildered as to why Taylor seemed to have lost her stride a few times when talking about Jez Tool. He suspected something, but hoped he was wrong. It was her one weakness, which could end a very promising career. He put it down to tiredness and pressed on.

"I'll be honest with you all now. I have directly accused Mandy Manning, the forensic pathologist, of leaking information to Polly Pilkington. A complaint has now been made against me."

There were a few audible gasps. He omitted to tell the team that he had accused them of having an affair.

"I'm still leading this investigation and I'm certain we can make an arrest before the end of the weekend."

He again opted not to share the fact that he was hoping to make that arrest sooner if he could."

"I want everything checked over again. I want something concrete on either Gleeson or Tool and I want it now. We'll meet again tomorrow morning at the same time, but if anything, no matter how trivial it seems, comes in then I want to be told straight away."

The briefing broke up and Fenton returned to his office, whilst Taylor distributed work to the rest of the team.

———

Taylor was left alone with Shirkham as the rest of the team got on with their assigned duties. Fenton had managed to give them a kick but had also got them gossiping about where Pilkington could be getting her information. He hadn't said he still believed the leak was coming from Manning: he had simply mentioned the complaint. It had been a clever deflection tactic. He didn't want the team being suspicious of each other at a crucial time in the investigation. This way they would come to their own conclusions that Manning might be the leak. It meant there would be no underlying tensions and they'd work together as a team and, hopefully, now the Forensics were concluded, there was no reason for Manning to know anything else about the investigation.

"Are you okay?" Shirkham asked Taylor.

"Sure, why wouldn't I be?" she replied vaguely.

"You seem a bit distracted, that's all."

"Just tired. You wanna grab a quick coffee?"

It wasn't unusual for officers to be friendly and on first name terms with those from junior rank, but it wasn't common practice. Taylor and Shirkham had known each other for a while and, despite their difference in rank, they got on very well outside work, keeping it professional whenever they were posted on the same investigation. This was regularly as Fenton usually asked for Taylor, Brennan and Shirkham on his team but, at times, Taylor was already being used elsewhere. As she was working towards promotion, Fenton had said it would be good for her to get exposure to as many different DCIs as possible.

Taylor and Shirkham opted to grab a coffee at one of the *independent* type coffee shops which seemed to be popping up everywhere. They claimed to be very green and have a stronger sense of corporate social responsibility than the mass-market chains. At the end of the day, coffee was coffee and all you were doing was paying through the nose for a coffee cup that had a picture of a lion roaring through the open African wilderness. Apparently, by buying their *responsible* coffee, you had saved the lion.

The place was empty – not surprising with a coffee costing a fiver. The advantage was that there was less chance of being overheard, owing to the constant stream of dire music and the fact that nobody was there to overhear them.

Taylor was reliving her conversation with Mrs White in the sanctuary of her own head. It was evident that Mrs White was quite hung up on Jez and had been upset when he stopped visiting. Taylor had probed about whether anything had happened between them and she had become flustered and denied anything, saying she loved her husband dearly. Taylor suspected she was telling the truth but believed she would certainly have liked something to have happened. Her physical description of Jez had been a little too vivid for someone who claimed to have not really had much of an interest in her husband's friend.

Taylor and Shirkham had been talking for a while. It had felt good to talk to someone without judgement. This had been the same ever since they had first met.

"God, it seems like only yesterday you were a Sergeant and the newbie on the team," said Shirkham.

"Why don't you go for Sergeant's exams? You'd get it easy."

She shrugged. "Do you reckon Fenton has any idea?"

"Possibly, there's nowt gets past him."

"Just be careful."

Shirkham cocked her head to one side, raised her eyebrows and then her face broke into a huge grin. They both laughed. In their fits of giggles, they didn't see Brennan walk in and approach their table.

"What did I miss?" he asked.

They both jumped and looked startled. He eyed them suspiciously.

"Just girl talk," replied Shirkham.

Taylor snorted into her coffee, trying to stop laughing.

"Suit yourselves," he said, shrugging dismissively. Where's the, Guv? My phone battery's dead so I haven't been able to get hold of him."

"In his office. Did you check out the alibi?" asked Shirkham.

He looked round sheepishly. "Hurry up and drink up. I'll just grab a coffee and meet you outside."

Shirkham and Taylor downed their coffees and got up to leave.

———

Fenton looked up, slightly annoyed when Taylor, Brennan and Shirkham walked in unannounced. However, judging by the look on Brennan's face he suspected it was for a good reason.

"I've been trying to call you," Fenton said to Brennan.

"Sorry, Guv, phone died."

Fenton took his wallet out of his pocket, removed a twenty-pound note and slapped in on the desk. "Buy another charger and keep it in your pocket."

Brennan glanced at the note and thought about taking it, but then changed his mind. His hand only flickered for a second, but he knew from the smile Fenton gave that he'd seen him consider it.

"Apparently Jez left the hotel earlier than he said, came back and then went out again, and he had a bag with him."

Brennan was out of breath, so the words were coming out rapidly and garbled.

"Sit down, Gary." Fenton signalled to a chair.

Taylor and Shirkham remained standing by the door.

"The manager told me that Jez went out shortly after the rest of the group sat down for dinner. He left in a hurry apparently."

"But that was before the murders took place?"

"Just getting to that. Then he came back, and, after about ten minutes, he left again, this time with a bag. He literally ran out the door this time."

"Could he actually kill three people in ten minutes? Maybe he just came to pick the bag up."

"Get this though, Guv. When he came back, he headed in the direction of the kitchens, before going up to the rooms."

"Go on," said Fenton, his pulse quickening.

"He left the hotel for the second time prior to the discovery of the first body, not after like he has been telling us."

"But he already said he never saw any police presence when he went outside, so that kind of makes sense," piped up Taylor...

Fenton found her reaction interesting and then signalled for Brennan to carry on.

"He claims to have left at nine thirty, which according to Forensics is after the murders took place, but the hotel manager claims he left before nine. If he had the perfect excuse to prove he was outside the hotel at the time of the murders, why didn't he use it, instead of putting himself alone in his room?" stated Brennan.

"Did you find out which shop he went to?"

"Yes, he did go in the shop. That was at around ten, after all the bodies had been discovered. He could have had the weapon in the bag."

"It still smacks of circumstantial though."

Brennan looked disappointed.

"It's good though, Gary. We just need to be absolutely sure of the time-lines." He was thinking aloud. "But we can work that out later... Right, let's bring him in!"

CHAPTER FIFTEEN

DIVERSITY SLAYER IS FAR RIGHT EXTREMIST
Polly Pilkington

Police have arrested a member of the far-right political group FREE for the triple murder that occurred in a London hotel earlier this month. Jeremiah Tool was apprehended at his home in Preston, Lancashire, late last night. He was transferred to Kentish Town police station in London. Investigating officers are to begin questioning him today.

Lead detective DCI Eric Fenton, 45, made the trip up north in order to make the arrest personally. Earlier today he called the arrest a "significant development" in the case. He wouldn't be drawn further on the exact circumstances of these developments.

Sources close to the investigation reveal that DCI Fenton was told he had only 48 hours before he was to be removed from the investigation. It is also rumoured that a complaint has been made against DCI Fenton for making unfounded accusations against a high ranking professional, intricately linked to the investigating team.

It is unclear on the exact nature of the complaint. A source close to Fenton has revealed that xenophobia is rife within this investigation with inappropriate jokes being made during team briefings. This latest development highlights further whether this is the right man for the job, especially with the next 24 hours being so crucial. There are concerns within the investigating team that the arrest has been made to save DCI Fenton's own skin. There is no guarantee that charges will follow. The public should remain on full alert. If Jeremiah Tool is guilty, but due to police blunders is released without charge, then nobody from a minority group will be safe.

Top criminal psychologist Dr. Deidre Peters, stated, "If this man is the guilty party and he is released back into the community then it is an absolute certainty that he will kill again. Serial killers have a purpose to fulfil and an arrest so early on would have affected his plans. Even if he gets a confidence boost from being released, he will be aware that the net is closing in on him. He will want to reach his climax. The pleasure he seeks in snuffing out those he feels are unworthy of life will draw him to kill again and again."

With the Queen's Speech due next week, it is still unclear if a debate on the death penalty will be tabled. The Prime Minister still refuses to be drawn on the issue and insists more research is needed. It is alarming that he is not listening to 85% of the public who support such a debate.

Dr Peter's comments are gravely concerning, and it is feared that a knee-jerk reaction by the police could have damaged the investigation beyond repair. Sources reveal that there are two other strong suspects. This could mean that the police have the real killer and could be about to let him go - or the real killer is still out there, no doubt already stalking their next victim.

———

The Leader of the Opposition read the article. He was impressed. Pilkington had obviously gone freelance, believing the story still had enough legs in it for her to get her name into the wider public eye. He wasn't a fan of journalists. They had a habit of twisting what you said or provoking you into saying the wrong thing and then leaping on it. He did admire ambition though and it was evident that this woman had a desire to get to the top of the pile. He just hoped that she would remain an ally when it came to his moment in the spotlight. It was clear that this was someone you did not want as an enemy.

He suspected that this DCI Fenton bloke was pissed off. He'd probably made an arrest over the weekend to give him some breathing space from her likely article in *London News*, which wouldn't usually surface until Monday. Given the way she had been gunning for Fenton, and their history, it was no surprise that he had tried to outsmart her. His chief minion had provided him with a full brief of the history between Fenton and Pilkington and the animosity was just intensifying. Had he been in Fenton's shoes, he would have probably tried something similar, but he would have been more underhand and gone to a rival paper with the story instead. These things always get out. It's virtually impossible to stop leaks, but you can at least control them.

Pilkington was a crafty woman, and he'd have to make sure he had her onside when it came to the no confidence vote, so he would keep agreeing to provide her with quotes for her articles, if it served his purpose as well. Success in the by-elections would mean a minority government. He was still working on schmoozing the smaller party leaders. They were irritated by that pompous little prick as well who had been in power for too long, but they weren't stupid and knew who the successor would be. One of them had given the *better the devil you know* line and they all had disagreements about policy direction. The Leader of the Opposition knew that if he couldn't swing them to back him in the vote then he would at least have to get their agreement that they would abstain.

It would be the perfect catalyst if this death penalty

debate blew up in the Prime Minister's face as the smaller parties would then have no option but to back him. He couldn't rely on that though. Public support was increasing for the death penalty and this was being driven by the media. Most of the smaller parties were dead against it. There were the two token far-right independent MPs, but they were more of the opinion that the Diversity Slayer deserved a knighthood.

Moistening his lips with his tongue, the thought of power being ever so close made his loins throb with excitement. It was an exhilarating feeling. He'd dreamed of this moment ever since he was a child. He'd watched previous leaders crush their subordinates like bugs. It took him back to the political debates at school when he had annihilated the competition with his two greatest weapons – intelligence and charm. It was the latter which would win him the votes. It was surprising how successful good-looking people could be. Ugly people did rise to the top occasionally based on their talent, but for them it was a constant struggle. He didn't have such battles to overcome. As long as he was *accidentally* photographed with no shirt on from time to time, then he would continue to ride high in the polls. There were parts of the electorate who would never vote for him because of what he stood for and there was no point trying to win them over. It was the fickle types who had no loyalty to a party which decided elections and that was where his attention would be focussed once his day came.

He remembered being asked once why he wanted to go into politics and had decided that the truth, "Power gives me a hard-on," was probably not the most appropriate answer. It was easy to spin bollocks to the public and the media, "I want people to know the real me," had been his most popular bull-shit phrase.

It had worked for those who couldn't be swayed only by

aesthetics. The public have always been gullible when it came to a bit of spin and cliché. Well, for about ten minutes. Their boredom threshold is exceptionally low, and they need something that will excite them. People don't like change when it's happening at work, or at home. It's distracting, uncomfortable and, frankly, a pain in the arse. But, in politics, it's all about change. Get a government into power and within a week people want them out because nothing new is happening. Governments get big majorities, become complacent, then corrupt with power. Suddenly one of your backbenchers is found dead in a brothel with a cucumber up his arse and you know your time is up.

The Leader of the Opposition frowned and looked at himself in the mirror. He didn't want to be a passing fancy, whilst the other main party spent five years on the other side of the house sorting themselves out, only to come back stronger. He was here to stay. There was only one way to secure a long time in office though, and that was to fight dirty. Especially as the current lot didn't seem to have a penchant for cucumbers.

———

"Can we not have this woman killed? Do I not get three kills for every parliament?" the Prime Minister asked his secretary. He was reading the latest Polly Pilkington article.

"No, sir, we don't

"How can she get away with printing such utter rubbish? I mean this top psychologist is about as plausible as a heroin addict working at Boots. How can she say that if this suspect is released, he'll go on a killing spree? I've never in all my life heard so much utter drivel. People are going to be terrified about this. I'm surprised she didn't name the other suspect that the police had."

"I believe Dr Deidre Peters has some excellent credentials, sir."

"Does she now? Well, she's not very professional when it comes to whipping up a moral panic."

The Prime Minister was in a rage. He didn't lose it very often and was pleased that only his loyal secretary had witnessed his outburst – therefore nobody would find out about it. Polly Pilkington had gone too far. He was flabbergasted that they had gotten away with printing the story.

"And what is this about me refusing to speak to her? She hasn't even asked me for a comment.

"Would you like to speak to her then, sir?"

"No, I wouldn't. Why, has she called?"

"No, sir."

"It's him trying to force an election. I've still got three years in this chair and he's not having it. A lot can happen in three years, you know. A lot can happen within three minutes in politics."

The Prime Minister was now quite worked up. He was reading the article again that was front page on one of the leading tabloids. At least when Pilkington was just local, she was a bit easier to control if need be.

He still had contacts though. He could find out if she had left *London News*. If she'd burned her bridges on the strength of this story, then she was stupider than he thought. From his conversation with DCI Fenton he suspected that Jeremiah Tool could be the right man, then again, he might not be. He secretly hoped that he wasn't. He was loath to ask Her Majesty to even mutter the term *death penalty* in her speech.

The State Opening of Parliament was on Wednesday and by Monday he would need to decide about which way he was going to go. Not to please the press, but the speech needed to go to print. It was all ready. It was a question of whether an additional paragraph was going to be added at the end.

———

The Leader of the Other Party appeared on *Sky News* to give his take on the latest developments.

"Sorry, we need to stop you just there. We're just getting some breaking news," interjected the newsreader.

WOOSH – went the flashing banner. The kind which caused Japanese children to have seizures.

BREAKING NEWS

"Debbie has survived being put up for eviction for a fourth time. Despite her eating binge, two of her fellow competitors gorged even more and they will face the public vote this week."

"I is doing this for all my fans innit!" screamed Debbie at the camera.

They never returned to the interview.

CHAPTER SIXTEEN

Fenton's plan to avoid press coverage, or at least coverage from Pilkington, had been scuppered. He'd had a blazing row with Harry Beeden about the planned interview. Fenton was clear that he would not be giving her an interview of any kind, only to be told that it was a direct order. Not only that, Fenton had been told to be on his best behaviour and was not to *lose his* shit with Pilkington. He'd requested that Taylor be present for the interview under the guise that he needed a witness in case Pilkington twisted what he said, when it reality, Fenton needed someone to give him a look, or interject if things started to escalate. Unfortunately, Beeden was not stupid and the request was denied – it was to be a private one-on-one interview.

The interview was to be conducted later that day; Pilkington had already sold the piece to a leading tabloid, sight unseen. Therefore, Fenton thought he should give her something, but then realised she'd make it up anyway. Nobody wanted to read the truth over their breakfast; the truth was boring. Sensationalism and scandal was what the public craved and the media were only too happy to feed that desire. The implications for the trial were irrelevant. If a murderer was acquitted then that would be the police, prosecutor, and Prime Minister's fault — the media were, of course, always blameless!

Fenton had still not told anyone about his private meeting with the Prime Minister, which was the only thing that hadn't leaked to the press. Suddenly he had one of those light bulb moments.

Oh yes, I've got you now.

He picked up the phone and dialled.

"Ms Manning, DCI Eric Fenton here. You've probably heard that we've made an arrest... I'm willing to let formal procedures deal with the matter, Ms Manning... It would be useful if you could carry out the tests as soon as possible... Shall we say two o'clock... Wonderful, I'll see you then."

He put the phone down. He hadn't felt this good in a while, even the arrest the night before hadn't given him the usual adrenalin rush. The circumstantial evidence was there — no alibi, history of violence and association with criminals. He had doubts, mainly about the motive, in that there didn't seem to be one; for Jez to have killed all the victims, it still didn't make any sense whatsoever.

———

Jez Tool stared at the ceiling of his cell. He'd been in the cells before, and it had never really bothered him. This time was different though. He was looking at spending the rest of his life in a place like this and it scared him. He'd not asked for a solicitor as he thought this would show he had nothing to hide. DCI Fenton had insisted that he have legal representation given he had been arrested for three counts of murder. It was obvious the chief copper was playing it safe in case Jez confessed and then tried to wriggle out of it later. They weren't just accusing him of triple murder; it was the murder of his colleagues and friends. Trudie was always pleasant to him – well, more pleasant that she was with most people. He got on with Nadeem and Carl very well and had even been out socially with them. He had no idea what the police knew, so he had to play it carefully and stick to his story. Nobody could know the truth; it would be the end of him. He'd managed to build a life for himself following his family's umpteenth term of imprisonment. This recent armed robbery was the last straw – he'd never eaten a courgette since. The *no comment* card would just make him look guilty, so that wasn't an option. He'd have to just stick to his story and find out what they knew first, before deciding on the best way to respond.

Jez sat opposite Fenton and Taylor. Something that looked young enough to still be in short trousers was sitting on his left, sweating, and looking out of his depth – his solicitor.

The room was an old-style interview room. Magnolia silk had been chucked on the walls, straight from the can by the looks of things. It was already starting to crack, and the room smelt damp. There was a modern tape recorder on the table, with a video camera in the top right-hand corner of the wall containing the door. The chairs looked like something out of a school canteen, designed in such a way that even children would find sitting for long periods on them unbearable. This was so they would leave the canteen as quickly as possible to entertain themselves, allowing the teachers to spend their lunches break bitching about the children in the staffroom, which was no longer the sanctuary it once was since the smoking ban. It was noticeable that Fenton and Taylor had comfortable padded chairs, so they could park their arses for the duration, waiting for Jez to crack – they would be waiting for a long time.

Fenton did the obligatory introductions and caution, before asking Jez to confirm his name and address. He was then asked to give his whereabouts on the night of the murders... again! He glanced at his solicitor to be sure he was right to speak, but the man was averting his gaze and seemed more interested in a crack on the back wall.

"As I said before, I weren't feeling hungry so decided not to join anyone for dinner like. The conference had been tiring. They always do loads of them interactive exercises. Walt likes to feel all the creative energy from everyone, so I spent some time in me room. Then I needed some fresh air, so I went to buy some fags. I went to the shops and had a bit of a walk and when I came back, I saw it were all kicking off."

"What time did you leave?" Fenton asked.

"I'm not sure of the exact time."

"Ball park."

"Between nine and half nine, I think."

"Can you be more specific than that?"

"I didn't look at me watch. I only went to the shops for a walk. I didn't think I'd need to give an alibi to prove I hadn't murdered three of me workmates."

"I have a witness who claims you left before nine."

"Maybe it were. Like I said, I didn't check the time."

"Apparently you also left the hotel earlier and then came back, before leaving again. Why was that?"

"I don't know what you're talking about, mate."

"Don't mate me. Do you realise the seriousness of these allegations I am making against you?"

"I haven't done anything. You got the wrong man."

Fenton banged his hands on the table, causing Jez to wince. His solicitor to jumped, which would hopefully remind him that he had a job to do. Jez had been arrested for triple murder and he thought it would be helpful if his solicitor absorbed the proceedings and tried to help in some way. Jez hadn't even wanted a solicitor, but now he had one, he expected the guy to at least speak up now and then.

Taylor took over the questioning. "Can you tell me about FREE?"

"I'm not a member anymore."

"We're aware of that. I still want you to tell me about them though."

"Is this really relevant? My client has already told you that he is no longer a member of this organisation," piped up the solicitor.

The detectives looked startled as they were reminded that there was a fourth person in the room.

"Political party, you mean."

"Again, I fail to see how this is relevant?"

"We are establishing a motive here. Three people who belonged to minority groups have been brutally murdered. Far right political parties are known for their less than favourable stance towards such minorities. Your client was a member of one. I'd say it's relevant," Taylor said in a manner that you could translate as *be quiet little boy*.

The solicitor looked like he'd just been scolded by his teacher in front of the whole class. Jez noticed that he started scribbling notes on what appeared to be a scrap of paper – maybe he couldn't afford a Filofax. He was bright red and looked like he was about to burst into tears. Jez looked at him with disdain but had found the outburst amusing. He found Detective Inspector Taylor very alluring, although he suspected she was not someone to be messed with, so he decided against any flirting... for now, even though it had often helped him to get out of trouble.

"So, tell me about FREE." she prompted.

"It's not what people think. It's just the name that makes it sound bad. There are a few knob heads, a few wreck heads, but Bill were all about the common man. He just thinks that in today's society, the common man has become the minority. He were never up for queer bashing and all that, it were just about preserving the interests of your common man. It weren't even about colour or being straight. We even had a few benders in the group. Hard bastards they are as well. I suppose they have to be with all crap they have to put up with. The names they call each other is worse than what any straight guy can come up with. It's weird that isn't it? You say something and you're homophobic or racist, but if they say it to each other that's alright – it's mad!"

"Can you get back to FREE please, Jez? I can call you Jez, can't I?"

"You can call me what you want, love," he said, and added a smile and wink.

She went bright red.

Maybe flirting will work.

Fenton stared straight at Jez with a contemptuous look on his face.

Maybe not!

"Jez, can you tell me about a typical meeting of FREE?" she asked, her voice cracking slightly.

"A typical meeting? Well I didn't go to all of them. They had one every two weeks usually. I were only down south once a month. Usually Bill would have an issue to talk about. It would usually be about something in that thing all the political parties have when they fight elections. That word with an M, never been able to say it."

"Manifesto?" offered Fenton.

He looked bored, but the Taylor woman seemed interested in what he was saying. Jez clicked his fingers and nodded.

"That's it. Well most often it would be about the common man. That's Bill's pledge or vision, or whatever, but we would all discuss the other issues. There were a couple of nutters who got confused by the name of the group, and thought we were gonna go and twat people, but Bill were a good family man. He never did anything like that. His wife were always nice to me when I stayed with them. I think she had a soft spot for me, but Bill were a mate and that's the golden rule, you see."

"What is?" asked Fenton.

"Don't bang your mate's missus."

"How noble!"

"These nutters would usually leave after one or two meetings and not come back."

"Where did they go?" asked Taylor.

"No idea, love. I mean they probably went to twat some blacks or gays. They were proper nut jobs. I don't agree with all that. If people want to come here and earn a living, then they should. If a bloke gets his rocks off with another bloke then that's his business. That's what I think and that's what Bill thought. He said that name were to do with being in East London cos that is to the right. He were gonna change it, but it attracted membership and he needed the money. He had loads of kids and his wife were always pregnant."

"Which meetings caused the most tension?" asked Taylor.

"Tension?"

"Disagreement."

"I suppose it were the football ones."

"What happened?"

"Well, nothing violent, but you know what men are like about football? They can get verbal. Bill wanted to put something in the manifesta thingy about what teams you could and couldn't support like. Well it got a bit heated as by this time he had people from all over the country. Men love their football clubs more than their wives. It's always mad though, as all the northern blokes support the southern teams, and vice versa. It's mad, but I got a theory about that. The men today do it without thinking. We follow what our dads and granddads did. I reckon when our great, great grandfather were around he decided to support a football club in the south. That way he could get away from the wife for a few days, like, to go and watch the match, as there were no TV or cars then, so you'd have to travel for days to get there and back."

The interview progressed for another hour or so when Jez's solicitor asked for a break. This was the first time he had spoken since Taylor had put him in his place. Fenton had agreed to a break so Jez could have some lunch, as it was already after two. He said they would reconvene in two hours.

Jez was taken to another room so he could talk privately with his solicitor. He failed to see the point and would have preferred to just have some alone time. His solicitor had now suddenly woken up and was making suggestions about how he might play it in the next round of the interview. Jez just wanted the whole thing over with and he knew he could end this quickly if he wanted to. He was just too scared to admit the truth. This solicitor was not a man he could respect, and he looked so inexperienced that Jez was certain that he wasn't someone he could trust to confide the truth in either. There was no clue as to what he would do with the information once Jez had revealed it. He needed some time to think, so asked to be returned to his cell. He wasn't hungry, but the custody sergeant insisted he ate something. She even offered to go out and get him a McDonalds if that was what he wanted, which seemed an odd thing to say. Jez was careful about what he ate and took particularly good care of his physique, but one dirty burger wouldn't do any harm. Besides, who knew what swill he could be subjected to if he did end up in prison.

———

"What were you playing at in there?" Fenton asked Taylor in the privacy of his own office.

"Sorry, sir," she spluttered, both shocked and hurt. He had never spoken to her like this before. It was a side of him she had only seen rarely, usually aimed at Manning or Pilkington.

"I felt like a gooseberry in there. For God's sake, Lisa, show a bit of professionalism, you're a senior officer."

"I don't know what you're talking about, sir," she said defiantly.

Fenton raised his eyebrows and his mouth flicked up to one side, before he exhaled loudly and shook his head.

"I thought a bit of false flattery would open him up a bit."

"False flattery, you were practically panting."

Taylor was getting irritated now. She would never act so unprofessionally. "I think you're exaggerating, sir."

"Lisa, I know the type you seem to go for and you're just asking for trouble. Just promise me one thing?"

"What's that?" she asked, sulkily.

"Even if he's not our man, he's released, and we get somebody else for these murders, stay away."

"I've no intention of going there, full stop, sir. Can I go now?"

He nodded and dismissed her with a wave of his hand.

She was trying to control the anger in her voice. She could feel herself starting to shake and she had no control over it. Her legs felt heavy and unsteady. She needed to leave. Her dignity meant everything, and she wasn't about to lose it in front of a man she idolised.

Once out of Fenton's office, she ignored Brennan when he asked her for something, and she just kept walking until she was outside the station. She needed some time to think, by herself. She wasn't sure where she was going, she just kept walking; she'd know when she got there.

CHAPTER SEVENTEEN

"Eric darlink, thank you for agreeing to see me."

Didn't have much choice in the matter – and why do you sound like a Swedish prostitute when you come from Camden?

"Ms Pilkington, always a pleasure."

There was no false sarcasm in his voice: it oozed nothing but utter contempt. She must have sensed it, yet she pressed ahead regardless.

"Call me Polly, darlink. I think we know each other well enough for first names."

Yes, but I didn't give you permission to use my first name, you just assumed it.

Fenton found these cutting statements, made completely in his own head of course, very therapeutic. What he wouldn't give to vocalise them and not worry about the repercussions. Sadly, the world didn't bend that way.

Their meetings always started off pleasant-ish, but her journalistic manner wasn't leading or persuasive like most of her peers; it was outlandish and personally offensive. Fenton lived in the vague hope that one of two things would happen; they would have a civilised conversation;

she would report the facts and make no personal or accusing remarks. The other was that one day she would get her comeuppance – hopefully involving a truck. Not that he was bitter or anything, but he hoped for the latter. It was one of the few things he still wished for when blowing out candles, pulling a wish bone, or throwing a coin in a wishing well. Taylor mentioned at one time that he might have become a tad obsessed with Ms Pilkington. He chose to ignore this. Women tended to over-dramatise anyway.

"I see you've moved to the nationals. Congratulations."

"Just freelance, darlink, Joey doesn't want to lose me, bless his heart. He knows I have ambition, but I stay loyal to my roots."

"You're still writing for the London News then?"

"Freelance as well. I promised them regular articles. Circulation has gone up and they wouldn't want to lose that, which would happen if I left permanently, darlink."

Fenton knew Joey, the Editor of *London News.* very well. He was a businessman who expected loyalty and he would be furious that she had just gone to a competitor overnight. Fenton suspected that, once this story blew over, Joey would drop her. That gave Fenton a warm glow as he relaxed back in his chair ready for the interview. He noticed she had switched to using a Dictaphone rather than just notes (although she had a notebook as well). He knew it was best not to say anything he'd regret when it could all be caught on tape. The risk of creating hard evidence was always a great deterrent from *losing your shit.*

"So, Eric darlink, how is the investigation going?"

"Progressing very well. As you know, we have a suspect in custody."

"Have you laid any charges yet?"

"It's too early for that. You know how these things work,

Polly. Even if they walk in off the street and confess, it can be a day or two before they are formally charged."

"He's confessed then?"

"I didn't say that." *Jesus Christ, she's already twisting it and we're only a few seconds in.*

"So, he's denied everything?"

"You know I can't answer that. Certain things I can't tell you, as it could prejudice any future trial."

"I'll take that as a yes then, darlink."

"Like I said, the investigation is still ongoing."

"Harry Beeden promised me that you'd give me a proper interview."

"Then ask me a question I can actually answer. You know how these things work, Polly. You've been doing it long enough. It isn't usual to issue press statements at this stage of an investigation, let alone give personal interviews." He noticed his voice was now an octave higher, but hoped he gave off the impression of being patronising.

"The public are very concerned about these murders."

"As we all are." He exhaled loudly and then counted to ten in his head. Well, he got as a far as three before...

"You see, if this is the wrong man, then the real killer is still out there and ready to strike again. If it's the right man then, based on his background, this supports our campaign and, with the Queen's Speech just a few days away, time is of the essence, darlink."

It didn't take you long to bring things round to this, did it? And what is all this "our" campaign bollocks? Like the public own it; this is your campaign, plain and simple.

"I won't be laying any charges until I'm certain we have a case that secures prosecution. The last thing we want is for the case to collapse when it gets to court."

"I guess that means your evidence is still only circumstantial then?"

"Again, that's not what I said."

"Not saying a lot, are you? Bit of a shit interview really!"

Her London lilt was coming through on the last sentence.

"I wouldn't want to jeopardise the case at such a crucial time, as I'm sure you don't either, Polly. I want to be certain we have the right man and to be certain that conviction is highly likely when the case goes to trial."

"Nice try, Eric, now let's cut the bullshit."

Her accent was now pure North London.

"What you've got here is a guy who is a member of a far-right extremist group. I'd say that's a pretty strong suspect."

"Again, you have sensationalism clouding fact, Polly my dear." He was hitting his stride now. "This far right group, as you put it, is nothing more than a gentlemen's club that gets a bit heated about football. They even let women in. And before you interrupt," he said raising his hand to silence her, "he is no longer a member of said club."

"Taking his word for it, are we?"

"I think we can carry out our own detective work, Polly my dear, without having to take the word of a suspect in a triple murder case."

"He's not your man then?"

"There you go again. I didn't say that. All I pointed out was that this far right group you are focussing on is nothing more than a social gathering of individuals who have chosen a ridiculous name to describe themselves."

"What else are you holding him on then? I know you Eric, you wouldn't make an arrest unless you had something. What is it?"

"And that, my dear, is where the interview must end. I informed the suspect that his interview would reconvene shortly, and you know what lawyers are like when you keep them waiting."

He got up signalling to her that the interview was over.

He'd managed to keep his calm and score a few points at the same time. He was rather pleased with himself.

"You're worried about some teenager in short trousers barely out of law school? I've seen you tell some of the top criminal barristers in London to go and fuck themselves, so why don't you sit yourself down like a good boy?"

He had no idea why, he obeyed – must have been a reflex.

"Now, I know his alibi is a bit shaky so is that what you're going on, or have you got something else?"

"I won't be drawn into compromising my case."

"Fair enough, darlink. I wanted to speak to you about another matter."

He nodded at the desk. She looked at her Dictaphone, nodded and turned it off.

"I don't wish to discuss the Davies case, and I know you've probably got another one of those hidden in your bag."

"I hadn't even thought about that case."

"Bullshit, you've mentioned it almost every day in your articles. How do you think that is for the family? For them to be reminded after all this time?"

"How are the family?"

"How would I know?"

"I know you still visit them regularly."

How did she know this? It couldn't be Manning. She didn't know this. He suddenly had a knot in his stomach. Had he got it wrong about Manning? No, he was certain. Pilkington had just admitted that she knew about the alibi and he'd deliberately told Manning about that earlier.

————

Manning had met Fenton in his office earlier that day. Even though she glided in with an air of authority, knowing full well that Fenton was currently subject to a formal complaint, she was still irked at having been summoned in such a manner. Nonetheless she decided to humour him, but also secretly anticipated that she may be able to provoke him into making some inappropriate comment yet again. Men were so easy to manipulate and bend to your will, she thought. Why women had agonised over what the species was thinking or feeling for centuries was bewildering. It was quite simple – men are cunts!

It was all relative anyway; she was here to do a job. They'd made an arrest, which was at least something. She'd seen far more brutal murders in her career, but it was the old woman. There was something about hers that had an unpleasant whiff about it, the sort that just hung there, pretty much in the same manner as men... always lingering.

"So, Eric, what can I do for you?" She paused for breath and carried on, not allowing him to speak. "DNA is going to be non-existent. We didn't find much on any of the deceased and the fact that he was a colleague of all three would mean it's likely to throw up reasonable doubt in the courtroom. You know me, Eric. I don't like to lose." She grinned broadly, flashing her teeth.

He beamed back at her. "Of course, Ms Manning, and I'd expect nothing less from you. That's why I insist on using you in my cases. Your evidence has helped me to put away a number of murderers over the years."

She wondered what the twat was up to. She knew it was true, he only worked with her because she was the best, but he wasn't the sort of man to say that out loud. He was up to something. Men were so easy to read. The false flattery was so transparent. Manning was not some vacuous bimbo who couldn't tell her arse from her elbow; she wouldn't fall for it. She'd just play along to see where he was going. Hopefully he'd hang himself when it came to them investigating her complaint.

"What can I do for you, Eric? I'm intrigued."

"Just between us?"

Here we go – he could at least make the effort to be subtle about it.

"Of course, Eric."

"We don't have a lot really. It's mostly all circumstantial. I suppose you saw in the papers that he was a member of a far-right group."

"Yes, I vaguely remember something. I only glanced at it."

"Well, this group's name is probably the most controversial thing about it. Not much to go on really. He has no alibi for the time of the killings. That's all we have concrete."

"That's not much to go on, Eric. I'm surprised you arrested him."

"Pressure from above. Besides, we've proved he lied about his whereabouts."

"You mean you've discredited his alibi?"

"Not quite. He said he left the hotel at a certain time, but we now know he left earlier and came back and left again. He could have done it."

"It's still not much. It won't convince a jury."

"I know. That's where you come into it."

"How do you mean?" A false smile plastered across her lips. *I know what you're up to.*

"I need some forensic evidence, even if it's not concrete. It will give me enough to get an extension."

"What sort of evidence? As I said, it's probably not going to be strong."

"Well, this guy is built like a brick shit house. Could you tell from the force of the stab wound, if the killer had a heavy build, or from the entrance of the wound how tall he was? Anything like that?"

"I might be able to get something from the tests done on the two men, but as the woman was sitting down and her assailant came from behind, it's going to be impossible to detect anything the like height or weight of the perpetrator."

"Just tell me what you need to know about the suspect."

————

Fenton had had two reasons for calling Manning in. One was to tell her about the alibi. He knew she'd spot what he was up to. However, Pilkington had already let slip that she knew this. There was something going on, despite Manning giving nothing away. He thought she was lying when she denied reading the Pilkington article. More like they were reading it over their coffee that morning and laughing about him. Did lesbians drink coffee? Maybe Taylor and Beeden were right; he was becoming a bit obsessed!

The other reason for calling Manning in was genuine. He had little to go on so was hoping some forensic evidence would give him more time. Otherwise Jez would have to be released tomorrow.

"So, Eric, what are your thoughts on the plans to bring back the death penalty?" asked Pilkington.

"I hadn't really given it much thought." He was aware that she no doubt had another Dictaphone in her bag.

"Don't be daft, darlink, everyone is talking about it."

"Not everyone is so easily led."

He couldn't stop himself; he just spat the words out. Although he did want to add *by the gutter press*, he managed to seal his lips tightly shut after the first part. It had still been enough to rile Pilkington. She looked like she'd been stung on the arse by a bee.

"Everyone is free to make up their own mind about this, darlink. It's an important debate that we must have. Now everyone is talking about it, darlink. We believe the Queen's Speech will refer to it. Her Majesty is going to utter the words *death penalty*. I think that is pretty ground-breaking stuff, don't you?"

"I don't think it will faze Her Majesty in the slightest. I mean the death penalty was still very prevalent when she first came to the throne."

"I think you are missing the point, darlink."

"Then do enlighten me," he said with feigned enthusiasm.

She glared back at him but wouldn't bite. "It's people power. The public are asking for this. Have you seen the latest opinion polls?"

"Is that the one where eighty-five people are speaking for the entire population?"

"Do keep up, darlink. The latest polls show two thirds of the public support the death penalty being reinstated, and the politicians are only talking about a debate here. The sample size was much bigger this time for the polling."

"There were two hundred people surveyed this time! Or was it three hundred?"

She ignored him. "The point I am trying to make is that the public have spoken as one voice, and their collective voice will be heard through just one – that voice is Her Majesty the Queen." She finished the end of her sentence defiantly.

Fenton burst out laughing.

"What is so amusing?" She was getting riled. The accent slipped again. The true Polly was showing herself.

"I'm sorry to laugh about something that you take so seriously, but I've never heard so much utter bollocks in my entire life."

"Excuse me but I'll think you'll find..."

He cut across her. "This is a press agenda. No, let me correct that. This is *your* agenda. You want to make a name for yourself, that's all. You don't care about these victims. They're just ammunition to you. Something you can use to get your stories in the paper and stoke up moral panic and political unrest, for the simple fact in that it sells newspapers."

"It's a shame you are so clouded, Eric. I think that was your undoing in the Davies case. You weren't looking in the right direction. You needed to look closer to home."

"This interview is over." He stood up, pointed at the door, and bellowed, "Get out of my office." He was aware that the murmur from the incident room outside had suddenly halted.

"I shall be making a formal complaint to your superiors."

"Join the queue, love."

"It won't help you to be against this, Eric. It's what the public want."

He muttered something under his breath, but unfortunately the word *lesbians* was audible.

"What was that, DCI Fenton? Is a senior officer of the Metropolitan Police making misogynous remarks about women?"

There was a loud knock and DI Taylor burst in.

Pilkington spun round looking startled.

"Everything all right, sir?"

He'd never been so happy to see her. "Ms Pilkington was just leaving."

"I don't think we've finished yet, darlink."

The annoying phoney accent had returned, probably because she had an audience.

"I think the DCI has made it quite clear that you are," Taylor added curtly. "My colleague DC Emma Shirkham will escort you from the building."

This wasn't Taylor delegating an unpleasant job to a junior officer, Fenton thought. Pilkington would be livid that she was being escorted out of the building by, in her view, a mere DC. It was clever. Pilkington paused for a second, pouted, swung her bag over her shoulder, put on her sunglasses, even though it was now early November, and flounced out of the office, barging past Taylor.

"This way please," said Shirkham, who had joined them.

"I know my own way out, thank you," Pilkington spat.

Shirkham ignored her and went to guide her arm, but she shrugged it off.

"Do you mind not touching me? I'm not some common criminal."

"Speaking to an officer in the manner you are is actually a criminal offence. Now shall we go, or would you like me to arrest you?"

Pilkington looked at Shirkham, and was clearly about to respond but then, scanning the room and seeing several witnesses, she obviously thought better of it and allowed herself to be escorted from the building. Taylor went into Fenton's office and shut the door behind her. There was a groan from the team in the incident room, evidently disappointed to be missing the fallout of the drama.

"She's good, Emma. Such a shame she's happy at DC level," said Taylor.

"Thanks for that," said Fenton, sitting back in his chair, running his hands through his hair.

"Do you wanna take a few minutes? Go and get coffee?"

"I'll just cool off in here if that's okay."

She looked a bit hurt but nodded and went to leave.

"I'm sorry about before, Lisa. I've only got your interests at heart."

He wasn't taking the piss, he genuinely meant it.

"I know, sir, we all have our weak spots. Perhaps Gary or Emma should sit in for the next stage of interview. It'll be good experience for them."

"No, Lisa, I want you in there with me."

He noticed her eyes water as she thanked him and then quickly left the room.

CHAPTER EIGHTEEN

Fenton had decided that if he was to break this case, he had to break Jez, without risking a broken jaw. No moron would attack a senior officer in a police station, but this wasn't just any moron; he was sixteen stone of solid muscle. He needed provoking into revealing his true whereabouts. Hopefully, this would result in a confession, but he doubted it. Jez was probably performing some altruistic act like stopping orphaned ducks from falling down a sewer, after their mother had been mown down by a black cab. There would be a hundred tourists as witnesses to this noble act of kindness, and Fenton would be a demon.

Pilkington would be disappointed that Halloween had passed. She could have run a *demon* headline as she liked to link her articles to current events. It couldn't just be a coincidence that she was utilising the upcoming Queen's speech and a wobbly government to fuel her stories. She had linked her articles to topical events in the past and in Fenton's case, very personal ones. In fact, the only thing Pilkington didn't link her articles to, was the truth.

Fenton hoped that Taylor would be back on form during

the second round of Jez's interview. She had that weakness for bad boys. Throw in motorcycle leathers, some tattoos and muscles and it was like he had another giddy teenage daughter. He supposed everyone had a weakness, but it was something she was going to have to deal with before it ended her career – she'd come close before.

———

In a prior investigation, Taylor had embarked on a stupid fling with a suspect's brother. It hadn't jeopardised the case in any way as the brothers no longer spoke. The suspect was tall, muscled, and brutish and had beaten his wife to death. He had confessed and then later retracted his story, coming up with some crap about an intruder. Fenton had still charged him with murder but had gotten a small team together to gather more evidence. It was obvious from the interviews that Taylor had the hots for the suspect, and they had been openly flirting during the interview. It got to a point were Fenton had needed to remove her from any direct contact. It had deeply affected her, but he knew any defence lawyer would have jumped on the interview when he saw the video tapes – it certainly wasn't subtle. Taylor had argued that it was an interview strategy, but Fenton was not convinced and had told her as much.

To get her away from the station and to still use her experience as a detective, Fenton had tasked Taylor with locating and interviewing the suspect's estranged brother – his identical twin brother! At the time of assigning the task, Fenton was not aware that they were identical twins. The brother wanted nothing to do with his sibling after a bitter falling out over a girl they had both loved many years ago. The suspect had also beaten the former girlfriend, putting her in hospital for a few days. Taylor demonstrated her prowess as a detective by convincing the brother to make a statement against the suspect. She also tracked down the ex-girlfriend who had not reported the original assault, and obtained the hospital records detailing her injuries, which were similar to that of the murder victim. She did it all in a matter of days, and it was that case which had supported her promotion to Detective Inspector. Once Fenton had presented all the new evidence to their suspect, he admitted the murder and was swiftly remanded back into custody.

What Fenton had not realised was that Taylor had also embarked on a stupid affair with the murderer's twin brother. It had been going on for a few months, in secret, before Fenton found out about it. He could always tell when there was a hint of scandal in his team. It was usually the officers shagging each other and that was easy to deal with. This was something else. If the murderer had changed his plea during the proceedings, the brother would have been a critical witness at the trial. Taylor's behaviour could have been uncovered by the defence and damaged the credibility of the witness. He did not understand why she could have acted so stupid. Fenton knew he would have to tackle the situation from two angles.

First, he hauled Taylor over the coals and made her take compulsory leave and told her to book a flight somewhere warm and piss off for two weeks. She was not to contact the brother again. He then went to see the brother and he was remarkably similar in look to the murderer, except this one had bigger muscles, more tattoos and drove a motorbike – Taylor had a type! Fenton didn't need to threaten the brother, which was good as he'd probably have been able to knock ten tonnes of shit out of anyone. Despite how he looked, the man was a very gentle and caring person. He had no idea of the implications to Taylor's career from the relationship. Once he was aware, he agreed not to see her again. Fenton had expected a battle, but the guy was basically a gentleman – in a different set of circumstances, he probably would have been the perfect match for Taylor. It would certainly make life easier if she had a man at home and didn't keep flirting with suspects and witnesses.

————

Fenton went down to the custody suite to ask for Jez to be returned to the interview room. As he approached, he noticed that there was a crowd of officers around the screens which showed the prisoners in each of the cells. They weren't aware he was coming as they were so engrossed in the screen and were all screaming with delight. It was like a girl's night out yet being held in a police custody suite. There were four female officers including the custody sergeant and one male officer, who Fenton knew was openly gay. He had a suspicion about what they might be looking at but hoped he was wrong. As Fenton got closer to the desk, they spotted him. They all had the look children have when they've been caught doing something they shouldn't. Four officers scarpered quickly, leaving the custody sergeant on her own. Fenton looked at the screen and saw that, for some reason, Jez was topless in his cell doing exercises. The officers were only human, but Fenton thought it would be fun to watch her sweat for once. This custody sergeant was the type who loved to utilise her power of being responsible for the suspects they were holding. She was like the Receptionist at the doctors surgery, who are supposed to ensure the patient gets the help they need, when in reality they acted like they had a medical degree and knew better than the patient, or the doctor.

"What was so interesting?" Fenton asked.

"Nothing, sir."

"So, why did everyone leave so quickly when I arrived?"

"They had to get back to work, sir."

"I see – nothing to do with my suspect working out in his cell then." He gestured to the screens

She shook her head, but went bright red.

"Okay," said Fenton. He noticed she was trying to cover her notebook. "What's that?"

"Nothing, sir," she said closing the notebook.

He held out his hand for her to pass it over, which she did – reluctantly. He went to the page she had been trying to cover up and saw she had written, *heating in cells*. He kept looking down for a moment as he was trying not to laugh. He put his serious face back on and passed the notebook back to her.

"Can you have the suspect brought back to interview room two please?"

"Yes, sir, right away."

Fenton started to walk away and then turned and walked back.

"One more thing…"

She looked nervous.

"Get a towel for him or something. I don't want him all sweaty in my interview room."

She nodded, going even redder.

Fenton walked away with a smile on his face, but also hoping she gave Jez a towel. Him arriving for the interview all sweaty would surely send Taylor over the edge.

———

Jez lay in his cell staring into space, unsure what his next moved should be. He knew bravado and backchat were not going to work with Fenton. He also knew, from his solicitor, when he went back into that interview room, they were going to ask him outright if he committed the murders. There was no way they were going to leave him alone until they knew everything. The truth was going to come out and Jez was just going to have to face the consequences.

It was a shame that woman copper wasn't in charge. He knew she had the hots for him, and she wasn't bad looking. Perhaps he could turn his charm on again if he got the chance. It had helped him out many a time before. He remembered flirting with Walt on the day of his interview with Training4All. Wearing a tight t-shirt, and stretching in the chair at the right time, just letting it ride up over his abs; you use what you've got. Women and men, he didn't care. It was only flirting, and you had to use all the skills you had at your disposal to get ahead in this world; he wasn't the smartest guy, especially with anything outside computers, so he had to use his other talents.

Jez didn't think flirting would work with Fenton though. Straight men could be flattered by a good-looking man flirting with them subtly. He'd tried it once with Nadeem and it had worked. Jez had fucked up a technical issue that Nadeem was having, and it had caused some problems with a client. Jez was still in probation at the time, but they had worked together to find a workaround, so the client was still happy. Jez had then taken Nadeem out for a drink to thank him and he'd promised not to tell anyone about the fuck up, even his wife, who was the HR Manager.

Jez was back in the interview room. Even though there were three other people there, DCI Fenton, DI Taylor, and his solicitor, he felt completely alone. Taylor appeared to be deliberately avoiding eye contact and Jez started to believe that he had imagined her behaviour as flirtations earlier. His solicitor was still completely out of his depth and offered no means of support. Even DCI Fenton appeared to be elsewhere and seemed to be regarding the interview as an inconvenience.

"Are you going to tell us the truth now, Jez?" asked Fenton.

"I already have. I ain't done anything wrong."

"Then I put three questions to you. Number one: did you murder Gertrude Longhurst?"

"No."

"Number two: did you murder Nadeem Jamal?"

"I've already told you I ain't done nothing," he said exasperated.

"Answer the question."

"No, and I did not murder Carl either."

"Number three: did you murder Carl Davenport?"

"I just said no."

"Would you like to know what I think?"

"Not really, but I'm sure you'll tell me anyway."

"I believe that on the night of the fourteenth of October you left the hotel and ensured you would be seen. You then sneaked back believing you had remained undetected. You then murdered Trudie Longhurst, Nadeem Jamal and Carl Davenport. After you had committed the murders you left the hotel, again thinking you had not been seen, and returned later during the commotion, giving yourself what you believed to be an alibi."

Jez went to speak but Fenton held up his hand to silence him.

"What I don't understand – and please enlighten me – is *why* you did it. I know it's got nothing to do with FREE. Or is there more to it than we've been able to find out? Did you have a personal vendetta against each victim or just one and you got a taste for killing? I just want to know *why*. For the families, murder needs make some sense, Jez, and this doesn't. *Why* did you kill them?"

"I didn't kill anyone. Why don't you believe me?" he pleaded.

"Then prove it. Where did you go?"

"I just went for a walk, and then to the shops. I wish I were with someone, but I were on me own."

"I give up," Fenton said raising his hands in defeat and then looking at Taylor. "You have a go."

"Let's look at the time you were away from the hotel," said Taylor.

"Again?"

"I think my client has already made his point on this quite clear," interjected the solicitor.

Taylor shot him a withering look and he duly retreated. Jez glanced at his legal representative with disgust and shook his head. He turned back at Taylor who was giving him a look as if to say *well*.

"I can't be arsed with this anymore. No comment."

Fenton leaned forward.

"Remind me again of the exact time you left the hotel," asked Taylor.

"No comment!" Jez spat. He cracked his neck and knuckles at the same time. He hoped it would be intimidating.

Fenton gently put his hand on Taylor's. It was obviously a signal that he wanted to ask a question.

"I ask you again, Jez. Did you murder Trudie, Nadeem and Carl?"

Jez felt his face flush. He looked to his solicitor, who was staring straight ahead.

"No comment," was Jez's choked response. He tried to say it with defiance.

"Okay, I think we have enough for now. I'm going to charge you with all three murders. Any comment now?"

Jez was flustered and looked to his solicitor for support.

The guy might be sat there, but from the look of him, he was in a place far away.

"Can I have a piece of paper and a pen?"

Taylor ripped a page from her notebook and passed it to him with a pen. He jotted down the name *Doris Dunkley* and added a phone number underneath. He passed it back to Fenton.

"Who's this?" he asked

"My alibi."

———

Taylor and Shirkham sat at the back of their usual coffee house haunt. Taylor had ordered a *regular* coffee, although the cup appeared to resemble the size of a wastepaper basket. She updated Shirkham on the interview with Jez and how it had concluded. No one knew who his alibi was and what she could say that would prove Jez couldn't have been responsible for the murders.

Taylor and Shirkham sat on the same side of the table. They wanted to see if anyone came in and it was easier to talk quietly. They liked this coffee shop as it was always quiet, possibly due to the exorbitant prices, but more likely because the counter assistant, who seemed to be always working, gave you a contemptuous look if you dared ask her to do something completely unspeakable, such as make you a coffee.

Taylor noticed Brennan walk in. He acknowledged his colleagues and sat down opposite.

"Get me another coffee," Taylor said thrusting her empty cup into his hand.

"And me," added Shirkham repeating the motion.

He shrugged.

"Fair enough. I can blow the best part of a score for a bit of gossip. Don't start without me."

He headed for the counter. They watched him start charming the counter assistant. She gave a look to imply that Brennan had said, *hey babe, how about we get some homemade coffee after your shift?* Her continued look of contempt after Brennan had finished speaking implied that Taylor's assumption was probably perfectly accurate.

"Right, before he gets back, let's keep the past case between us girls," Taylor said with urgency.

"Naturally. He wouldn't blab though."

Brennan had finished schmoozing and was heading over with the coffees on a tray, trying to look cool by balancing the tray on one hand.

"I'd love him to go flying," whispered Shirkham.

"Too smooth that one to make a tit out of himself."

"Ladies, your coffee," he said putting the tray down and then plonking himself down. "So did the Guv give you a bollocking then?"

"Jesus, you don't waste any time. No, just a friendly warning."

"I wouldn't worry about it. Every policewoman in the station has had their tongue hanging out, as well as Dominic from the robbery squad."

"Excuse me, not all of us," added Shirkham.

"Yeah, okay. Anyway, I don't see the appeal. All muscles and no brain if you ask me."

"The best way. Who wants a man who can think? Too much like hard work," retorted Shirkham.

"I thought you weren't interested?"

"I'm not, I was just making a comment."

"Anyway, can we move the conversation on from idle gossip," clipped Taylor.

"Yes, ma'am," replied Brennan with a mock salute.

"So, do you think it is him then?" Shirkham asked Taylor.

"All depends on this alibi, don't it? I suppose it might be, but gut reaction – no, I don't think it's him. I've been wrong before though."

"What does the Guv reckon? He's never wrong," Brennan asked.

"I wouldn't be sure of that. He doesn't let people know when he's been wrong, that's all. I think he's keeping an open mind. Jez was definitely hiding something. This alibi could be it. Depending on what it is though."

"Jez wouldn't say anything about the alibi then?" asked Brennan.

"Nope, just told us to call her and ask where he was."

"Sounds like an old woman's name. Could be a relative or something?"

"No, they're all inside or dead. We checked everyone," interjected Shirkham.

"Perhaps it's his bit on the side. Proves he likes them on zimmers so couldn't have murdered Trudie?" added Brennan, still grinning. "Unless they were having an affair and it all went tits up."

They all looked at each other for a second and then laughed, causing the coffee shop girl to glare at them.

———

Fenton put down the phone and sat back in disbelief. This had to be some colossal joke or piss take. He glanced at the calendar on the wall. No, it was November, not the first of April.

He pinched himself hard. Not dreaming either. He'd interviewed a lot of murderers and suspected murderers over the years and never had he heard something so ridiculous. It couldn't be true, but then who the hell would make up something like that? It wasn't plausible. A man that looked like Jez would not be seen dead doing something like that – would he?

He thought back to the situation he now faced with Jez. Doris Dunkley was on her way to the station at Fenton's request. This had to be seen with his own eyes and he suspected that was the same for the rest of the team. If it all checked out, Jez would be free to go. Had they gone for the wrong man? Should Fenton have gone for Peter Gleeson or Wendy Baxter instead? There was nothing concrete for either of them to make a viable arrest. It was why he had gone for Jez. He had the background, which had now turned out to be as extreme as an old lady's tea party. The big thing holding it together, was that he had no alibi, but now he did. Doris Dunkley swore Jez was with her and not only that, she had several witnesses, who were also on their way over. Perhaps there was going to be a tea party after all!

CHAPTER NINETEEN

"I don't mean to be rude, Guv, but are you taking the piss?" asked Brennan.

"No, Gary, I'm deadly serious."

"It's got to be a wind-up."

"Do you see me making something like this up?"

"Well, it's original, I'll give him that."

"In all my years of dealing with murderers, I've heard every excuse and alibi in the book. This is a first for me though."

"Let me get this straight..."

"According to Doris Dunkley at the time of the murders, *our Jez*, was training for the *National Needlepoint Championship*. He's going for his third successive title," Fenton added, with a mock sense of being impressed.

"I still think it's got be a wind-up."

"We'll soon find out. She's on her way, with a gaggle of other witnesses. They all swear Jez was with them."

Fenton was visualising hosting a Bridge Tournament as they discussed Jez's untapped talents. He suspected this was going to be one of the most bizarre days in his entire career.

Taylor and Shirkham were also in Fenton's office but hadn't said anything. It was the first time Fenton had ever known two women to be completely lost for words. He embraced the silence of such a wondrous once-in-a-lifetime event as he contemplated how he should handle Doris and Co. when they arrived.

He needed to try and break the alibi, but he couldn't be seen to bully an old lady. What was bullying these days though? It appeared that whenever somebody was given an instruction that they didn't like they'd claim it was bullying – another redundant word which had lost any real meaning. A bit like management!

Management wasn't easy, and he didn't really see himself as a line manager as the team could be quite different from case to case. He had his regular team and they were sitting in the room with him now, as well as a few others. That was what he liked about police work, you got to meet new people all the time, not just suspects and witnesses. It was getting more difficult to do the job he was supposed to do with the added *management* responsibilities. His job was to find out who had murdered three people. In the middle of that he must ensure that the woman who did the photocopying prior to the briefings has a *regular dialogue* with him. If he asked her to pop into his office for some dialogue, she'd probably have a coronary. It's that old cliché with the boss. You want the feedback, but if they ask to see you or book an appointment, you spend the intermittent time completely paranoid and wondering if you're going to get fired. It can't happen. People don't just get fired anymore. Well, they do, but usually with the help of the employer's cheque book, to keep it out of the press.

Fenton had also lost track of the amount of management meetings or peer support group meetings he'd wasted time on. If he was a bit stumped on a case, which of course rarely happened, he'd have a quick chat with another DCI at the time. You can't wait for a monthly meeting. You needed to catch the killer now. He suspected this might work well in other types of organisations but guessed that when people needed advice on a situation, they tended to need it in the moment, not at an agreed time through facilitated discussion forums and committees.

Fenton was a bit old fashioned in some of his methods, then very advanced in others. He was a good copper, well so he got told, and people showed him the degree of respect that would justify such an assumption. They knew were they stood with him. He could also be quite charming when he needed to be; it was charm that was going to help in the current situation. Fenton had to find a way of questioning the validity of this alibi, without actually questioning it. The last thing he needed was another complaint; he was getting quite a collection of them now.

Doris Dunkley was short and stumpy with tight curly grey hair. Part of it had gone white. She wore spectacles on a chain that gave her a rather severe look. When she took them off, she looked like butter wouldn't melt. She was wearing a floral dress, with a lavender coloured handbag held tightly under her arm. When Fenton asked if she'd liked to put it down, she tightened her grip and muttered something about the place being full of criminals. She had a matching hat as the pièce de résistance of elegant mature lady attire. Fenton felt she had pulled it off to a tee.

Fenton was determined to get the full story from her, despite how endearingly she came across. She might look like a sweet old grandmother, and possibly was, but he suspected this was a very shrewd woman who had been around the block a few times. She'd brought along three friends: Hilda,

Agnes and Breeda. Taylor, Brennan and Shirkham were taking individual statements at the same time, under the guise that they didn't want to keep the ladies any longer than they had to. Fenton just wanted to check that their stories matched.

"When are you going to release our boy?" Doris asked bluntly.

Her voice was loud and booming cockney. It made her sound tough and flippant. Fenton would have to approach this cautiously, to catch her off guard.

"We still have a few things to clear up, madam. He is being held on serious accusations."

"I'm aware of that, dear. Take it from me, our Jeremiah wouldn't hurt a fly. He's a big softie under all that muscle."

Fenton somehow doubted this, but he was keeping an open mind – had had no choice, his mind had already been blown today.

"If you could just explain what time you were with Jez on the night in question, what you did, who else was there..."

"Yes, dear, I know what an alibi is. I do watch a lot of shows, you know. And please don't call me madam, my dear; it comes across as very patronising."

Fenton raised his eyebrows, although thought better of saying anything about being called *dear* and the fact that real police work was different to what was written to entertain people on television.

"And don't think I can't see you raising your eyebrows there, my dear. My eyesight is as sharp as anyone's. Don't let the glasses fool you."

"Now if we could just..."

"And let me tell you this. Our Jeremiah is a champion. The things that boy can do with a needle are out of this world. I've never seen such a talent."

"So, what time..."

"Now listen, dear. Jeremiah couldn't possibly have

murdered anyone. He's not the type. Have you even met him?"

Fenton was finding the whole situation completely bizarre, hilarious, and irritating all at once. This woman could talk for England.

"Of course, I've met him. I'm the lead investigating officer, and..."

"Well done, dear, your wife must be so proud. Are you married?"

Fenton nodded.

"Stay at home-type, I expect. Kids?"

"Three girls."

"Oh, how lovely. Boys are a pain in the arse. Take it from me, dear, I've got four of them and the oldest must be about your age by now. What are you dear, early fifties?"

"Forty-five." Fenton was slightly miffed but couldn't help smiling.

"Oh dear, you look like you need a break. I expect the work ages you something terrible. Although it's not dangerous, I suppose. You don't use guns or anything in England."

Fenton decided not to add that, although he might not use a gun, some murderers were inclined to use them and other weapons on occasion He let her ramble on for what seemed like hours and every time he tried to steer the conversation back to the reason they were there, she just spoke over him and went off on tangents.

An hour and a half later the interview concluded. Tucked away in a constant stream of pointless waffle were the details of Jez's alibi. Fenton was miffed. It seemed very genuine and although deep down he had suspected Jez was not the killer, it was a blow to the investigation, nonetheless.

Jez had arrived at a local community centre in Kings Cross. Rehearsals were underway for the National Needlepoint Championship. He was in the individual event, where he was trying to win the title for the third year in a row and he was also part of a team event. There were five in the team: Jez, Doris, Hilda, Agnes and Breeda. They had taken Jez into the fold to replace Sylvia. She was Jez's grandmother. She'd died a year ago – not before teaching Jez all she knew.

Jez had arrived shortly after eight and then, realising he had left his best needles in the hotel, had rushed back to get them. He had then been with the women until after nine thirty. They would all back up the story. There were also other people at the community centre who were connected to the needlepoint association. In total, there were another twelve potential witnesses. He assigned the interviews of the other witnesses to the more junior officers in the team to give them some field experience, rather than all the back office work they had been doing; well, that was his reasoning for delegating the task anyway!

———

Brennan found the whole situation both bewildering and utterly hilarious. In a warped way he was hoping that the latest development would leak to the press because he was fascinated to know how it would be reported. Numerous headlines flew through his mind involving crochet bobble hats linked to brutal slayings. He couldn't think of any catchy straplines himself. That's why he didn't work in a creative environment. He was about hard methodical working and facts. He was a copper for genuine reasons; he wanted to catch the bad guys. Despite being a short arse – thankfully, they changed the height restrictions, he hadn't just become a copper for the uniform. Granted, that hadn't done him any harm with the ladies when he used to wear a uniform, but he took his job very seriously, even if he did come across as a jack the lad at times. His colleagues would ask him how he could be such a cheeky twat and yet witnesses and suspects would still find him utterly adorable, so much so that they would spill their secrets. Fenton had told him it was a gift that couldn't be taught, and that he should use it well.

Brennan was interviewing Hilda. He liked her instantly. She was feisty and a little bit flirty.

"You're a bit of a cutie, aren't ya, love?" she said. "I bet you're a right dish in ye uniform. How come you're not wearing one now?"

She spoke in a similar accent to Jez and Wendy, although she didn't add *like* or *fact* after random sentences, which was a great relief. He liked her even more for it.

"Detectives don't wear uniform," he said, flashing a smile.

She giggled like a schoolgirl, clutching her pearls. "Oh, a detective, I do feel special."

Hilda was well into her seventies. She dyed her hair a rich auburn colour – this was an assumption, that was no doubt accurate. She wore very contemporary clothing, including a low-cut top that would just look wrong on anyone else of that age, but Hilda had the character and bust to pull it off. Brennan couldn't help but glance at them; he quickly looked away and suddenly felt very dirty. This woman was old enough to be his grandmother and more, but she had spotted him.

"Oh, don't be shy, look away, dear, God blessed me with them, so it's my duty to share them with the world. Even my own son can't help it and he's a woofter." She roared with laughter. "That's how I know our Jeremiah is innocent. I read in the paper that one of those that got done in were a woofter as well, and my Jeremiah don't have a problem with woofters. He gets on really well with me son."

Brennan hadn't heard the word *woofter* for years. He was

of the age where you didn't use that word unless you were a woofter. It was the same with anyone from a minority group. If you're in that group, you and only you can use those terms, otherwise its offensive. This woman wasn't offensive, she was just old school and honest. Brennan adored her.

"I'm afraid I will need a bit more information though about Jez's movements on the night in question."

"Fair enough, love, you're the detective." She giggled, batting her eyelashes, and clutching her pearls again; pearls that were clearly worn to bring attention to that impressive cleavage.

———

Shirkham was perplexed by the latest development, although took it in her stride. Not much fazed her and she didn't like to show herself up as the more junior officer. Even though she could easily have progressed by now, she was doing something she enjoyed. It was part of her life, but it wasn't her whole life. She took pride in what she did, but it wasn't who she was. It was just a job that she liked doing, and she'd sort of fallen into it. She had first applied to annoy her father. However, the recruitment stage had taken so long that she was working in an office by the time she had her first interview. The whole process took months and when she was offered a training placement it coincided with her being made redundant, so she took that as a sign to go for it. Her father had said he was immensely proud when she told him, which was a mild irritation, as her plan had backfired. That didn't matter in the end as she'd really enjoyed her training and time in uniform, so she'd stuck with it and trained as a detective, before moving into the murder squad.

. . .

Shirkham was interviewing Breeda. Fenton had thought it a stroke of genius to put two Irish women together, as she would extract more information this way. Shirkham decided not to question this tactic, however she knew that a once in a lifetime event had just occurred – Fenton was wrong! Breeda inquired as to why such a beautiful Celtic charmer needed to work, when a man could be looking after her.

Breeda was a rather squat woman, with white hair and dazzling blue eyes. She had the look of a woman who had led a busy life raising a family. Shirkham found out that was true. Breeda had eight children and two dozen grandchildren.

"Such a stunning beauty, aren't ya? Your mother must be a looker too. It's down to good genes and it's always the women. Men have their uses, but most of the grafters look like shite. I don't go in for all these pretty boy types meself. All moisturiser and plucking. Give me a real man any day. Our Jeremiah, now that's a real man, don't you think, dear? I could get you his phone number if you like?"

"I don't think that would be appropriate."

"Why ever not, dear? He's gorgeous and he's a grafter. A real man!"

Shirkham doubted Breeda's vision of a real man. "It wouldn't be appropriate considering he's a suspect and I am a police officer."

"I told you already, dear, he didn't do it. He was with us the whole time. And besides, if you find yourself a good man, like our Jeremiah, you won't have to do all this man's work."

Shirkham was reaching the end of her tether, but Fenton had been quite clear to all of them. Charm and smiles, and whatever else it takes to get a clear statement. Make sure you probe on everything without making them feel like you are accusing them of lying. They would then reconvene at the end and compare notes. A briefing was due before they went home for the night as a decision was needed on whether they were going to let Jez go or apply to the magistrate for an extension.

Through gritted teeth she fought off Breeda's countless offers of a husband from her various nephews and friends' grandsons. In the end she got the information that she needed. It was looking promising for Jez, but not so good for the investigation. If the others backed up this version of events, it was about to come to a shuddering halt.

———

Taylor sat across from Agnes. Agnes looked a little bewildered and hadn't appeared as feisty as the other three when they had all been waiting in the reception area. She was noticeably quiet and hadn't spoken much when they were a collective. At first, Taylor was slightly concerned that perhaps Agnes wasn't in full possession of all her faculties. That was an incorrect assumption.

"What do you need to know? I am rather busy."

Her voice was bossy, yet soft. Taylor could detect a faint southern lilt to her accent.

"I just need you to tell me what time Jez joined you on the night in question? How long he was with you? Did he leave? Was he with you the whole time? Who else was there?"

"Steady on, girl. I'm eighty-two. I'm not Rain Man. One question at a time please!"

It was a long process, but Taylor got everything she needed. It corroborated everything Doris had told Fenton earlier on the phone. It was possible that they were covering for him as friends of his grandmother. She doubted it, but that was up to the boss to decide. Taylor brought the interview to a close. Agnes was collecting her things together and Taylor had her hand on the door before Agnes gently put her hand on top to stop her from opening the door.

"You're a very bright girl, but can I give you some advice?"
Taylor shrugged.

"Jeremiah is a fine-looking man, and he's an adorable gentle soul. He's had a very tough time with all the trouble that family has caused for him. At least now they're behind bars. I'm asking you to keep your distance. I can tell from the way you look when you talk about him. He likes a woman who can dominate him a bit and I suspect you're someone who likes to be in control. We, and I mean me and the others, we don't want our boy exposed to the rough types you come across in your work. Now my boy is innocent, and the other girls will back me up. Plus, the other witnesses I told you about. He's associated with some very unpleasant people. That's not through his own doing. It's that family of his. I don't think that sort of association would do your career much good either. I suspect you're the ambitious type. Yes, you look it. Well, good luck to you. I always admire women who want to make a career for themselves because you've got to be a tough bitch to make it in a man's world Just keep your distance, I think that's best for both of you."

Taylor was stunned and found she was incapable of speech for the second time that day. All she could do was nod and lead Agnes out to the front desk to join the rest of her friends. Doris was missing, so she knew the boss was still busy. Still in shock, she decided to get some fresh air before she compared notes with the others. As she left the police station, she could feel tears welling up in her eyes. She quickened her pace; she needed some time alone to think and she couldn't let anyone see this vulnerable side of her – they'd see it as weakness.

———

Fenton was in Beeden's office explaining that now the team had fully checked out Jez's alibi, he was going to be released without charge.

"I don't like it, Eric. I don't like it one little bit. The press will have a field day."

"Should we really care what the press thinks, sir, especially someone like Polly Pilkington? We can't hold a man who is clearly innocent. The magistrate won't grant the extension."

"Stop making this personal, Eric. You're obsessed with Pilkington and it concerns me."

"Has she made a complaint then?"

"No, why would she?"

"Just an empty threat, sir. Things got a little heated."

"I asked you to give an interview, Eric, not have a slanging match."

"I thought she hadn't spoken to you?"

"She hasn't – I know you!"

"Oh!" Fenton shifted uncomfortably. He didn't like being caught out.

"Oh, indeed. I really don't need any more crap from this investigation Eric. You shouldn't have arrested him until you were sure."

"You told me to make an arrest."

"Yes, but make it stick, not make us look like a bunch of tits who don't know what they are doing. You know the Queen's Speech is tomorrow"

"I thought they usually did all the pomp and circumstance on a Thursday."

"The Prime Minister wants to wrong foot the opposition. I bet Her Majesty is a bit miffed having her schedule changed."

"I suspect she probably had a say in it, sir."

"No doubt. A shame we couldn't have somebody charged beforehand though."

"I'm not rushing it again, sir. If you want to bring in another DCI that's fine, but I won't jump the gun and be made to look, as you put it, a tit, again."

"I won't replace you, Eric. Too late in the day for that. It won't look good in the papers."

Fenton seethed. He could have said it was because he had faith in him. It showed that when people got into their expansive offices, they forgot the friends who had helped them get there. It was one of the reasons why he never wanted to progress any further. If that was what you became then he was better off where he was. At least his team still respected him.

"Can I release him then?"

"I don't suppose we have much choice. What do you propose to do next?"

Fenton explained in which direction he wanted to take the case, now they had exhausted the original motives. Beeden wasn't happy and kept raising concerns about the press attention; although even he realised there was no use in flogging this very dead and decomposing horse. Fenton had requested some time off for the team to have a breather from the enquiry, so they could come back refreshed, as they had just worked another weekend. Beeden grumbled again about what the press might say, but reluctantly gave permission and told Fenton to keep him updated daily whilst the investigation was ongoing. That was unusual as Fenton knew Beeden was overseeing about two dozen murder investigations. He suspected the political implications of this one would ensure more photo opportunities. He then noticed the tinted face moisturiser on the desk and there was no doubt – that was the appeal.

. . .

Fenton called the team together for an evening briefing. It was late and everyone was tired out after a long day, some of them working since the early hours following Jez's arrest the previous night. That included Fenton, who had forgotten what his bed or wife looked like and wondered if his daughters had left home and gotten married yet. In real time the case had only been going for a few weeks, although it felt a lot longer. There was a unanimous cheer when he told them that they could have the next two days off, but the mood soon waned when he confirmed that Jez was to be released.

The team knew it was the right decision, but it was still a blow after all the work they had put in to checking out his history and alibis. It felt like the case wasn't just back to square one, in fact it was even further back and square one was sticking up two fingers.

Fenton summarised what had happened over the last twenty-four hours. The Jez needlepoint saga became too hilarious for everyone in the end and a laugh was what they all needed. Brennan and Shirkham's descriptions of Hilda and Breeda had everyone in fits.

Taylor was unusually quiet, which didn't go unnoticed by Fenton. She didn't offer any anecdotes about Agnes, so he didn't share any about Doris. He didn't want to bring attention to her sombre mood when the team was jovial for the first time in days.

Fenton explained that once everyone was back from their short break, he wanted to go back to the beginning and check everyone's story again. He would be travelling up north with Taylor to conduct some further face-to-face enquiries. Brennan looked a bit put out, but Fenton explained that he wanted him and Shirkham to co-ordinate the rest of the team in the incident room. He suspected a lot more information was going to have to be thoroughly checked so it was a better use of manpower for them both to stay behind. He knew that energy would be high again once the team was rested. Fenton would also use the trip to get some time with Taylor alone. He had noticed her distance herself more lately; she probably needed a pep talk, rather than another bollocking.

"Watch yourself with Wendy, Guv," joked Brennan.

"Don't worry, I've got a great way to keep her at bay."

"Oh yeah, what's that?"

"Your phone number!"

For once in his life Brennan was lost for words, as his teammates laughed again.

Fenton sat opposite Taylor in his office. The rest of the team had left. He'd asked her to stay behind on the premise they would discuss their trip to Preston in more detail.

"Lisa, what's wrong?"

"Nothing, sir, just tired like everyone else."

"You've been a bit distant ever since this ridiculous Jez thing kicked off. Since the interview with Agnes it's like you've not been here."

"Nothing, sir. Can I go home now? I'm really tired." She stood up.

"Sit down please."

She looked visibly upset as she sat back down.

"Now what's all this about? Is it because I balled you out?"

"You hardly balled me out, sir. You had every right. I weren't acting very professional."

The tears came. It was so unlike her to show any sign of vulnerability.

"Lisa, I didn't bring you in here to give you another bollocking. I'm just concerned as a friend. I've seen officers crack before and I'd hate that to happen to you. It won't go any further than these four walls, even if you've done something you shouldn't have. I promise."

She shook her head, still crying. Fenton had never been a good one with tears. You don't want to seem cold or patronising. You can't comfort them either as a friendly hug could always be misconstrued. You just had to sit there awkwardly, hoping it would soon be over.

"It were just something Agnes said."

"I wouldn't pay any attention."

"It were nothing bad. She just told me the facts of life. Sometimes it takes a stranger to point out the obvious."

"You're right, sometimes it does." He gave her a look that he hoped showed the empathy he felt for her.

Fenton went inside his desk drawer, pulled out a card and put it on the desk in front of Taylor.

"She's good. Give her a call. She's private and her rates are reasonable as well. That way nothing will be on your record. She really helped me after the Davies case, and she still does from time to time."

She picked up the card. "I'll call her."

"Tomorrow?"

She nodded, stood up and left.

Fenton would not be taking time off, as he was planning to get everything set up for their trip. He suspected that tomorrow was going to be an eventful day – it was the Queen's Speech.

CHAPTER TWENTY

SLAYER SUSPECT FREED ON EVE OF HISTORIC
SPEECH
Polly Pilkington

Jeremiah Tool was released from custody last night, following his arrest for the brutal triple murder in a London hotel last month. The victims were all from minority groups. Tool was arrested because he had no alibi for the time of the killings, and his association with the far-right political party, FREE. He works for the same company, Training4All, as all three victims. It is not known whether he will be returning to work today.

It is understood that he was not released on police bail. Tool has now been eliminated from police enquiries. Sources also indicate that the police investigation is considering dropping the hate-crime motive and pursuing other avenues of investigation. This is another indication that the Metropolitan Police is vehemently opposed to public demand for a House of Commons debate on the reinstatement of the death penalty for hate crimes. Sources indicate that the views about the importance of tackling hate crime is not one that is shared at the top level of policing. Their abstention from making a formal statement only adds weight to these allegations.

The Queen's Speech will be delivered today in an historic move, which sees the speech moved to a Monday. Sources close to Number 10 reveal that the speech will contain a "few surprises."

The decision to move the speech has meant that nobody yet knows the full detail as the final draft was only given to Her Majesty late last night. It is believed that there will be additional tough crime measures included as well as the proposed debate. It is likely that such a debate will be tabled in the form of a draft bill, which means the matter only needs to be raised in the House of Commons, not put before a vote.

Sources close to the police have revealed that Jeremiah Tool claims to have been taking part in a National Needlepoint Championship at the time. This has raised many questions, because he is over six feet tall and has a history of violence. All his living relatives are currently in prison, some of them for offences as serious as armed robbery. It is understood that several elderly ladies came forward and gave an alibi for the time of the killings. All these witnesses were friends of the accused's deceased grandmother, also a known criminal.

It is rumoured that Tool left FREE, as the party started to allow people from minority groups to join and he is starting up his own more extremist branch. This "Championship" is not known to other people within the needlepoint industry – yes that is a real thing readers! It is thought that this is merely a cover for something far more sinister.

Last night Tool and all his "witnesses" could not be contacted, and it is understood that they have gone into hiding, no doubt at the taxpayer's expense. A witness has revealed that this 'association' consisting of Tool and the others could be more disturbing than the activities of FREE. A small dark brown teddy bear was found, in the community centre used for these meetings, with pins sticking out of it. Some of them in unmentionable places. It raises serious questions *about what this group is really doing, under the guise of needle-pointing!*

Sources reveal that DCI Fenton, 45, was so desperate to make an arrest in the case over the weekend, and to avoid further reports in London News, that he may have alerted the real suspect, and informed them what little evidence the police have against them. People are still being warned to be vigilant, particularly those from minority groups. It is now feared that after a dormant phase the killer could strike again soon. Despite a serial killer still being on the loose, Fenton has decided to give the investigating team two days off – let's hope nobody else gets murdered whilst they are enjoying their rest at the taxpayer's expense.

———

The Leader of the Opposition was muttering to himself – he was angry.

"What's that bastard up to? Trying to wrong foot me, the conniving little shit."

Today he had to focus. It was normal protocol for him to see a copy of the speech beforehand, so he could prepare his attack in the House of Commons. This new approach was highly unorthodox, and for the Queen to agree to a last-minute date change made him even more anxious. The Prime Minister was up to something. This was nothing unusual, the furtive little shit. The fact that he didn't know what he was planning from his many sources was what unnerved him. He'd even asked his chief minion to arrange a little dalliance with the Prime Minister's secretary, but that was not an option. The Prime Minister had sent him overseas on a business trip. The timing was suspicious, and the Leader of the Opposition wondered if it was because the Prime Minister knew his secretary had a, so called, loose tongue.

Even the Cabinet appeared to be at a loss as to what the

speech would entail in its entirety. He suspected that the Home Secretary would know, as it must be linked to crime, although he was another pompous twat. Thinking he owned the place. He wasn't even elected; he was a Lord. What was he doing holding one of the four most senior positions in government? He was never in the House of Commons to be challenged by MPs; it was ridiculous and would be one of the first things he would change when he was Prime Minister.

One thought had occurred to him and it was the only thing keeping his cool. Had the Prime Minister decided to go a bit further with the death penalty debate? If that was the case, then it could backfire. That was what he wanted; the Prime Minister to go too far and for it to be his undoing. However, with public opinion so volatile on the subject, it was getting harder to predict how best to get onside with them. He hoped the Prime Minister would not propose putting it to a referendum. That would be a disaster, as they would then have to openly choose sides; if it was kept in the House of Commons then he could continue to play both sides before deciding which way to fall, when the time was right. He was determined that he was going to be the next Prime Minister. He just needed his counterpart to do the right thing, and metaphorically hang himself!

———

The Prime Minister was alone in his office reading over the speech, feeling satisfied and relaxed.

He sipped his coffee and gently closed his eyes. It was going to be an eventful day, he knew that. It could make or break his term in office. It was a gamble, but he was fed up with being labelled a pussy. He needed to regain his authority and stranglehold on the opposition and subordinates. Not literally of course – he had professional decorum... most of the time.

It would be interesting to see how his opposite number would respond after the speech. It was a good feeling to have the upper hand for once. Considering he was the head of the government, he felt like all he did was fend off attacks from the opposition, his own MPs, the public and the media. It was time that he hit back. He had won two elections and he needed to find that person who had won those fights. This new Leader of the Opposition was different to the others. He was a slippery bastard and was obsessed with power. Most politicians were, particularly the senior ones, but this one was different and the thought of that man being in the most powerful political position in the country made the Prime Minister extremely nervous.

———

The Leader of the Other Party sat at a hot desk. He didn't have an office. It wasn't poverty; it was trendy. He had no idea what was happening with the Queen's Speech as he hadn't seen a copy. The others were fighting amongst themselves and to be honest nobody seemed to be listening to him. He was used to this, although he could usually muscle his way on to the news to voice his opinion. At present, he was only certain of one thing. He wanted to become Prime Minister for one reason and one reason only. Was it to lead the UK to a better tomorrow? Enshrine equality as a way of life? End child poverty? Provide free education for all? No – he wanted to have Debbie killed.

———

The pomp and circumstance of the state opening of parliament began. It had its highest viewing figures ever. News channels showed their usual blanket coverage, all claiming to know what was in the speech with various panels of *experts* offering their pearls of wisdom and insight into what the speech would contain. There were breaking news banners flashing every few seconds, but in all honesty, everyone was just guessing, and nobody had a clue what the speech would contain. That was the way the Prime Minister liked it. He didn't like this new generation of media leaking. Politics had become like soap operas. What the hell was the point in watching something if you had found out what happened in the newspapers three weeks earlier? He liked that everyone, including the media was going to have to do what he had to all the time – react in the moment. Think on your feet and don't let your real feelings show. That was bloody difficult and now everyone else was going to have to do the same as him.

The House of Commons was called to the House of Lords. The Prime Minister and the Leader of the Opposition did their obligatory walk together trying to look all chummy and matey for the cameras.

"What the fuck are you up to, you little shit?"

"You'll just have to listen to the speech like everyone else," replied the Prime Minister.

"I'm supposed to see a copy beforehand. That's the protocol."

"It's not a written rule. Perhaps you'll have to think of your rebuttal on the spot like a real politician for once, instead of having your press secretary do it for you."

"Wanker."

"Prick."

"My Lords..."

The Queen began her speech. The usual policies: education, defence, immigration, and the economy. The Prime

Minister noticed some of his backbenchers were already yawning. Why become a politician if you aren't even interested in the government that you're a part of? He'd saved the juicy bit for the end – make them stand it out.

The news channels would continue with their speculation and analysis. The Prime Minister had heard of people taking the day off to watch the news and employers appearing baffled when their employees asked for TVs in the staff rooms.

"Is there a football match on or something?"

"No, it's the Queen's Speech."

"Blimey it's not Christmas already, is it?"

The Prime Minister was pleased. It was good that the public were getting interested in politics again. The Parliament Channel had never had so many viewers. In fact, it usually never had enough viewers to register on the BARB ratings. People were opting to use the parliament channel as it was just showing the speech raw. No analysis or flashing banners. Children convulsing was distracting, and the volume could only go up so far before the sound was distorted.

Her Majesty was nearing the end of the speech; soon would come the moment when everyone would need to try and control their natural reaction to what was about to be said. Hopefully that odious cretin next to him would be caught on camera looking agog.

"My government will introduce a bill to reinstate capital punishment for cases of murder with a discriminatory motive."

"Reinstate?" everyone was asking. "Not debate, did she say reinstate?"

The Leader of the Opposition gave the Prime Minister a glance. He looked surprised. The Prime Minister was singing inside. He'd finally got one over on him. This was his day. His moment. He wanted it to last forever.

Within a few seconds his stomach knotted, and he started to sweat. He noticed a grin appear on his counterpart's face. The Leader of the Opposition turned to look at him, covered his mouth so it couldn't be seen by the cameras and whispered; barely audibly so only the Prime Minister could hear...

"Gotcha!"

CHAPTER TWENTY-ONE

Taylor was walking along Marylebone Road towards Baker Street tube station. A November chill was finally in the air, even though the afternoon had consisted of glorious sunshine, which had convinced her not to take a jacket. Now it was freezing. If it was still warm, she'd have walked back to her flat in Ladbroke Grove. Instead, she decided to brave the chill and get to a tube station; one which would mean she wouldn't have to change lines. It was one of her pet hates. There was always some vacuous, self-absorbed moron, who would shuffle on to the tube and then stop in the doorway, completely oblivious to the people behind.

She'd spent her day off running a few errands and caught up with some friends. She'd also met with the counsellor whom Fenton had recommended. Fenton had been right; she was incredibly good, and they had arranged to meet again in a week. The team hadn't had any time off for a while and it was unusual for the them to be given time off on weekdays, but given they had just worked another weekend, Fenton had ensured that Beeden had cleared the time off. They had expected there to be a comment from Pilkington in the press about it, but no other newspapers or news channels had picked it up as an issue.

Taylor suspected that Fenton would not have taken any time off. He wouldn't have been involved in any off the fallout from the Queen's speech, but Beeden would have wanted him close by, in case there was any press enquiries linked to the case. Taylor had received a call from Polly Pilkington but had just given the *no comment* line and hung up. She'd then had a few missed calls from an unknown number. She had ignored them, working on the assumption that if it was anyone important, they would have left a message.

Just one day away from the case had allowed her to reflect on what had happened with Jez. Could something have happened if Fenton hadn't stepped in? Would she have been tempted to contact him, especially now he had been exonerated? She liked to think she would have still been professional. He was a suspect, and that last incident had only been with a suspect's estranged brother. Even she had limits! That relationship could have turned into something special. They'd had an instant connection, but it wasn't to be. She was fed up with being single. One of her friends had offered to set her up again, but she was so sick of going on dates with men who were too clean-cut. That wasn't her type. However, her friend had said this guy was a biker, so that had piqued her interest. She'd agreed to be setup but said it couldn't be until after the case was over. Now they no longer had a suspect, she had no idea when that could be.

She was just about to cross the road to the tube station. She never used the underground walkway at night. She wasn't scared of being mugged or anything, but the smell of piss tended to put her off her dinner and she had some salmon in the fridge that she needed to cook, as it went off at midnight. She glanced over at Pizza Express on the corner and was tempted for a second to get a takeaway but decided to stick with her plan. She did a double take as she was sure she'd seen someone familiar. She looked again and she wasn't wrong. She moved out of view as they were sitting by the window. She took out her mobile and dialled.

"Boss, how quickly can you get to Pizza Express opposite Baker Street tube... That thing you asked me to do... No, that thing on my own... Yeah, that's it... Well, guess who's having a cosy dinner right now... Right, bye."

She hung up the phone and went to put it back in her bag, then stopped. She held it up and zoomed in on her target and took a few photos. She checked her handiwork and gave herself a smug smile of satisfaction. This would get her back into Fenton's good books and could come in handy if he didn't make it in time. She was slightly apprehensive as she wasn't sure what he was going to do when he got here. There were several options; the majority were too embarrassing to even comprehend.

By the time Fenton arrived, Taylor was turning blue. She hadn't dare nip in somewhere to keep warm in case the target moved, and she needed to follow. Hopefully, that wouldn't be the case. What if they split up? Which one would she follow?

She was glad that Fenton arrived, and she wouldn't have to make that decision.

"Where are they?" he said, trying to catch his breath.

"Bloody hell, did you run here from the station?" She asked, pointing to the window of the restaurant.

"No, I got a cab as far as Regents Park tube and jogged the rest of the way. Traffic's a bitch."

He glanced at the window and his eyes narrowed as he focussed. He smiled. "May I take you to dinner?" He offered his arm.

She smiled, linked his arm, and they strode over to the restaurant. The salmon would have to go in the freezer!

They walked into the restaurant. It was moderately busy, so they weren't noticed entering. The other patrons were engrossed in their food or conversations, including the targets. Taylor got a waft of pizza and realised how hungry she was. She wondered if they were going to eat, or if Fenton was just going to flash his badge and then march over to their table and cause a scene!

"Table for two. Something by the window if you please."

Fenton had put on a posh accent for some reason. The waiter raised his eyebrows, nodded, and then escorted them to a table, furnishing them with menus. They were four tables behind their targets, who were so engrossed in their conversation they hadn't looked in their direction as they were seated.

Taylor started to scan the menu. She assumed Fenton would want to get the waiter away from hovering near the table before they discussed the best way to proceed. Fenton was sitting so he could see the table of the target, whereas Taylor had her back to them. She decided what she was going to order and then put the menu down, so this indicated to the waiter that they were ready to order. Fenton hadn't even looked at his and was watching the other table.

The waiter came over and asked if he could take a drinks order. Taylor went to speak, but Fenton got in first and ordered a bottle of red wine and two glasses. She had intended to have a soft drink as she'd had a few glasses of wine with her friends at lunch, without any food. That was why she was so hungry. Fenton said they would need longer to decide what they wanted to eat, so the waiter left to fetch their drinks.

"I got some photos," whispered Taylor.

"No need to whisper, Lisa," boomed Fenton.

The result was as he must have hoped. Manning and Pilkington, who had been enjoying a quiet dinner, whipped round to see where the loudmouth was sitting, as did everyone else. They all went back to their meals, a few shooting contemptuous looks, but Manning and Pilkington glared for what seemed like an age and he gave them a little wave. Manning, who had a direct view of Fenton gave a smile and then went back to her food. This clearly didn't please him, so he stood up, carried his chair over to their table and sat down with them.

A waiter who was dressed in a suit, different to the rest of the staff, so was probably the manager, had rushed over. Taylor couldn't hear what he was saying, but she heard Polly's response. She was speaking at a volume that ensured everyone in the restaurant could hear it as well.

"Don't worry, Eddie darlink, we can take care of this."

The manager seemed placated and moved away.

"Not going to invite your lady friend over, Eric?" asked Manning, pointing at Taylor.

Fenton looked miffed that they didn't seem in the slightest bit bothered that he had caught them, okay it was hardly intimate, but at the very least, they were meeting socially.

"Leave her out of it. This is between us."

Taylor was conscious that people were now looking at her. She was mortified and wanted the ground to swallow her, but she hoped the ground also had pizza.

"What is between us, Eric?" asked Manning. "What do you think you have got here?"

Fenton then spoke to them both in a quieter tone, so Taylor couldn't hear. She guessed this was a tactic by him to try and bring their tone down as well. It didn't work.

"Wait by the bar. I think we should be allowed to finish our meal," snapped Manning.

Fenton nodded and got up. He left his chair where it was and signalled for to Taylor to follow him. Fenton sat down at the bar and asked the waiter to bring their wine. He stated that they would no longer be eating. Taylor was wondering if she was ever going to eat tonight. She really hoped that whatever conversation was to happen with Manning and Pilkington would be done somewhere else. Although the restaurant was busy, she knew everyone would be interested to know the latest instalment in the saga. They were all watching them both and looking at Manning and Pilkington who were eating their food and chatting away like nothing had happened. After a few more seconds they realised they weren't going get any more drama, so the other patrons went back to their meals; the usual restaurant murmur resuming.

———

The next morning, Taylor and Fenton made an early start up the motorway. It was going to be a long day. Fenton had told her that he wanted to be back in London that evening as the rest of the team were due back the next morning – so much for having two days off! The press were still panting over the Queen's Speech so, thankfully, attention appeared to be diverted from their case for the time being, but after last night who knew how Pilkington was going to respond.

Fenton was bombing up the M6 and Taylor was concerned they might get pulled over. She pondered why men tended to do this when annoyed. Speeding in their cars, darting in and out of traffic and causing their passengers to repeatedly take sharp intakes of breath; the driver glaring at you from time to time, daring you to comment on their driving ability – something you must never do to male drivers.

They were approaching a service station and Taylor glanced at it longingly.

"What?" he barked.

"Coffee?"

He nodded and pulled over to the outside lane, ready to turn in. Taylor couldn't help but exhale loudly with a sigh of relief.

"What?" came another snappy response.

She shrugged and shook her head to signal she hadn't said anything. He grunted and signalled to turn into the services. She was relieved but kept her face completely straight as she could feel him watching her closely. She was very aware this meant he was not looking at the road and was thankful when the car finally came to a stop.

Fenton gulped down his scalding coffee in one. This was another thing about men she found fascinating; their ability to conceal pain. The exception is when they've got a cold, in which case they claim to be dying.

"You never said how you want to play it when we get there," she said, feeling the need to speak.

"What?"

"Which way do you want to play it?"

"I heard you the first time."

She let it go.

"I want to start at the company again. Elizabeth and Derek are still both off on extended compassionate leave or something."

"That's been weeks."

"Apparently Elizabeth was back part time, but Jez's arrest and then release sent her over the edge or something, so she's off again."

"And Derek?"

"He's not been back to work. Too distraught, apparently."

Taylor raised her eyebrows.

"Just what I've been told."

"But we're still going to speak with them?"

"Oh yes. I've appointments for this afternoon. Local plod is fine for us to get on with it. We need to give them a heads-up before we make any arrests."

"Is that likely?"

"I don't bloody know, do I? That's why we're going, isn't it?"

She didn't say anything.

"Sorry, I don't mean to snap, but last night really go to me."

"I gathered. You wanna talk about it?"

"No, it will just get me steamed up again. I was so certain."

"I think we all were."

"Anyway, let's forget it. How did your session go with the erm..."

"Very well. I think it'll be erm..."

"Useful?"

She nodded.

"Well, you'll be fine today. Muscle-boy's gone into hiding from the press, as well as all the old ladies. It's really screwing my budget on this case, giving them police protection like this."

Taylor said nothing, but she concluded that men, even the good ones like Fenton, could be bastards sometimes.

―――――

Fenton was not looking forward to speaking with Walt again. The guy was always *on,* and it was tiresome to have *dialogue* with him, or whatever it was called these days. Fenton would have preferred it to be a straight-forward interrogation in a police station. That would scare him into speaking normally and drop his dying swan routine.

Fenton had been annoyed the other day when the team burst into hysterics after he told them the investigation must be *fit for purpose*. He had no idea why he said it, as he had no idea what the hell it meant. It was just one of those soundbites that people love to hear – the kind that excites advertising executives even more than a bulk discount on cocaine.

Fenton knew he wasn't going to get anything out of Walt. It was just a starting point. He was still convinced the murderer was someone from within the company. Peter Gleeson seemed the next logical choice, but he wasn't about to make a fool out of himself again. They still hadn't completely ruled out Wendy. Walt's rent-boy or rent-man as he was now over forty, had verified his whereabouts. For now, Walt was in the clear.

"How wonderful to see you again, Inspector. How may I help you?"

"Sit down, Mr Channing, please, and it's Chief Inspector."

Walt looked a little miffed for a brief second, but dutifully obliged. If Fenton hadn't been eyeing him so sternly, he wouldn't have noticed the slight flicker of the eyes. It was a cheap shot using his rank, but Fenton knew that Walt was being passive aggressive when he said how *wonderful* it had been to see Fenton again.

"Would anyone like a drink?"

"No, thank you, this isn't a social occasion and we don't have all day. Now please will you sit?" he insisted.

Walt looked irritated that someone twenty years younger than him could scold him like a child. Walt sat, or it was more of a swoon. Fenton sighed. Picking her cue, Taylor started the questioning.

It was as Fenton predicted: a waste of time. All it succeeded in doing was winding him up further. He was especially irritable when Walt burst into floods of tears and it took some time to calm him down. Taylor gave Fenton a look that said *piss off*. This had caused a mini stand-off; however, when she made her eyes bore into him, he relented and went outside to cool off.

She came out and confirmed she hadn't got anything more from Walt. He was shocked at Jez's arrest and still didn't believe any of his staff could have killed someone in cold blood. His belief was that if someone from the company was responsible then it must have been a spur of the moment thing, a rash act of madness. He knew these people and he didn't think any of them were capable. Fenton felt there could be some logic to that summation. However, since the three people had been killed, all in different locations, temporary insanity would be a bit of a stretch.

———

Nothing new was gained from Peter Gleeson. Fenton gave him a hard time and all but accused him of murder. It was dangerous ground and Taylor was worried that Fenton seemed to be grasping at straws. She felt that they might get more insight from Wendy, but she was out training at a client's premises. It was only local, and they could talk to her at the end of the day.

Fenton wasn't interested though. He felt she would just utilise another interview as another bit of gossip and believed she was incapable of keeping a secret anyway, so there was nothing new she could add. Taylor let it go as he was in the wrong mood to challenge, but she decided that if he wanted to go back to London that afternoon, she would hang on and get the train back after talking to Wendy. She kept this to herself for the time being, as she was now starting to get wound up herself, and it was best that one of them kept themselves in check.

Peter Gleeson had acted very smug. He had openly criticised Fenton for his blunders with arresting Jez and suggested he look at some of the nutcases in London, rather than hounding him and his colleagues. Fenton was about to respond, but Taylor had swiftly kicked him under the table. By the time they left Training4All Fenton was hobbling from the amount of times Taylor had used this tactic to shut him up. The only thing she did agree with Fenton on was that their morning had been a complete waste of their time.

CHAPTER TWENTY-TWO

Taylor was starving, yet Fenton dismissed the idea of having lunch, as he had decided to head over to Derek's house early.

"I thought he wasn't expecting us for another hour or so," said Taylor.

"I like to surprise people."

"What if he's not in?"

"Then we visit Elizabeth."

That was stretching it a bit as they weren't due to see her for a couple of hours at least. She could understand Fenton's determination, but these were grieving relatives and their actions could be considered as bordering on harassment.

When they arrived at Derek's house, they were astonished to see a SOLD sign in the front garden. Taylor was immediately suspicious as nobody had mentioned anything at Training4All. The suspicion was intensified further when they got out of the car they had been loaned by the local CID. Walking down the driveway, was Polly Pilkington!

Taylor did not want to a rerun of the night before, she also wanted to know what the hell that woman was doing here. Fenton had gone bright red, so she prepared herself for the explosion. Derek was nowhere to be seen, which was just as well if there was going to be a shouting match between the Fenton and Pilkington

"What the hell are you doing here?" snapped Fenton.

"Eric, darlink. How lovely to see you! I think the question really is what are *you* doing here?"

"I asked first."

"So masculine and forceful! I thought you'd be hiding somewhere after last night's humiliation."

"I have nothing to be embarrassed about."

"Delusional as well I see."

"You still haven't answered my question. What are you doing here?"

"Following the story, darlink. Why else would I be here?"

"I'd appreciate it if you could not harass the families of the victims."

"You sound just like him," she said pointing back at the house. "Anyway, I best be on my way. Those articles don't write themselves and I am in such demand after yesterday's historic speech. Bye darlink!"

Without another look, she walked over to her car, got in and drove off. They just stood there watching. Fenton was still bright red and looked like he might explode at any moment. This was not the time to be knocking on Derek Longhurst's door, but that SOLD sign needed an answer. Taylor suggested they take a few minutes and get back in the car. He agreed, probably realising it was best that he calmed down before spaking to Derek.

———

Fenton was reeling!

What was Polly Pilkington doing interviewing the family

of the victims, and less than forty-eight hours after they had released the only suspect in the case. He was tempted to drive over to Elizabeth Jamal to see if Pilkington was heading there as well. Maybe he should call to warn her. Fenton suspected Pilkington would get short shrift from Elizabeth, but wondered if Derek had spoken to her, and if he had, what had he said to her. Had the sale of the house been discussed? The last thing he needed was that hitting the press before they had even found out what was going on.

"Right, let's go," he said.

They'd been sat in the car in silence for ten minutes. He did feel calmer, but they needed answers. They walked up the drive and knocked on the door. At least they knew he'd be home.

"Detective Chief Inspector Fenton and Detective Inspector Taylor," Derek said warmly. "I wasn't expecting you for a while yet. Did I get the time wrong?"

"Our other appointments concluded a little earlier than anticipated, so we thought we'd pop by on the off-chance. Is this a convenient time?" Fenton didn't really wait for an answer and barged his way in.

After Derek had gone through the rigmarole of making coffee he sat down, and Fenton was able to begin. "I see you are moving?" It was a clear question.

"Well, as you know, DCI Fenton..."

"Eric, please..."

"Well, Eric, as you know, my Trudie was my light. Now that light has gone out, I doubt if it will ever come on again. I have no choice, you see. I must depart, so that I may heal."

Fenton was fighting two urges at once – laughing and throwing up.

"Have you found a new home? Are you staying in the area?" Taylor interjected.

"I've decided to have a completely fresh start. My sister lives in Australia. I'm going to go and live with her."

"Australia?" Fenton asked, his ears twitching.

"I know it seems a bit drastic... Eric, but it would just be too painful to stay round here and at Training4All. I'd be reminded of it all the time."

"When do you plan to leave?"

"No immediate hurry. I've found a buyer, but I wouldn't leave Walt in the lurch. I'll work my notice and help him find a replacement."

"Does he know yet?"

"Yes, of course. I told him a week ago of my plans."

"I don't mean to sound rude, but you do seem to have sold up very quickly."

"Cash buyer. Said if we could get everything through in a month, he'd pay the full asking price. Couldn't turn that down really. It gave me the kick I needed."

Fenton was livid. Walt had mentioned nothing of this when he had spoken with him earlier and Taylor hadn't got it out him when he'd left the interview either. He wondered who else in the company must have known what was happening. His wife was barely cold in the ground and he was moving halfway across the world. It might look suspicious, but it still didn't make any sense. If he was sitting here talking to Trudie's killer at this very moment, then why had he killed the others?

Taylor was obviously thinking along similar lines because she suddenly piped up, "Can you tell us what you thought of Carl Davenport?"

"Carl?" He looked a bit surprised. "Any particular reason?"

"Mr Davenport wasn't married like your wife or Mr Jamal, so it's been difficult to get a clearer picture of type of person he were. If that makes sense?"

Fenton was pleased; plausible excuse, the false modesty of asking what he felt. The whole business with her getting the hots for muscle-bound murder suspects had somewhat clouded his judgement and he'd forgotten how good she was. All the women in the station had been panting, so she wasn't alone. It looked like Taylor was back on form.

"Yes, I see what you mean. What would you like to know?"

"Just what sort of person he were, in your opinion. What were he like to work with? Did you ever meet socially? What were he like out of work? You know what I mean."

"Well I never socialised with Carl out of work. There's a bit of an age gap between us. I'd only usually see him at the monthly office social. Walt's quite keen that we interface off site from time to time. It ensures that the creative energy continues to flow outside the work environment. Especially important for a company that relies on innovation and creativity in the way that it does. He was mostly friendly with the younger men in the office and he was immensely popular with the girls of course. I suppose they all thought that they could turn him. I never understood women's fascination of trying to turn gay men straight. It's not likely to happen, is it?"

Taylor smiled and signalled for him to go on.

Fenton was doing his best to keep quiet, although he was already growing impatient.

"Let me see. Well, we never worked together really. He had a different training style to me. He liked to be very inter-active, game-based and use a lot of new methods. I'm more traditional and like to use theoretical models. We had vastly different client groups. I think we must have worked together only a handful of times. He was always very amiable and professional."

"Was he seeing anybody at the time of his death?" asked Taylor.

"Goodness, I wouldn't know. Not likely to tell me anything like that..."

Derek paused and looked like he was thinking deeply about something.

Fenton was getting twitchy.

Taylor gave him one of her looks, whilst Derek wasn't looking. He shrugged and sat back in the chair. They still hadn't asked Derek what Pilkington was doing here.

"Now I'm not a big fan of office gossip... but I did hear a rumour that Carl was currently involved with a married man. Now that doesn't necessarily mean a man that was married to a woman, these days."

"Have you any idea who it was?" Fenton demanded.

"Haven't a clue, but Wendy should be able to tell you."

"Wendy Baxter?"

"Yes, she and Carl used to talk about it all the time. Very secretively, I might add, or so they thought. I overheard them a few times."

"Wendy!" Fenton said aloud, feeling furious.

———

Taylor and Fenton were now at the company were Wendy was delivering training. Fenton had barely spoken on the way over. He'd looked annoyed when Wendy's name had come up and quickly wrapped up the conversation with Derek. It was only when they were leaving that Taylor remembered to ask him about Pilkington. For a split second he looked flustered, not something she had seen with Derek before. He then stated that she had wanted to interview him as part of a piece she was doing on the murders. He had invited her in for a cup of tea, but politely declined to be interviewed. She hadn't seem bothered by his decision and left shortly after, declining his offer of tea.

Taylor had been to see someone from the company to find out how quickly they could speak to Wendy. She was delivering training and they couldn't just burst in and drag her out, although she wasn't sure if Fenton was really joking when he had suggested it.

"She's still training, be out in bit for dinner."

"Dinner? It's half twelve?" grumbled Fenton.

"Lunch then."

"Well, that is the correct term."

"Then why do they call them dinner ladies?"

"We don't have time for this. Where's the woman who runs this place?"

The Managing Director, Suzy Manky approached them looking a little bewildered by what was going on. Taylor felt sorry for her for two reasons; that name and that she was about to get a full blast of Fenton.

"Are you in charge here?"

"I am the managing director, officer. How can I help you?"

"We have been informed by one of your staff that Wendy Baxter cannot be disturbed until the lunch break. I am sorry but that is unacceptable. You need to go in there and tell her that she needs to speak with us now!"

"Excuse me, Officer, but I'm not comfortable with your tone. Ms. Baxter is training my staff at considerable expense. They are due to break for lunch in around twenty minutes. Surely you can wait, or do I need to make a complaint to your superiors?"

"Third complaint, third complaint, third complaint," Taylor whispered in his ear.

"Is there a room where we can wait until she comes out?" Fenton beamed.

"Of course, follow me."

"I'd like to stay and observe the training session discreetly."

"Suit yourself," replied Fenton skulking off, after a brief hesitation from Ms Manky.

Taylor sidled up to the door of the training room and sneakily peeked through the glass.

Wendy appeared to be in her element. She seemed to feed off the attention she was receiving. You can't get more attention than standing at the front of the room with all eyes and ears firmly on you.

"Before we break for lunch, we're gonna have a thought shower," remarked Wendy, bouncing around at the front of the room.

Whatever she was doing it seemed to be working, Taylor thought, as she had everyone's attention.

"What we're gonna do is list stereotypes. List as many as you can. Think about what we talked about this morning."

"You said that stereotypes were wrong this morning," piped up one of the delegates, or *learners* as they appeared to be called these days, something Taylor had found out at her last *learning event*.

"But they still exist. Fact. I mean there are probably stereotypes in this room right now."

Taylor saw a few of the learners share a smile, the irony evidently lost on Wendy. She'd seen enough and went to join Fenton whilst they waited for the group to break for lunch.

————

Fenton glared at Wendy as she sat down and shifted nervously. She said it was lucky this training wasn't a working lunch, or they'd have had to wait until the end of the day.

Fenton was all too familiar with the term *working lunch*. It was created by employers to ensure that their employees never leave the premises and take the breaks they are legally entitled to, under the guise of there being a *free lunch*. The phrase still rang true to this day – there was no such thing as a free lunch!

Fenton was furious with Brennan. It had been his job to get information about Carl Davenport and, unless Derek was lying, then he'd failed. Fenton had asked Wendy immediately about Carl's affair and her look had said it all. She gained her composure very quickly, but it was enough of a wobble for Fenton to know it was true.

Fenton had bellowed into the phone at Brennan, who feigned ignorance, much to his dismay.

"She never gave me any indication she was lying, Guv."

"She wasn't lying, was she? You just didn't find out everything that needed to be found out."

"I told you, Guv, she was just interested in trying to jump me."

"If this turns out to be true then we need to have a serious talk when I get back to the office."

"Are you still coming back today...?" Fenton terminated the call before Brennan could finish.

"Let him stew for a while."

"Are we going back today?" Taylor asked.

"No idea yet. It depends on what Wendy tells us. I've got an idea what she might say."

"What's that?"

"Prefer not to say just yet," he retorted bluntly.

"Not a great impression of teamwork there, sir," she joked.

"You can talk," he snapped.

"But I didn't…"

His glare cut her short. She went deep red and looked completely humiliated. He'd never spoken to her like that and regretted it instantly. Was he upset about missing something that could be crucial to the investigation? Or was he still fuming over how things had gone with Manning and Pilkington the night before? It wasn't like him to be beaten so easily. He was worried that he might finally be losing his touch – the last thing he wanted was for Pilkington to be right. He needed to shake off this self-doubt.

"So, Wendy, who was it?" asked Fenton.

"I don't know," she protested.

"Don't give any more lies. Why didn't you tell Officer Brennan at the time?"

"I don't know." She was getting flustered, then she just burst into tears.

Fucking brilliant!

Fenton took a minute to absorb his surroundings. They were in the room that Wendy was using for her training, whilst the learners were at lunch. Almost every inch of wall space was covered in flip charts, and he suspected this was not how it looked normally. Nothing to do with the company itself, but not even Training4All had such buzz words littering the walls. *Professionalism* seemed to be a clear favourite. What this meant in this context was anyone's guess. Fenton wasn't sure how to take this room. He wasn't against training. As someone from the old school, he was very progressive with personal development, he thought. There was just a difference between training where you learn something and training which was a load of wishy-washy bollocks.

Little name cards littered the table. He suspected there was more to it, otherwise it was a very unfortunate bunch of people who were being trained. Lucy Orange, Paul Apple, Bob Apple, *perhaps brothers*, Matilda Peach, Alex Grape and Jamila Strawberry. The last one convincing him it was no doubt in relation to some pointless icebreaker exercise that added no value to the training which was to come.

Taylor gently put her hand on Fenton's shoulder in such a subtle way that Wendy didn't notice. It was such a delicate touch that he relented and leaned back in his chair, allowing Taylor to take over.

"Wendy, what's with all the different types of fruit on the name cards?"

Fenton didn't care about the name cards. He had a theory about who their killer was now, and he just needed it verified. He suspected Taylor was going to do her circle the airport routine for a while, before initiating brace procedures and bringing it down for a crash landing. It was always highly effective, but it did take a bloody long time.

"Well we're talking about culture today. Fact. A lot of culture can be associated to a person's family name. Now everyone picked a new one for today based on what fruit they would be, so we don't make assumptions based on people's social identity."

Fenton bit his lip hard, puncturing the skin. It was a *fact* that he had just heard the most ridiculous thing in his entire life. People made assumptions on what they can see first and foremost. The name was only relevant if you couldn't see the person.

"Thanks for clearing that up. I were just curious. Sounds really interesting!"

Wendy beamed, missing the sarcasm that was sweeping through the room like a tornado.

Fenton suddenly found something interesting out of the window to avoid sniggering.

"Well it's good to keep things fresh."

"Absolutely."

"I really don't know who it were, you know."

"Who?"

"The guy Carl were having affair with."

Fenton continued looking out the window.

"I thought you shared everything together?" asked Taylor gently.

"We did, but he said it were top secret. I'm not known for keeping me gob shut." Her voice was quivering with emotion. "It's not that he didn't trust me, ya know," she added quickly, no doubt more to reassure herself than anyone else.

"Of course, it's obvious you were a very dear friend to him. It must be such a terrible loss."

Fenton thought she was laying it on a bit thick; it was working though. He stopped looking out the window and looked at the two women, keeping his physical and emotional distance. Wendy was more relaxed in her posture now. She was still blubbing, there were no hysterics.

"Do you think it's got something to do with why he were killed?"

"We don't know, Wendy. We don't know who it was. Are you sure you don't know anything? Even the most insignificant little detail could be helpful. Nobody will know it's come from you."

She looked at Fenton who agreed with a nod of his head. He'd moved forward in his chair, letting Taylor take the lead. He just needed some little clue that would prove his theory.

Wendy was choking back the tears, although her face was now badly streaked with mascara; she looked like hell. Hopefully, she'd be able to pull herself together before everyone became potatoes, courgettes, and carrots in the afternoon.

"Well, the only thing is the reason why he couldn't tell me who it were, why he'd hardly ever talk about it in the office."

Go on that's it, tell me what I want to hear

"Why was that?" asked Taylor.

"It were a guy from work."

Bingo!

CHAPTER TWENTY-THREE

Elizabeth Jamal opened the door to Fenton and Taylor. "You're late!"

"Very sorry, Mrs Jamal, we got held up."

"I have things to do this afternoon."

"We won't keep you long."

Fenton wasn't sure how he wanted to play this. He'd watched Taylor use empathy and compassion to get the one bit of information from Wendy that he needed to be certain of his suspicions. He'd felt guilty about not sharing them with Taylor. She was right. Fenton believed in working together as a team and sharing ideas, no matter how stupid people thought they were. He'd always let people prove or disprove their theories within reason.

He'd shared his theory with Taylor on the way over to Elizabeth's. She'd agreed with him. It made sense. He'd been right all along. There had been more to these murders than some moral panic bullshit created by Pilkington. She might not be bedding Manning, but she'd still created a panic with the public over these murders and had a lot to answer for; sadly, it was all ethical and nothing criminal... yet!

"I'd like to make a formal complaint," remarked Elizabeth.

"What?" replied Fenton. She'd thrown him.

"That horrible woman, Polly Pilkington, had the audacity to knock on my front door and request... no, demand an interview. She wants to do a Sunday page spread on each of the victims. She says she has already got agreement from Wendy Baxter and Carl's sister. She also says that Derek is on board, which I can't believe. She has called me several times and has been told that I will not be giving any interviews. Every other journalist has paid attention and never asked again, but that woman is relentless."

Fenton wondered what Pilkington was up to. He had known her hound the police and politicians before, but never the families of the victims. Perhaps her final moral scruple had evaporated. Elizabeth had raised an interesting point about Derek. Had he just lied to their face, or was Pilkington manipulating Elizabeth into agreeing to the interview, which she could then use to convince Derek to agree as well. As for Wendy Baxter, Fenton was now certain that he wanted to charge her with obstruction of justice as this was something else, she hadn't bothered to mention. Wendy was craftier than Fenton first thought. She had not outright lied to the police; she had simply not shared relevant information unless she was directly asked for it. To Fenton this was still obstruction and they would be paying her another visit in due course. This time with uniformed officers to arrest her.

"Mrs Jamal. I will speak with Polly Pilkington and ensure she leaves you alone. We have just spoken with Derek and he informed us that he had not agreed to be interviewed."

"Thank you. I didn't think Derek would. I knew she was lying. Well you tell her that if she contacts me again, I'll get an injunction out against her."

Fenton nodded. She asked them to take a seat in the lounge whilst she made some tea. Fenton considered his next move. Elizabeth was still giving off a very frosty energy, even though Fenton had placated her about Pilkington This was a clever woman who would spot false flattery and fake empathy a mile off. She worked in HR. Her whole career was based on mediation and bullshit. Fenton was also fed up with being told how he should and shouldn't speak to people.

He looked at Taylor and gave her a signal to let him take the lead to start and for her to come in when needed. Elizabeth came back into the living room carrying a tray with cups of tea and biscuits. She put everything down on the coffee table and finished making tea to everyone's requirements. She then sat back in her chair, and Fenton knew he had to just go for it.

"Mrs Jamal, I have reason to believe your husband was having an affair with Carl Davenport. When you discovered the affair, you murdered them both. I suspect Trudie Longhurst witnessed your crime or was aware of it in some way, so you murdered her in order to silence her."

The allegation hung there for a few seconds.

Elizabeth didn't react at first and then suddenly her face crumpled. She broke down into floods of tears. Was this finally going to be an admission of guilt, or was it simply another bash at getting the Oscar?

Elizabeth Jamal was pacing up and down the room. Fenton and Taylor were now standing. If she was the killer, they didn't want to be seated, as they would be in a very vulnerable position if she was to suddenly launch an attack. Fenton knew they should have arranged backup, but he was partly going off a hunch and some circumstantial evidence.

Elizabeth was slowing her pace and the tears had stopped. She was taking deep breaths as if to calm herself so she could speak. Fenton hoped that this would finally be the truth about what happened that night. She stopped and turned to face them.

"I never intended to kill them at first. I just wanted to catch them together."

"Shall we sit down?"

She nodded. Taylor discreetly excused herself. Fenton suspected she had gone to call for backup now they were certain. They were in the presence of a triple murderer of course, no matter how dowdy she looked. Mutton can be dangerous. Fenton decided to just let her talk in her own time.

"I suspected my husband was cheating on me for some time. I then received some anonymous phone calls telling me my suspicions were true and before you ask, I had no idea who the caller was. They disguised their voice so well that I couldn't even tell if it was a man or a woman. It wasn't until the lead up to the conference that I started to believe my suspicions were correct. At first, I thought nothing of Nadeem and Carl being away so much together. Their training styles were so similar that they were a natural pairing. It was when a new trainer joined the company that I had my first suspicions. I call them trainers as that job title Walt gave them is ridiculous."

Fenton smiled and nodded his agreement. It encouraged her to keep talking.

"This new trainer was another of Walt's hire. All cock and muscles, or style over substance as we would say in a professional environment. Anyway, given my role, I should have a say in the hiring decisions, but Walt is ridiculously impulsive and is known to create new roles to accommodate his latest acquaintance. We are all used to it now, and like the others, this one didn't last long – fucking useless."

Fenton was surprised at her language. Taylor walked back into the room and sat down. She gave a look that told him backup was on its way. He signalled for Elizabeth to continue.

"This guy, Elliot, was his name. He was also openly gay. Evidently he and Carl got on very well."

"Because they were both gay?" Fenton asked sarcastically.

"Don't be so facetious. It was because they were two good-looking men with egos the size of aircraft hangers."

"Please carry on," said Fenton.

"Walt had paired this guy Elliot up with Carl as he felt he was doing me and Nadeem a favour. It would mean fewer trips away from home. Nadeem started to act very oddly at that point and would be grumpy at home all the time. Walt asked Nadeem to do a supervision of Elliot's training. Part of the probation process that I introduced. I tend to prefer them to have skills and competencies as it's less earache later if you need to get rid of them. Like I said, Walt bases his judgement on other talents!"

Fenton was getting a little edgy. He noticed the more she spoke, the angrier her tone was becoming. He didn't want to interrupt her flow. They were getting a confession, with motive by the sounds of it, but he also didn't want her to explode. He was also not sure how subtle backup would be when it arrived. He didn't want her to get spooked and then clam up before she'd revealed anything. She may have confessed, but they still didn't know why and how she had done it. All they had was circumstantial evidence; they needed this confession. Thankfully, she was still sitting down, although Fenton was conscious of how close to the kitchen they were and wondered if there was a knife block on the kitchen sideboard!

"What happened with Elliot then?" prompted Fenton.

"Apparently he wasn't the best trainer. I think Nadeem took it to extremes when he did the assessment. If it had been that bad, we would have had complaints from clients,

Still, Walt trusted Nadeem's judgement and Elliot was out. Nadeem and Carl were paired up again and his mood changed instantly. At this point I knew something was going on. I wanted the proof so I could be certain. Like I said, I never intended to kill them, just expose them, and humiliate my husband."

"What changed that?"

"I would prefer to tell the story in my own time. Are we against the clock or something? Are Special Branch en route?" she asked looking at Taylor.

"Erm... Please continue," replied Fenton. Nothing got past this woman.

"How terribly kind of you. Where was I? Right. I wanted to make a bit of a weekend of the conference trip to London and stay on. Nadeem agreed readily to this and was excited about it. I thought I might have been wrong. Perhaps I was seeing something that wasn't there, or I'd wrongly identified my husband's lover. On the second day of the conference Nadeem made out he was unwell, although I caught his lapse in acting at times. Men are crap at lying. Carl made out that he wasn't hungry and skipped dinner. Nadeem had already done the same due to his alleged illness. I knew they were planning to spend time together right under my nose. I had never felt so angry in my entire life. I felt that at least doing it whilst they were away together was subtle, but this was just rubbing my face in it, especially as this was supposed to be doubling up as a romantic break with my husband.

"I slipped away from dinner and intended to confront them. I went to Carl's room. They weren't there, so I assumed they must have gone somewhere away from the hotel. I went to our room to get something and before I opened the door, I heard them. They were doing it in our bed, the bastards." She burst into tears.

Fenton signalled for Taylor to not attempt to comfort her,

or they could interrupt her need to unburden herself. That's what they were experiencing. Fenton had seen it many times with other killers. Those who killed impulsively. They'd act rashly in the moment and they would regret it instantly. Even those that would try and cover up the crime. They are still acting on instinct; an instinct to protect themselves, rather than the initial instinct to lash out. Most killers immediately regret what they have done, and it eats away at them until it all comes out, like it was doing now. It was the other type of killer; cold and calculating, that unnerved Fenton. They had no emotional response to what they'd done. They were also the least likely to confess.

Fenton let her cry it out for a while, until she was ready to continue. It didn't take long. She wiped her eyes and looked at Fenton. He could see in her eyes how betrayed she felt.

"I burst into the room and confronted them. I told Carl that I wanted to speak to my husband alone. He wouldn't leave. He said he wanted to be there to support the man he loved. Can you believe that?"

She wasn't asking a question. It was more of a statement, and she was getting angry again.

"Nadeem asked Carl to go to his room and that he'd be along soon to talk to him. I couldn't believe what I was hearing. When Carl left, Nadeem confirmed what I already suspected — it had been going on for almost a year. He said he still loved me. Can you believe that? The filthy hypocrite. I told him he disgusted me. He got incredibly angry. He told me I was only disgusted because he was with another man. How dare he accuse me of such a thing? I have ethics and principles."

"You weren't shocked that your husband was cheating on with another man?"

"It was the fact he was cheating on me, full stop. Why

should I think any differently that it was a man? What are you accusing me of?"

Fenton wasn't sure how to respond. This had nothing to do with equality or being homophobic. Fenton had no such prejudices, but if he came home and found his wife in bed with another woman, it would feel like a double whammy to him, but maybe he was just old fashioned. He suspected someone like Brennan would probably give a thumbs up and then join them for a threesome.

He wondered when Elizabeth was going to get to the actual murder. They had been talking for around twenty minutes, so backup had to be waiting outside. He guessed Taylor had told them to hold back until they were given a signal to enter, but if they left it any longer, they might assume something was wrong and just come piling in. He wanted to prompt Elizabeth to get to the point. He looked at Taylor who was avoiding eye contact for some reason. She was looking at her phone – hopefully telling backup to keep their distance... for now. He gestured for her to continue.

"It made no difference who he was cheating on me with, unless it had been a family member or friend, then that obviously would have been a double betrayal. His accusation was the last straw for me, I just snapped. I stabbed him right in the heart. It seems symbolic now. At the time it just meant he was more likely to die."

Fenton wondered how spur of the moment it could have been if she had a knife on her. They were in a hotel room and this was not usually something which came with the tea and coffee making facilities.

"Where did the knife come from?" asked Taylor.

Elizabeth didn't seem perturbed by someone else asking a question. She was in full flow now and nothing was going to stop her getting it all out.

"I had the knife in my bag. One of those irritating little

men with a Madonna mic was at a market selling them. He was quite rude to me. I was speaking to someone at the time and he had the cheek to ask if I came with an off switch. Wish I'd stabbed him as well."

"Excuse me?" remarked Fenton.

"Just a little joke to lighten the tension."

Fenton smiled, but wasn't convinced. He'd known people use humour around death as a coping mechanism, but something in her tone implied she was not joking. They had still not got onto the murders of Carl and Trudie. It may have been a spur of the moment decision with her husband, but with the other two, it would be harder for her to claim that. Besides, he still wasn't convinced that she just happened to have a knife in her bag that she had bought that day. It all seemed too convenient. Taylor had also picked up on this.

"So why did you buy one, if the man selling them was so rude to you?"

"It was an exceptionally good deal. It could cut through steel and not blunt the blade. Like the ones you see on late-night television."

Fenton wasn't about to ask why she needed a knife which cut through steel. It was the sort of purchase his wife would make. The number of things they had which she had only used a couple of times was ridiculous. The under stairs cupboard was full of gadgets and he wasn't allowed to throw any away or put any in the loft in case she needed them.

"Where there any witnesses with you when you purchased this knife?"

"There was but you can hardly ask her."

"Why?"

"She's dead."

"Trudie? I thought you weren't a fan."

"I wasn't, but I was still civil. She wanted to go out. Derek was busy. Some of the conference was reserved for trainers only. We went out to Camden Market."

"Is that why you killed her, because she knew about the knife?"

"I've nothing to say on that matter."

Fenton interjected. "Mrs Jamal, you have just told us how you killed your husband. You are going to be charged with three murders. It is very much in your interest to tell us everything now."

"You're going to charge me with *three* murders?"

"Of course."

"May I continue with my version of events? Or are we still on the clock?"

She wasn't angry anymore. In fact, she appeared to be showing no emotion. Maybe Fenton was wrong, and she was just a cold-blooded killer.

"Well I suppose I best get to the bit you've all been waiting for, hadn't I? My husband turned his back. He mocked me. Told me that he was going to leave me for Carl. I got the knife out ready. I was not about to do what he had done to me and just stab him in the back. Once he turned back to face me, I stabbed him. I watched him die. I wasn't sure what came over me in that moment, but I knew I had to go and tell Carl what I had done. I had no intention of killing Carl. I just wanted to tell him to his face what I had done, so I could cause him the same pain he had caused me. I took the knife with me as it had Nadeem's blood on it, so I could prove to him what I'd done. I didn't think he'd believe me, and I knew he was a strong man, I might need to protect myself."

Fenton wasn't convinced with her explanation and believed that Carl's murder was pre-meditated. No matter how she spun it, a jury wouldn't buy that she had killed all of them in the spur of the moment. What about Trudie? She hadn't been mentioned yet and according to the forensic report there was no blood evidence to link her to the other crime scenes. Elizabeth's explanation that she had killed her husband first and then moved on to Carl had corroborated the forensic report, but with Trudie she must have used a clean knife or cleaned the knife she had. That moved her from being a spontaneous killer, to a pre-meditated one.

"I went straight to Carl's room. He was apologetic and seemed upset. It was obvious that Carl had loved my husband very much. For a moment I felt sorry for him and empathised with him. I saw us as both being victims. I was hesitant to tell him what I'd done. Can you believe that I wanted to spare his feelings in that moment? After what he had done to me."

The anger was coming back into her voice and the coldness disappeared. Fenton believed he had her figured out. She had killed in anger, but her feelings about the murders afterwards had become detached. It wasn't an unusual reaction for a killer. It did not do them any favours with the jury, but it was a coping mechanism. They had done something so horrific that they had to emotionally detach themselves from the situation. This was a woman with a quick and dangerous temper, and he wondered what the other two victims had done to provoke her. He was about to find out.

"At that moment I could have just walked out, but he just turned on me. He had the audacity to accuse me of emasculating Nadeem. Turning him into a pathetic and needy man. He said it was because of me that Nadeem would never be with him. I was the one holding him back from being his true self. How dare he blame me. After everything they had done to me. I was furious. I told him that Nadeem was dead, and they wouldn't be getting their happily ever after."

"What did he say?" asked Fenton.

"He didn't believe me. He laughed at me. Said, he thought he was the drama queen."

"What did you say."

"I fucking stabbed him!"

She broke down sobbing and flopped onto the floor. She was inconsolable. There was no way they were going to get onto Trudie's murder until she'd been seen by a doctor. Fenton asked Taylor to call a doctor as well so they could be waiting at the local station. She would need to be transferred to London, but that would probably be the next day once she was deemed fit to travel. Whether they could get onto Trudie's murder today was doubtful, but he wanted to know what had happened to provoke another murder. Fenton could understand why she had killed the two men. It didn't excuse her actions, it just explained them. There was something different with Trudie that Fenton couldn't quite put his finger on. He guessed he would just have to be patient.

Elizabeth Jamal never made an application for bail. She gave a full confession to the murders of her husband and Carl. When asked about Trudie she replied *no comment*. Fenton gave up after six hours of interrogation. Fenton suspected she had been killed because she would have known about Elizabeth buying the knife. That murder had no justification and had been done simply to protect Elizabeth from prosecution. The woman was nothing less than a cold-blooded murderer and he hoped the judge would sentence her accordingly. Elizabeth Jamal was remanded in custody to wait for trial on three counts of murder. She had no idea what she had done with the knife. Fenton knew he had enough to convict her without it.

CHAPTER TWENTY-FOUR

Elizabeth Jamal had been on remand for two weeks when she made her first request for Fenton to visit her. It was unusual to receive such requests. The case was being wound down with just a few officers putting everything together ready for the case going to trial. Brennan and Shirkham had already been allocated other cases. Taylor was on leave. Fenton was also due to take some leave, although he had been given some time to revisit the Davies case whilst overseeing the trial preparations. He ignored her request.

He was staring at all the files spread out on his desk, but there was nothing new. No new leads. No further lines of enquiry. It was frustrating. He knew he was missing something obvious. He had this gut feeling. He was trying to remember something someone had said to him recently that he felt was relevant, although he couldn't remember who it was or what they'd said.

Fenton remembered the articles from Pilkington during the case. She was vicious, but aside from crossing the line by using Fenton's personal tragedy against him, she was right. His mind was not fully on the case and things were not as thorough as they should have been. This was his opportunity to put things right. He owed it to the family and if he was being honest, he'd love to stick it up to Pilkington. She'd been quiet since the arrest of Elizabeth Jamal. No doubt disappointed that the outcome of the investigation did not fit her narrative of creating moral panic. He suspected he had not heard the last from her regarding this case, and most certainly their paths would cross again during his career.

———

The Leader of the Opposition felt elated. The feeling of victory could beat any tantric massage orgasm. A small pastime he dabbled in to relieve tension; it was absurd to think that someone so close to power should do it themselves. The general public should feel that their future leader was provided with high quality relaxation; after all, they were paying for it. The expenses scandal had been a bit of a bugger when it came to what he could and couldn't claim. There were many things that he could still claim for, but somethings were best not for public record. He was fortunate that he had a masseuse who also doubled us a yoga instructor, so he was able to funnel a few expenses through under the heading of *mindfulness and spiritual wellbeing.*

His plan was working. Public support for the death penalty was waning. He knew that the Prime Minister was keen to get the bill out for debate as soon as possible before its chance of success completely slipped away. There was no way that such an issue could be anything but a free vote. There would be outrage if either side tried to force their MPs to vote a certain way on an issue like this. There was a place for whips and the Capital Punishment Bill was not one of them.

It was important was that he didn't misjudge the public

mood, which can shift as quickly as the weather. It only took another high-profile case to emerge or for something to happen in a soap opera and attitudes would change within a second. It was amazing how influential soap operas could still be, but he'd heard it first-hand when campaigning on the doorstep. The electorate were a strange bunch. You could show the indisputable evidence from a field of experts and they'd say you were lying, but if it had happened to Chantelle on EastEnders then it was gospel.

His strategy had to be subtle. He couldn't come on the attack. The public weren't keen on that either, even when you were right. You had to be clever, but not too clever as then you weren't relatable. He knew that he had to give off the impression of selflessness, no matter which way the debate went. It was tiring work!

———

The Prime Minister did his usual cheek puffing and exhaling loudly. He liked to sigh loudly, and then make out everything was okay. When people showed concern and asked if there was anything they could do, he felt better. Some people might describe that as being a tad needy, but it was a very lonely job at times and it was nice to know that people cared for his wellbeing, even if they were just phoning it in.

He was exhausted. Having to second guess people all the time was draining. It was easy enough to see what the Leader of the Opposition was up to. Using murder as a way of muscling into his abode was a low blow, but he knew his counterpart had played his part well and would come away from the scandal unblemished. In all honesty, the Prime Minister couldn't give a shit what that odious toad was thinking. He was more concerned with the public. They were being duped by a master con artist and they were falling for it. The Prime Minister would be fine if he was voted out of office. He'd be disappointed, but he'd move on. It was your average voter who would suffer under the new regime. It was those voters that were being swayed to the dark side by the moral panic whipped up by the media.

He had an idea of how he could tip things in his favour. It still wasn't over. The mood hadn't completely shifted. The sheep, otherwise known as the electorate, could still be swayed with a bit of propaganda. He didn't like to do it, but this was no longer about doing what was honest, it was about doing what was right. Sometimes you had to stoop to the level of the enemy in order to get the right result; some people just needed to be helped to make the right decision.

He picked up the phone and dialled hurriedly before he changed his mind. He arranged a private meeting with the person on the other end of the phone and then rung off. He smiled; it wasn't just the Leader of the Opposition that could fight dirty. Now, it was his turn.

DISCRIMINATION AT HEART OF TRIPLE MURDER
Polly Pilkington

It is understood that discrimination will play a central part in the forthcoming trial of Elizabeth Jamal, who was charged with three counts of murder earlier this month. It is alleged that Jamal murdered her husband and his gay lover, as well an elderly, disabled colleague who, it is believed, was murdered in order to silence her after she witnessed the other murders.

Jamal, who works as an HR Manager at Training4All, the company which employed all three victims, is alleged to have used her knowledge of equality legislation in order to deflect suspicion after she committed the murders.

Sources reveal that Jamal was aware of her husband's infidelity for some time and it was only when she discovered that he was having an affair with another man did she take such drastic action. It is also believed that Trudie Longhurst did not witness the crime and was killed in order to lead the police enquiry in the wrong direction.

As an HR professional, Jamal is aware of the different equality laws and is alleged to have murdered Longhurst, in order to "complete the set." A leading employment law firm have stated that there are only six main protected characteristics, and the three new ones introduced in 2010 were already covered elsewhere and are therefore "nothing new."

Her husband, Nadeem Jamal, and his lover, Carl Davenport, were both from ethnic minority backgrounds; Davenport was openly gay, and her husband was also a practising Muslim. It is understood that Longhurst being female, elderly, and disabled completed the "Equality Umbrella", which protects people in the workplace from discrimination.

The police investigation led by DCI Fenton, 45, has been scaled back following Jamal's arrest and her being remanded into custody. The prosecution is planning to use the discrimination angle at her forthcoming trial.

This raises serious concerns about the forthcoming bill on the reinstatement of the death penalty, for which support has been waning. If a conviction is secured on these grounds then Jamal would be likely to receive three life sentences with a high minimum tariff, yet one day she could be released back into society.

With the bill's first reading due in a matter of days, sources reveal the government are to push ahead with what they believe are crucial crime reform measures.

Elizabeth Jamal had managed to develop a distinct prison pallor within the short time she'd been inside. Fenton suspected she was being segregated from the other women. This was not so much for her own safety, as killing your husband tended to be something of a status symbol in prison, especially if he was cheating on you. Fenton suspected that her plainness unnerved the warders, given the crimes she was accused of. They probably expected her to suddenly go on another killing rampage. They liked their murderers to fit the stereotype. Fenton knew from experience that there was no stereotypical look for a murderer.

Fenton was never keen on visiting prisons. They were such depressing places. Women's prisons were even worse. Despair lingered everywhere. The thought of women being wrenched from their children on visiting day was an unpleasant feeling. They were in prison for a reason. They'd done something wrong. Well, most of the time. Fenton had put several women away for long stretches, but it still didn't make the place feel any better.

He was still curious why she wanted to see him. He'd offered to send Taylor who was due back from leave. Elizabeth was insistent that it be Fenton. She didn't want a lawyer present, which he thought was a little odd. Even when she'd confessed, she had still requested a lawyer for her formal statement. He was hoping she wouldn't inform him of a change of plea. A not guilty plea would mean a long-drawn-out trial that would probably span a month at least and warrant excessive press attention.

The press had been largely quiet since the arrest, except for Pilkington's recent article. The snake had finally resurfaced, and Fenton wondered if that was the reason Elizabeth had asked to see him again. He had ignored her first request, well not ignored it, he had just said he would visit her as soon as he could and not prioritised. When he saw the article in the paper, which was followed by another message from the prison, he knew he had to make time to see her straight away.

She might just be worried about how the press attention could affect her sentencing, or she could finally be ready to provide some details on how Trudie had been murdered. At present it was a lot of speculation, but the crown prosecution service had been comfortable with charging her with all three murders.

Following her arrest, the press had reported the story, but it was not as excessive as the reporting had been during the investigation. The general press had been surprisingly honest about the whole thing. There didn't seem to be an outpouring of sympathy towards her from the public. She wasn't portrayed as the victim in any way. They simply reported the truth. That was, until Pilkington's article.

"Thank you for coming to see me, Chief Inspector Fenton."

"Well, I have to say, I am a little curious. My apologies for not getting here sooner. I have been working on another case."

"Well you're here now, that's what matters. I suppose you have seen yesterday's papers and what that woman has written about me?"

Here we go, Fenton thought. He knew Pilkington had gone too far this time. The article could certainly jeopardise the trial if there was a not guilty plea. He wished he had managed to silence Pilkington permanently, but the whole Manning debacle had spectacularly blown up in his face. He still cringed when he thought about that evening.

Fenton had wanted to silence Pilkington in such a way that no other newspaper would hire her. That was the only way to shut her up. He didn't want any physical harm to come to her. He just wanted her to bugger off out of his life, and her career as a journalist to coming to an end was the only way to ensure that. Sadly, Manning was not the person Pilkington was using as her source. Fenton was still determined to find out who it was and hoped that Pilkington would slip up one day. He could be patient when he needed to be.

"I was very upset by some of the accusations in this article."

"I understand that."

"I don't think you do. I mean where did she get all this information? It's slanderous."

Fenton thought this was a bit of an exaggeration. Pilkington had gone overboard, yet the bare bones of the article were that she had killed her husband and his gay lover, then a disabled old lady to silence her. It was pretty much what happened.

"I can assure you that it was from nobody on my team, Elizabeth."

"Well, this article has made my mind up, Inspector. I was always going to plead this way anyway..."

"But you confessed, Mrs Jamal."

"To the murder of my husband and his lover. Yes, I do not deny that. I will plead guilty to those crimes. I will however be pleading not guilty to Trudie's murder."

He'd been waiting for something like this. This investigation had already been a ball ache and now it looked like the trial would be the same. At least Wendy would be pleased; she'd get her day in the spotlight to sob in the court about being a GBBF.

"Why will you be pleading not guilty to Trudie's murder?"

"Well, astonishing as this might sound, I didn't actually kill her."

Fenton looked at her directly in the eyes and he knew in an instant that she was telling the truth. His mind started racing at the possibilities.

"You admitted it," he said with conviction, although he knew she hadn't.

"I did not. I made no comment about her murder if you remember."

She was right; whenever he had tried to get anything out of her about Trudie she had remained silent, even despite advice from her lawyer.

"Don't you think it would have been prudent to mention this to us at the time? If what you're saying is true, then Trudie's killer is still out there."

"This is why I am telling you now. How did you find out about my husband's affair?"

"You know I can't answer that."

"You see, Inspector, sitting alone in a cell for twenty-three hours a day gives you time to think. I have a feeling I know where you got your information and why. If you want to know who killed Trudie, I suggest you look a little closer to home."

That last sentence resonated with Fenton. He'd heard it somewhere more recently. He was sure it was about something different. He couldn't think right now, his mind was focussed back on the case; a case he assumed was now closed. Deep down he had known something about Trudie's murder still hadn't sat right with him. When Elizabeth had described what she had done he could understand it; it made sense. It was something he would never say to the victim's families, but most murders make sense. It doesn't justify the murder at all, but there is a reason for why it has happened. With Trudie, it didn't make any sense; it just fit, and now Elizabeth's statement had reopened the investigation.

It was Wendy who had told them that Carl was having an affair with someone at work, but what link was she to Trudie? It suddenly dawned on him. Who was it that had sent him in Wendy's direction? When the investigation seemed to be going nowhere following Jez's release, there had been someone who had pushed them in Elizabeth's direction, albeit through Wendy. Fenton also knew that person had the most to gain from Trudie's death.

"Thank you, Mrs Jamal. I need to take this away and investigate further."

He was flustered and knew time could be against him, if it wasn't already too late. He got up and had his hand on the door handle.

"DCI Fenton, I murdered my husband and his lover because they hurt me and made a fool of me. It would have been the same if it had been another woman. What that horrible woman is saying about me is not true."

"I know that Mrs Jamal. I also thank you for being honest with me now."

He looked her in the eyes, which were brimming with tears. He knew she was not the hateful woman the press had made her out to be. Yes, she'd done a terrible thing and she'd pay for it. Her motive had been one of the classics – a good old-fashioned crime of passion and revenge.

As Fenton was leaving, she made one last comment which made him turn back.

"I hope you catch him."

She knew who the other killer was!

Why hadn't she bothered to tell him this information before today? Was this his fault for not coming sooner. Was it hers for holding this information back? Was it the teams' fault for not covering every avenue of investigation? No, there was only one person whose fault this was, Trudie's murderer – Derek Longhurst!

CHAPTER TWENTY-FIVE

Taylor dashed from her flat when Fenton pounded his fist on the horn. They drove in silence for a while, whilst he navigated his way out of London via the A40. It was the middle of the day. The M25 was astonishingly clear and Fenton was able to pelt at top speed weaving in and out of traffic like they had done on their last trip to Preston. The silence was making the situation tenser than it needed to be.

"Are the locals on standby for when we get there?" Taylor asked.

Fenton remained silent. His eyes fixed on the road in front.

Taylor was annoyed as well. She'd been duped, as had everyone. The only person who had first suggested two killers had been Fenton. That hadn't made any sense at the time as the killings were so identical. It still didn't really make complete sense. If they hadn't been in it together then Derek had to have witnessed the murders or known about them, so he had killed Trudie in the same way. That was cold and calculating and it made her feel uneasy. Elizabeth Jamal had done a despicable thing. She'd reacted in anger at the hurt and betrayal, which was right under her nose. She could relate to that. This was another matter. It was more pre-meditated, more calculated, and as far as she was concerned, pure evil.

"How did we miss it?" grumbled Fenton.

"We didn't miss it – you suspected him at the start."

"Yes, but why didn't we pursue it?"

"Because we were looking for one killer and it didn't make sense for him to kill the other two."

"He must have seen Elizabeth and took advantage of the situation. There's no way he could have just reacted in the moment and it be identical to the other murders. He must have been planning this for ages. I wouldn't be surprised if he made it, so Elizabeth found out about the affair."

"How would he know that she would kill them though? She didn't even know that's what she was going to do. It was spontaneous."

"Maybe he just hoped she'd be pushed over the edge and was ready to take advantage. If that's true, then that is one cold twisted killer."

Taylor nodded. It was exactly what she thought. She also considered that if he was planning to kill his wife, then it might not have been his first attempt. Had there been any other incidents? Nobody had mentioned anything during the investigation, but they hadn't asked. It was something they would need to investigate. She sent a text message to Shirkham. They had spoken shortly before Fenton had picked her up. Shirkham and Brennan had not yet been recalled to the case, but it was possible they could be, so she thought she'd give them a heads up. Shirkham had said that Fenton had already called her and asked about her current case as he didn't want to request her be pulled off if it would be too disruptive. He had also spoken to the DCI to be sure that if he needed to take both Brennan and Shirkham back, there wouldn't be any issues. That was classic Fenton. He had respect for his peers and would never just assume he could have officers back without question. It was why he was so respected – he got results, he was considerate, and he was a team player. It would be the qualities she would need to demonstrate if she was to be successful in moving up to his rank.

"Sir, don't shout but I think we should call in the locals, get them to keep an eye out..."

Fenton glared at her and held it. She didn't want to bring attention to the fact that he wasn't looking at the road again. She stared him out. Eventually he nodded. She quickly made the call before he changed his mind and barked instructions into the phone. They were going to arrest Derek Longhurst for the murder of his wife. The local police were to go to his place of abode and keep watch. They were not to move in until they arrived. She hung up the phone.

She hadn't given them an opportunity to press for any further details. She didn't want to give them enough information so that they could make the arrest themselves. They drove in silence for a while. Her phone rang. The local police had gone to Derek's house to find the new owners moving in. They had approached them. He had apparently handed over the keys that morning. They had no idea where he had gone.

"Bollocks – tell them to get to Training4All. Someone there must know something," said Fenton

They were still a good ninety minutes away from Preston and were steadily moving up the M6, now on the outskirts of Manchester.

She relayed the instructions down the phone rapidly. There was not much more they could do. She then had a thought, and quickly dialled the incident room back in London. As some of the original team were still pulling together the case files for Elizabeth's trial; she asked them to check flights to see if Derek Longhurst was booked on anything that day or tomorrow. She told them to start with Manchester, Liverpool, and Leeds airports and then to move outwards from there.

"Good idea, but I hope it comes to nothing," remarked Fenton.

Taylor nodded in agreement. If only Elizabeth had spoken up sooner, they wouldn't be this mad panic. Perhaps this was his plan. Once Elizabeth had been charged, there would have been nothing to stop him getting his hands on Trudie's money. That must have been all he was waiting for. Then he'd be gone. She wondered if he really was going to Australia, and if he even had a sister there. She quickly made another phone call instructing them to check that out as well.

She sent a text to Brennan and Shirkham to keep them updated. It would be up to Fenton to request they be pulled off their current case. That was above her pay grade. She just wanted to keep them in the loop so they would be ready when the call came, as she knew it was coming. If Derek had already left the country, then there wouldn't be much they could do other than issuing an international arrest warrant, but if he was still in the country, Fenton would want as much of the old team back as possible. It would be easier for the old team to pick up the investigation again straight away. They would be highly invested in tracking Derek down quickly. They would be feeling the same as Fenton and Taylor; that they'd be taken for mugs.

The call came back from the local police. Derek had requested that he forfeit the rest of his notice period and *some old guy* at the company had been only too happy to grant such a request to be rid of the whole *frightful affair*. Taylor took this to mean that they had spoken to Walt. They had no idea of Derek's plans or where he was going. He hadn't mentioned any plans of emigrating. They were only aware that he was selling the house and leaving the area.

"Do you think he would be trying to go Australia or somewhere else abroad?" asked Taylor.

"It makes sense. If he stays in the UK, we'd find him eventually. Maybe Australia was just a ruse though. He could be heading somewhere with no extradition treaty."

Fenton pulled into a service station. He told Taylor that he needed to get his head clear.

"I don't think it's worth us heading up to Preston now," he remarked

"I dunno. We're not far from Manchester Airport. If the team in London come back with anything, that's the most likely place he's gone if he's heading abroad."

"Too obvious, I think. Our Derek might be a lot of things, obvious isn't one of them."

The phone rang and Taylor quickly answered it. Derek wasn't booked on anything out of any of the airports in the north-west for the next week. This was on the proviso that he was using his own name. They had also checked his card activity with the bank, and he had made a purchase at Manchester Piccadilly two hours ago. He was potentially heading down south. Taylor told them to check the London airports immediately.

"Bollocks – it will take us three hours to get back. He could be on a plane by then."

He phoned Chief Superintendent Beeden and gave him a quick update on the latest developments. He requested that Shirkham and Brennan be pulled off their current case and be ready to head to the airport if word came through. He had already squared it with the DCI and knew they had already made an arrest in that case, so there shouldn't be a problem. If nothing was booked in Derek's name, he suggested they start with Heathrow as a first port of call. Beeden agreed to the request and said he would recall them immediately.

They drove in silence for the next two hours with no updates or new information coming through. It was like a pressure cooker in the car. The next update revealed that Derek was booked on a flight to Sydney, via Bangkok leaving Heathrow. It appeared he was going to Australia. He must have believed that they would never discover the truth. Brennan and Shirkham were already en route to make an arrest. The flight wasn't due to leave for another hour and airport security had been told to hold him at the gate if the police couldn't get there in time.

It was such a relief to know they had got him. Taylor suggested they head straight back to the station to prepare for the interrogation, but Fenton wasn't having any of it. He had changed course and was heading towards Heathrow. He wanted to make the arrest himself if he could. Taylor could understand that. She wanted to be there when he was nicked as well; she just didn't think they would get there in time.

The call came through half an hour later. Brennan had spotted Derek in the terminal building and moved in straight away for an arrest. He wasn't to know that he'd just pissed the boss off. He was following orders. Fenton turned the car round and headed back to the station in stony silence.

CHAPTER TWENTY-SIX

Fenton was informed that Derek had spoken to his solicitor and was now ready to be interviewed. Fenton asked Taylor to accompany him. He thanked Brennan for the arrest, and he meant it; his ego was now firmly back in check. Derek looked very relaxed when they walked into the interview room. He was dressed very casually, probably so he'd be comfortable for his flight. After the house sale and getting his hands on Trudie's money, Derek was now technically a millionaire, although he had still been intending to fly all the way to Australia in economy class. It was another insight into the sort of man he was.

Fenton started the interview with introductions and then reminded Derek that he was still under caution. Given what he had been arrested for, he decided there was no point in dithering around the issue.

"Derek. Did you murder your wife?"

"No comment."

Great – this is going to be a long fucking day!

"Derek. Elizabeth Jamal has denied murdering your wife and I believe her."

He gave no reaction.

"It was you who suggested I speak with Wendy Baxter regarding Carl Davenport's affair with a married man. Did you know that man was Nadeem Jamal?"

"No comment."

"I believe that you witnessed Elizabeth murder Nadeem and Carl and then copied her when you murdered your wife, in the hope that she would be blamed. Is that true?"

"No comment."

"I have enough evidence to charge you with her murder, regardless of whether you answer my questions or not, and I will charge you. So, I ask you again. Did you murder your wife?"

"No comment"

Fenton was irritated. He did have enough to charge him, but knew it was borderline on whether a jury would convict him. He kept on putting accusations to Derek over the next two hours. Derek's solicitor would only interject every so often to state that Fenton was repeating himself. He was aware of that but was hoping that Derek would finally give him something. Even if he kept saying *no comment*, it was possible that his non-verbal reactions could give away something else. There was usually something that could indicate a question had triggered a reaction. You would then know to focus in on that point, as that was more likely to get the suspect to crack. With Derek there was nothing. He kept his face impassive the whole time. The guy would make a great poker player.

Derek's solicitor requested a break and Fenton agreed. Taylor had passed him a note saying that Shirkham had wanted to see them urgently. He wasn't sure what it was about, but he needed a break himself and it was not as if they had Derek on the back foot.

Shirkham was waiting in Fenton's office and she looked

excited. He learned that Taylor has asked her to investigate Trudie's past to see if there was anything to indicate that there might have been other attempts on her life. What she had discovered was shocking. Fenton had to think about how he was going to present this information to Derek. Technically, he should disclose it to the solicitor, but it wasn't unheard of, for the police to hold a few things back. The last thing he wanted was for Derek to have time to prepare a response, or lack of one, when Fenton presented this new evidence to him. Fenton thanked Shirkham for her quick and diligent work. He asked Taylor to help him prepare for their next round with Derek – this time they were going to get a reaction from him.

The interview resumed and Fenton reminded Derek that he was still under caution.

"Derek, I put it to you again. Did you murder your wife?"

"No comment."

"If that's how you want to play it. I'd like to know what you were doing on twelfth of August last year."

"No comment."

Derek's solicitor interjected and asked for the relevance of the new line of questioning. Fenton ignored him.

"It was the night that your wife crashed her car when her brakes failed."

Derek shuffled in his seat. "No comment."

There had been a reaction.

"Your wife wasn't injured in the accident, although the car was a write off. In fact, according to the report she was incredibly lucky to have escaped without any injury. Where you in the vehicle with her at the time?"

Derek hesitated and looked at his solicitor, who gave a slight shake of his head. "No comment."

"Moving on. Do you remember where you were on eighteenth of November last year?"

His eyes flicked to his solicitor, but other than that there was no reaction.

"That would be the day you wife's wheelchair malfunctioned and she rode round the city centre for three hours until her battery ran out. Again, she was not injured. Do you have any comment about that incident?"

Derek shook his head

"For the tape, the suspect has shaken his head. On Valentine's Day of this year, you had to call out an electrician late at the night when all the power blew in your house. My colleague has spoken to the engineer and they state that a massive power surge caused the fuse board to blow. He also remembered the incident very well as your wife was in the bath at the time as she made a joke that she had fallen asleep and woke up to a loud bang. She said she wasn't affected by the blackout as her husband had made her a lovely bubble bath with candles."

Derek was really squirming in his seat now, but he still wasn't biting. Fenton hadn't finished yet though.

"Any comment about that incident?"

Derek shook his head. His face was going red. It looked like he was trying to control his anger.

"Again, for the tape, the suspect has shaken his head. Well I have a more recent example for you. On the third of June, this year you and your wife were admitted to hospital with suspected food poisoning. This was allegedly from her birthday dinner the night before at a local restaurant. Your wife was discharged from hospital after a few hours, but you were in hospital for three days. Do you have any comment about that?"

He was clenching his hands together and his knuckles were turning white. He looked like he was about to explode with rage, but he still shook his head. Fenton had one more card to play.

"Again, for the tape, the suspect shook his head. Do you know what I think, Derek? I think you have been trying to kill your wife for some time. There are at least four incidents here which we believe were attempts on her life. There could be other attempts that we are not aware of, it wouldn't surprise me. Your attempts to kill your wife and make it look like an *accident* failed on numerous occasions, so you had to change you approach.

"You found out that Nadeem Jamal and Carl Davenport were having an affair and you were disgusted about this behaviour so you thought you could, and pardon the pun, kill two birds with one stone. You hoped that you could provoke Elizabeth into a jealous rage so she could take the blame when you murdered your wife. You witnessed her commit two murders and did nothing to stop it, instead you crept up behind your unsuspecting wife and stabbed her in the heart in a way that mirrored the murders committed by Elizabeth."

Derek was looking down at the table and shaking his head and wringing his hands. Fenton upped the ante.

"You had achieved your goal and you didn't care about the collateral damage of Nadeem and Carl. A couple of dead poofs was no big loss."

"How dare you!"

"How dare I what, Derek?" Fenton knew that would needle him.

"I'm not homophobic."

"But you are a murderer."

Derek looked directly into Fenton's eyes. The man looked close to tears and he nodded, finally confirming his guilt.

"For the tape, Derek. Are you saying that you murdered you wife?"

"Yes," he said calmly. "I murdered my wife."

Fenton was relieved. He glanced at Taylor sitting next to him and she flashed a quick smile. They only had circumstantial evidence, albeit a lot of it, but they needed a confession, and now it looked like they were going to get it. Derek's solicitor asked for some time alone with his client. Fenton was loath to grant it, given he didn't want to break the momentum, but he didn't really have a choice. He just hoped his solicitor would not advise him to revert to the *no comment* response when the reconvened.

It was only thirty minutes before Derek's solicitor asked to see Fenton and explained that his client was ready to make a full confession. It looked like they would finally have the missing answers to the case which had received such widespread media attention. They all took their places back in the interview room and following the necessary pre-amble for the tape, Fenton asked Derek to give his side of the story. He could tell from Derek's body language that he was ready to unburden himself.

"I admired Trudie when we first met," he started. "I saw a vulnerable side to her that she never showed to anyone else. It was what caused me to fall in love with her. Not long after we were married, she started trying to control me. To the outside world we were an odd, but happy couple. Behind closed doors my life was miserable. She constantly made comparisons between me and her previous husband. He was responsible for her disability. He killed himself by driving his car into a bollard, trying to take her with him, but she would not hear a bad word against him."

"Why didn't you just leave?" asked Taylor.

"I wanted to. I tried several times. I worried about how it might look to other people."

Fenton thought this was an odd statement. The fact that,

had Trudie been the only one murdered, they would have had about sixty million suspects was a good indicator that, if he had left Trudie, most people would have described him as very sensible.

"Was it the money?" Taylor asked.

He nodded. "I was never interested in her money at first. After she emasculated me over the years, I felt I was owed my due."

"Why didn't you just divorce her?"

"She made me sign a pre-nuptial agreement. At the time I'd have done anything. I loved her. In the end I knew the only way to get hold of the money would be for her to die. That wasn't likely to happen naturally so I thought I could fix it, so she had an accident. The woman had more lives than a cat though."

"What sort of accidents?" Fenton asked.

"You got them all DCI Fenton. The first was the old standby, a car accident. I tampered with her brakes on the car. She totalled the car without a scratch on her. I tried to electrocute her in the bath and all it did was blow the power in the house. I tried to poison her and I'm the one who ended up throwing my guts up. Then I fixed that bloody scooter of hers. She went on a tour of Preston all afternoon and came back claiming she hadn't had so much fun in years. There was nothing I could do to get rid of the damn woman."

"Were there any other incidents we're not aware of?" asked Fenton.

"No. You got them all. Very clever detective work."

Fenton nodded to acknowledge the compliment. He'd already thanked Shirkham for the pulling all that together in such a short space of time. If only they had investigated Derek thoroughly from the start, they may have resolved the case sooner. Fenton signalled for Derek to continue.

"I suspected Carl and Nadeem were having an affair for

some time. After years of working so closely with people every day I can pick up on things relatively easily. I've no idea how Elizabeth missed it for so long. She suspected something, it was obvious, yet had no idea who it could be.

"That night I wasn't planning anything but thought with a bit of a nudge she may react rashly – she always struck me as the type who had one hell of a temper which she kept bottled up. I made a throwaway comment about the hotel being a bit sleazy and wondering how many people carried on their affairs here, given the hotel was cheap and had such a good central location for a quick tryst. Elizabeth look annoyed and I saw her slip away from the dinner. She was visibly upset, so I decided to follow her. I noticed Carl and Nadeem were also missing and had a fairly good idea what she was about to discover. Imagine finding them in your own bed, even if it was a hotel bed. It was bound to sting a bit. I kept my distance at first and then watched as she checked through her bag and took a knife out of a box and placed the knife back in her bag. It was a similar knife that Trudie had bought that day from some annoying little man shouting into a microphone. She'd told me that he had been very rude to Elizabeth, so I thought it was very strange that they still purchased the knives from him!

"She burst into the room. I couldn't hear very much, not that I was trying to listen anyway. It wasn't my business. I saw Carl emerge and return to his room looking flustered. I was about to go back to dinner when I saw Elizabeth emerge alone, still with her bag, and make her way down to Carl's room. I wasn't sure what had gone on, so I followed her. Carl was also on the ground floor, as we all were, so I managed to sneak round the back of the hotel and, although there were net curtains, I could still see into Carl's room.

"I couldn't hear what was being said. I was horrified when I saw her stab him in the heart. She just stood there and watched him die before putting the knife in her bag and casually leaving as if she was going to a cocktail party. I wouldn't be surprised if she went back and had dinner. She's a cold one that Elizabeth."

Fenton considered what he had said. If it was true, then she had gone into her room with the knife ready to use. Perhaps it was not as spur of the moment as she had made out in her confession.

"I assumed that she had killed Nadeem in the same way, although I wasn't sure. Still, I had to take an opportunity when it was presented to me... Trudie was asleep in her wheelchair when I got back to the room. She was a very deep sleeper so didn't wake when I entered the room. I went into her bag and took out the identical knife that Elizabeth had used. I went behind her and towered over her. She didn't wake up when I plunged the knife into her heart. There was a slight reflex jerk. She died pretty instantaneously."

Fenton let him speak. He showed little emotion. There was no hatred in his voice. In the end it had been another good old-fashioned motive for murder – greed.

"I waited for a minute or so to be sure and then her body fell forward, and she ended up in a crumpled heap on the floor, with her wheelchair upended. I washed the knife with soap in the bathroom. There was little blood on it anyway, and I dried it and put it back in the box. I went out into the hall and there was nobody around, so I threw it one of the hotel bins out the back I then went back to the room and made out that I had just discovered her body. I then made sure to check for a pulse, so my DNA was on her body. Then I raised the alarm."

Fenton was annoyed that the murder weapon had not been found during the search unless Derek was lying. They would probably never know. He wondered if Elizabeth had done the same thing, even though she claimed to have no recollection of what she had done with the knife.

"What about when Jez was arrested?" asked Taylor.

"I did feel a bit guilty about that, but I'd suffered enough, and it was only fair that I was free. When he was cleared, I was worried that the investigation might lead to me. You had evidently suspected me early on. After Jez was released, I decided to deflect suspicion towards Elizabeth. I knew she was guilty of two of the murders. She was going to get two life sentences. What was one more?"

Fenton asked Derek whether he had been the one making anonymous calls to Elizabeth about Nadeem's affair. He denied this and Fenton was inclined to believe him, based on how he reacted to the question. Given what he'd admitted, he also had no reason to lie about it. For now, that mystery caller would have to remain just that − a mystery!

A week had passed since Derek Longhurst's arrest. He had also been remanded in custody, owing to the serious nature of his crime and because he was a flight risk. The case was truly over, except for the trials, but they would be some months away.

The press had been favourable towards the police investigation. There had been no article from Pilkington. Fenton was on his last day before going on a two-week break with his family. He hadn't had a Christmas and New Year off for years.

Winter was finally here. A humid October and mild November had resulted in a freezing December. Although it was too cold to snow, whatever that meant.

Fenton was still looking over the Davies case. He knew he was missing something. A throwaway comment said recently more than once. What the hell was it? A junior officer popped his head round the door.

"I'm off, Guv."

"Thanks, Anthony."

"Good to see Pilkington hasn't written anything about Derek Longhurst. Maybe she got fired for causing all that panic for nothing?"

"I doubt it – besides, she was freelance."

Anthony nodded and then left.

That was it. Pilkington and Elizabeth had both said the same thing. "You need to look closer to home."

Fenton was outside Beeden's office bursting with excitement. He was looking around for Beeden's secretary. She was nowhere to be seen. He listened at the door and couldn't hear anything but knew that Beeden tended to keep his door open when he wasn't there.

Fenton knocked and opened the door. The files he was holding dropped out of his hand. It was one of the few times that he had ever been genuinely stunned. There was his mentor Harry Beeden and his worst enemy Polly Pilkington in a deep embrace.

They jerked apart at the sound of Fenton walking in, making a sucking noise like a sink plunger. Fenton just stood there in the doorway. Pilkington hoisted up her leg, so she was no longer straddling Beeden. She slung her bag over her shoulder and smiled at Fenton. He shuddered.

"I'll leave you boys to talk... bye, darlink."

She squeezed Fenton's cheek. He felt ill. The door clicked behind her as she left.

"Sit down, Eric."

"It was you, sir, wasn't it? That's where she's been getting all her information."

"Sit down, Eric."

"I'd rather stand, thank you, sir." He tried to say it defiantly, although it just came across as pathetic.

"Sit down!"

Fenton decided to sit. Not out of fear, but he was afraid his legs were going to give way after what he had just witnessed.

"I'm sorry, Eric. I know how you feel about her."

"I just don't understand how you could tell her everything to do with the case. She's made the investigation ten times more difficult and my life a misery. Did you tell her to make those comments about me as well?"

"Of course not. I told her not to. She said it would be a good diversionary tactic. You wouldn't suspect me. You'd probably suspect Manning."

"Did you know that they were sisters?"

He nodded.

"And you didn't think to tell me! Harry, we've known each other for nearly twenty-five years."

"What can I say?"

"Do you know what a twat I looked like when I confronted Manning and Pilkington and accused them of having it off with each other, only to discover that they were sisters?"

"I'm surprised that didn't make you suspect Manning more."

"I tend to know when people are lying."

"Point taken. What did you want to...?"

"Can I just ask why?"

He shrugged. "She's a very talented woman."

Fenton felt even more nauseous. He stood up, losing his balance for a second. Clutching his forehead – it was clammy. "I need to go now, sir."

"You wanted to see me, Eric?"

"Oh right, the Davies case. I'm going to arrest the uncle."

"I thought he was ruled out early on?"

"We overlooked something."

"Take who you need."

Fenton nodded and left Harry's office.

He was going to close his only unsolved murder, but after what had just happened it didn't feel like a victory. He had to push that out of his mind though as even though it was a betrayal, it paled into insignificance compared to what he was just about to do.

All those years ago, he'd made a promise to Jack's parents – he was about to deliver.

EPILOGUE

Elizabeth Jamal was convicted for the murders of her husband and his lover. She was given two life sentences and told that she would serve a minimum of twenty-five years in prison.

Derek Longhurst was convicted of murdering his wife, two counts of failing to report a crime and four counts of attempted murder. He was also given a minimum tariff of twenty-five years.

The death penalty bill was defeated in the House of Commons. The Leader of the Opposition triggered a no confidence vote in the government which resulted in an election being called. He now resides at 10 Downing Street and has a relaxation room where he indulges in his tantric delights. The former Prime Minister has retired from public life. The Leader of the Other Party... well, nobody has any idea what he's doing. He keeps wandering around muttering to himself and all people can make out is the words *bitch* and *cakes*.

Walter Channing continues to run Training4All. His *business associate* is now part of the team working as a Performance Enablement Facilitator. Walt felt that their synergy could be utilised for profit. The creation room has undergone a makeover and been dedicated to the three murdered employees. Walt feels now that the creation room truly is *fit for purpose.*

Wendy has left Training4All. She now works as a trainer at a media company in Manchester. She is delighted to be GBBF to twenty of her colleagues. Twenty-one people work at the company.

Jez has moved on and left his family behind. He continues to work in IT but has moved to London in order to pursue his passion for needlepoint. Doris is now training him up for knitting competitions as well and victory is within their grasp. He is also dating one of Breeda's nieces.

Manning is still reeling from the shock of Fenton apologising to her and saying he'd like to start afresh with their professional relationship and that she had his utmost respect. She had been so taken aback as she knew that it was genuine this time, that she had unintentionally told Fenton that he was also the police officer she respected the most. It had been a rather awkward moment. She also withdrew her complaint against Fenton She has recently started a relationship with renowned criminal psychologist Dr. Deirdre Peters.

Pilkington continues to work freelance, although her articles are rarely seen anymore. She is thinking of moving overseas and starting afresh.

Beeden managed to convince Fenton to keep quiet about his affair with Pilkington. He went back to his wife and, due to his wife's lack of sexual adventure, Beeden has managed to keep case details confidential ever since.

Shirkham continues to work at DC level despite numerous recommendations for promotion. She has a happy home life but continues to keep her work very much separate.

Brennan is still at DS level but hopes for promotion one day. He is currently enjoying the company of a certain female coffee shop assistant whenever he gets a weekend off work. Unfortunately, he has also developed a serious caffeine addiction.

Taylor was promoted to DCI, much to Fenton's delight. She found the therapy useful and now only focuses her other desires in the direction of the non-criminal classes. She is currently learning how to ride a motorbike with her new beau and can often be found accompanying him in the free weights area of the gym. They have also booked in a session to get joint tattoos.

. . .

Fenton was pleased to secure the conviction of Jack Davies' uncle for his murder. He had been the early suspect, but he had a solid alibi. Fenton had worked on the assumption that it was a random kidnapper, but he had been jolted into looking at the family closer and managed to discredit the uncle's alibi. His record now remains unblemished. He had a wonderful Christmas and New Year with his wife and girls in a lovely villa in Lanzarote. He wondered why she had chosen to go away for Christmas and cook until, on Christmas Day, they broke with tradition and she served up enough cottage pie to feed an army.

And finally...

Debbie won Cake Shop Hell. She retreated to her home with a life-time supply of cakes and hasn't been seen since.

NOTE FROM THE AUTHOR

Thank you for reading my book – I hope you enjoyed it!

I cannot thank the family, friends, peers, and professionals enough for helping to make the DCI Fenton Murder Trilogy a reality. However, the biggest thank you must go to all the readers of my books. Without your support, I would never have pushed through the procrastination and self-doubt to finish the series and make this dream of becoming a published author a reality.

If you enjoyed this book, then please consider leaving a review on the online bookstore you purchased it, or anywhere else that readers visit. The most important part of how well a book sells is how well it is endorsed by other readers. Even a line or two would be incredibly helpful. Thank you in advance to anyone who does.

If you would like to find out about my other books, and read my short stories then please visit my website:

www.nicklennonbarrett.com

ALSO BY NICK LENNON-BARRETT

Murder for Health and Fitness

Murder for Social Media

Printed in Great Britain
by Amazon